D0917914

Dog Dreams

Fact & Fantasy

Ron Cook, PsyD

This is a work of fiction. All of the characters, organizations and events portrayed in this novel are either works of the author's imagination or are used fictitiously. Any resemblance to actual persons, living or dead, or actual events is purely coincidental. If you believe any of the references in this book are about you personally, seriously - you really do need to get over it.
This is not about *you*; it's about the *dogs*.

DOG DREAMS

Copyright © 2020 by Ron Cook

All rights reserved.

Visit us at DogDreams.us

Cover photo by
Susan Richey-Schmitz under license agreement from 123RF

ISBN 978-0-9854526-4-3

In memory of the dogs we have loved and lost.

Prologue

All his life he tried to be a good person. Many times, however, he failed. For after all, he was only human. He wasn't a dog.

~ *Charles M Schulz*
(cartoonist and creator of Snoopy)

Imagine being able not only to peer into the minds of sleeping dogs, sharing their vivid dream experiences, but also to use some exciting new cutting-edge technology, which for the first time allows us to actually talk to our dogs and understand them when they talk to us. This incredible breakthrough was made possible by the work of a team of dedicated researchers, scientists whose talent and expertise have combined to accomplish what we would have never imagined possible. This is the story of that research team and their journey.

If you are a dog lover like me, you have probably marveled at the seemingly endless capacity of man's best friend to impact our lives in so many positive ways. There is nothing like the wag of a tail, an excited welcome home or a loving touch when we need it most to let us know we are loved. That bond may be difficult for others to comprehend, but we know our relationship with our dogs is strong and unbreakable. We enjoy their steadfast loyalty and companionship, mourn their passing, and we know in our hearts they mourn ours.

This book will take a look at this very special relationship, detailing the biological and psychological elements, comparing and contrasting the dog-human bond with those we share with loved ones. We will examine the various ways our dogs show affection and how we communicate. We will then take a fanciful journey to an imaginary realm in order to peer into our canine companions' most intimate thoughts, emotions and imagination. During the voyage, we will meet several interesting and memorable dogs, each with its own story and, thanks to some amazing technology and our dog fanatic research team, you will have the opportunity to view the world through their eyes, as we em*bark* (see what I did there?) on a quest to answer the questions we desperately need answered. Do dogs feel love? Do dogs *dream*? As you follow this story, you will learn the scientific basis for love and affection and similarities in human relationships as compared to the relationships we share with our dogs.

In this book, we will be using definitions, descriptions and terminology that are not meant to offend, but rather to frame the story in a simple and understandable way. In referring to the relationship between a dog and its human master, I have chosen to use the word "owner" to describe that relationship. I did so for two reasons. First, and while the anthropomorphists among us might seek to ascribe human attributes to our canine companions, I recognize that this is, in fact, a relationship between man and beast. But I also choose the word because it is the most accurate in this case. If in the future we see animals as true equals and not as property, we can agree on different terminology.

Of course, my anthropomorphic friends and, I suppose, possibly *YOU* may occasionally try to remind me: "Come on, man! You know, dogs are people, too." NEWS FLASH, FOLKS: No, they are not! Humans are humans. Dogs are dogs. Trust me on this one! If you are thinking that is a cold and heartless response, rest assured it is not meant to in any way diminish our love and affection for our canine friends. They are absolutely an integral part of our families, no doubt loved more than some relatives we will not mention, and always as close to our heart – possibly more so – than many humans. We love them dearly, grieve their loss as intensely as we do our family and friends, and keep them in our memories forever. Love is everlasting, and that is true with our love for our dogs.

As with any story that involves references to humans or animals that may be of different sexes, I may alternatively use examples that refer to *he* or *she*, rather than *it*. These are purely generalizations and are not intended to suggest a preference for either sex. When the sex of an animal may have a direct bearing on our research, I will point out how that impact should be considered in evaluating the research findings.

As you are introduced to our research subjects, I will be revealing information gleaned from a research study that is both intimate and private, typically out of reach from sharing with the public. In this case and in this regard, several factors are at play. It is obviously not possible to get informed consent from a dog. That is not to say that the dog did not willingly consent to and benefit from the research, but let's be honest – in each case the *owner* signed the release allowing me to share this information with you. In no case was any dog or owner in any way coerced to do so, no participant was compensated in any way, and advance consent to share information was not required for participation in the research study. On the contrary, as we shared the research findings with each participating owner and dog, we offered the opportunity to keep the findings confidential and respect each dog's privacy, just as we would do with human subjects. We are especially pleased and that all participants enthusiastically supported including the results in this book. For that I am eternally grateful.

Finally, *this is a work of fiction, not an actual scientific study*. While many of the concepts discussed have a factual scientific basis, the majority of the story asks you to use your imagination to ponder "what if" and envision a world in which we can directly communicate with our beloved pets. As pet owners, we already enjoy very special relationships with our dogs, and we feel a bond and level of communication those who have never owned a dog may never comprehend.

Join me now, as we venture into an imaginary world, a world where humans and dogs can share their innermost thoughts, where dreams blend with reality - a world of *dog dreams*.

One

How it all began

Outside of a dog, a book is a man's best friend.
Inside of a dog it's too dark to read.

~ *Groucho Marx*

For years scientists have searched for the origin of what are today the domesticated dogs we know and love, and a complete history of this evolution would more than fill the pages of this or any other book. Evidence suggests that today's domestic canines can trace their roots to a group of wolves that interacted with humans as much as 40,000 years ago, or a whopping 280,000 in dog years! While it is unclear precisely where this occurred, fossils and DNA evidence have revealed two possible wolf populations, one in Asia and another in Europe. More recent research suggests that as of about 7,000 years ago, dogs were common in most areas of the globe, including North America.

Theories regarding early human-canine interaction suggest that less aggressive wolves may have become tolerant of human hunter gatherers over time. Is it also possible that early dogs may have simply tricked humans to allow them to come inside out of the cold? We may never know the answer, but over time the once aggressive wolf and pack mentality gave way to less menacing but still feral dogs, and eventually domestication and bonding with human companions. We may have domesticated dogs, or perhaps they domesticated us. Regardless, the question of who is really in charge is certainly something to think about when you are next in the toy aisle at your local PetSmart plopping down twenty bucks for the perfect dog toy.

One interesting alternative theory of canine domestication comes from a story passed down over the ages in a small village in Moldavia. The village elders recount with vivid detail how their ancestors were tricked into domestication by a cunning pack of feral village dogs. According to the legend, it all started when the pack's alpha male called a pack meeting on an especially cold night as a massive winter storm was approaching. The dogs converged on a large bonfire set by village leaders near the edge of town, as the villagers moved to their homes to retire for the night. Witnesses to the meeting observed the alpha dog seeming to bark orders (sorry) to the other dogs, who appeared to listen attentively as the Alpha held court. After eavesdropping on the canine conference, thc village Shaman summoned the village elders, claiming that while witnessing the get-together he experienced an ecstatic trance, gaining the psychic ability to hear and understand the entire discussion. As the astonished elders listened, the Shaman presented the verbatim account of what he heard. He described the Alpha's guttural, low pitched "voice" and the focused attentiveness of the pack. A rough translation follows:

> *Brothers and sisters of the pack. Thank you for coming. Like you, I sense the approaching storm, and we need to take action to protect our families. (barking, howling and frenetic tail wagging in apparent agreement)*
>
> *Over the past few years we have called this village our home, living close, but not too close, to the village humans. We have not attacked them, being careful to keep our distance and have given the humans their space. Now they hunt us no more. (more barking and howling) In fact, they often share the meat from their hunts, and we gladly accept their kindness. So today we hunt less and can raise our pups in safety. This coexistence has grown from mutual respect.*
>
> *Tonight, my feral friends, and even as the storm draws closer, we must take this opportunity to take the final step, a historic move from our open exposure to this harsh environment to move inside with the humans.*

(agitation and nervous barking) Wait, don't get your fur in a bunch! This is not their idea, it is ours! (howls and tail wagging)

We will neither sacrifice our freedom nor deny our heritage. We lose nothing by accepting the invitation to move into the warmth and protection the human structures provide. As you have seen with your own eyes, they even puppysit our young, especially the human children. (tails wagging)

Warmth and protection, food, free puppysitting. My fellow canines, we can befriend these humans to our great benefit. We only agree not to bite the hands that feed us, and while our pups may retrieve inanimate objects thrown repeatedly by these humans to annoy us, surely this is a small price to pay. Are you with me? (full-on, head-to-the-sky howling erupts, excited shaking, jumping and tail-chasing)

The Shaman continued to describe the scene. The celebration continued for quite some time and, as the dogs became less excited, they moved to surround the Alpha, as a show of respect and solidarity. Then an amazing scene unfolded. As though driven by some unseen force, the pack slowly began to disperse, with each dog selecting the home whose owner he or she found most acceptable, or perhaps simply the least distasteful. Then, as though directed by an invisible conductor, each canine made their presence known at their chosen doorway – a simple, well-placed paw scratching the door, a soft whimper calling out to human occupants – each dog seemed to intuitively know just the right approach. And slowly but surely, doors opened one after another, with light and heat escaping only momentarily, with each dog's silhouette disappearing quickly from head to tail, with doors closed securely behind.

Whether this age-old story, handed down through generations, is a true and accurate account of a significant historical event or a fantastic concoction from the imagination of a mystical spiritual leader matters little, I suppose. What matters most is that this evolution did occur in some form or fashion, and it continues to this day. Whenever and however humankind and dogs may have come together, and however that symbiotic relationship may evolve in the future, we can be sure that the affection and companionship we share with our dogs and they feel for us will only continue to grow in the years ahead.

Of course, the story, real or imagined, also serves to validate the old saying "*You can't teach a cold dog new tricks.*" That *is* the old saying, right?

In 1872 Charles Darwin published *The Expression of the Emotions in Man and Animals*, his third published research and support for his theory of evolution, following his most famous work *On the Origin of Species* and shortly after his *The Descent of Man*. Darwin's work inspires the field of evolutionary psychology, applying his theory of natural selection and *survival of the fittest* to the inner workings of the mind. In the simplest terms, Darwin's theory suggests that humans and animals of all species adapted over time in response to changes in their environment. Those that adapted increased their chances of survival and reproduction. As a result, these adaptations are passed on to the next generation, the process of *natural selection*. Those that failed to adapt failed to survive such that, over time, only those who adapted and evolved contribute to future generations. Applying natural selection to the evolution of the human mind, we consider that we adapted and evolved like other animals, and those adaptive changes supported our procreation and survival.

An example of how Darwin's theory of evolution and natural selection is found in *The Expression of the Emotions in Man and Animals*, with Darwin citing a situation in which a dog approaches a strange dog or man. Instinctively anticipating potential danger, the dog prepares for attack, an understandable survival instinct and something we often refer to as preparation for *fight or flight*. This preparation includes certain mental and physical changes – head raised and alert, eyes in a fixed stare, ears directed forward. If the dog continues to approach, then realizes that the other dog is a sibling or part of the pack or that the human is not a stranger but, in fact, his master, the dog experiences what Darwin refers to as the *Principle of Antithesis*, assuming mental and physical conditions completely opposite from the previous aroused state. The body relaxes, the tags drops and wags, the ears relax, the eyes no longer stare and take in the overall surroundings. Darwin notes that, while the initial hypersensitivity and aggressive preparation have significant value in natural selection, the antithetic actions do not, suggesting: "It should be added that the animal is at such times in and excited condition from joy; and nerve-force will be generated in excess, which naturally leads to action of some kind. Not one of the above movements, so clearly expressive of affection, are of the least direct service to the animal." It is notable that *Darwin specifically refers to joy and affection*, based on his direct observation of the dog's behavior, with a series of illustrations supporting his theory.

As the human and dog relationship has continued to develop over time, we have seen the seemingly infinite capacity of dogs to serve us unselfishly in so many ways. What began with "seeing eye" and guide dogs soon grew to include so many other functions – assistance dogs, guard dogs, police dogs, dogs of war, bomb and drug sniffing dogs, emotional support dogs – the list goes on. Stop to imagine the commitment required for a dog so well trained and committed that he does not hesitate to lead his handler into a life-threatening combat situation or take down an armed assailant in a robbery. Instinctively, these amazing canines follow their training to the letter, without regard for their own safety. In the military, a longstanding tradition is that every type of military working dog (MWD) is unofficially a non-commissioned officer, making it one rank higher than its handler, signifying a true partnership.

Think about it - a guide dog devotes its entire life to the service of others, in many cases quite literally responsible for the life and safety of his human assignment. Whether helping a blind person cross a busy intersection, accompanying an elderly shopper home from the grocery store, or simply a faithful and loving companion for someone dealing with severe personal trauma, a dog assumes huge responsibility for our safely and aiding in our wellbeing. Outside of the military or law enforcement, today we use the term *service dog* to refer to dogs specifically trained to provide any type of assistance for people with disabilities. These include those already mentioned – visual or hearing impairments, issues with mobility and other physical limitations, as well as providing comfort and support for individuals with a range of mental disorders such as post-traumatic stress disorder (PTSD) and other categories of anxiety disorders or depression. As we will learn in later chapters, there are psychological, biological and hormonal factors at work in these important human-dog relationships.

We know that dogs are both loyal and obedient, and we can present ample evidence to support that assertion, but how can we prove Darwin's theory regarding affection and joy? How can we know with absolute certainty that our dogs truly love us as much as we care for them? Searching for such evidence and answering those questions is what this book is all about. To begin the journey, we need to understand the science behind affection, love and the bonds that exist between humans and between us and our dogs.

Two

For the Love of Dog

A dog is the only thing on earth that loves
you more than he loves himself.

~ *Josh Billings*

Now that we know a bit more about the history of the relationship between man and dog, my goal was to create a comprehensive research study, with a goal of further exploring those relationships, searching for answers to a series of thought-provoking questions around three key topics:

1. Do dogs feel love? It seems such a simple yet complex question. Do dogs display affection? Absolutely! But do they *love*?

2. Dog owners have a certain level of communication with our furry friends. Can our dogs actually understand us? Can we understand *them*? How can we improve that communication?

3. Do dogs dream? If so, what do they dream about? Are dog dreams similar to ours?

How can we find those answers? Before we delve into the formal research study, let's begin with the obvious observable behaviors. We know that dogs display affection in a variety of ways and, while we cannot then presume that these behaviors are indications of emotional love, they are a logical and observable place to start.

Here is my "Top Ten" list:

1. They look you straight in the eye.

Your dog is demonstrating a deep emotional bond with you when he looks you straight in the eye. Some say it is as though they are peering into your soul, and it is a way to let you know that you have their full and complete attention. Neurologically, when dogs make direct eye contact with us, have physical contact through petting or hugging, or are playing with us, the same chemical that is released in bonding between babies and their mothers, oxytocin, is also released through our canine/human interaction. From personal experience, I can share that when my dog challenges me to a stare-down, it is generally because he wants something and/or anticipates that something is about to happen, letting me know he is ready for a play session, ride in the car, trip to the park – whatever is about to occur, I have his full and complete attention. Admittedly, it can occasionally be a bit annoying, but once playtime is over, he can return to that blissful state we affectionately refer to as UDD (upside-down dog).

2. They wag their tails.

Most people think a dog's wagging tail is a friendly gesture and expression of a calm, relaxed state. A tail wag can have a variety of meanings, almost like a type of canine sign language, if we know how to interpret it. When your dog offers a full-body wag with his tail up midway, he is sending a clear message: he is happy to see someone he knows, and you are OK to approach and interact. While many tail wags do indeed indicate happiness, others may signal fear and apprehension. The height of the tail is also an important signal, sort of an emotional meter. As a simple rule, a tail wagging at middle height is a sign the dog is relaxed. As the tail height moves up, it signals a relative degree of alertness, while if it drops lower, it signals submission, or perhaps the dog is feeling poorly. A tail tucked underneath the body signals a state of fear. Conversely, if the tail moves up to a most vertical position with little movement, it is a signal that the dog is becoming threatened, signaling everyone to back off.

Research by an Italian neuroscientist and two veterinarians used video to track the angle and height of the wagging tails of 30 dogs to record their reaction to their owner, to a person they had not met before, a cat and finally a dog they had never encountered before. The interesting results were that when the dogs saw their owners, their tails wagged more vigorously and with an angle to the right side of their body. An unfamiliar human caused the tail to wag to the right, but more moderately. When the dogs saw the cat, the tail wag was still to the right, but the wag and their overall movements were more restrained, as if to say: "This is interesting and doesn't appear to be a threat, but I'm checking it out." When an unfamiliar dog is introduced, especially one who seems potentially aggressive and a threat, the tails all wagged to the left. The study concluded that right-biased tail wagging signals a positive approach and acceptance, while a wag angled to the left was consistently seen as a negative response and a signal of avoidance.

Now that you know the secrets of "tail language", you will be better equipped to gauge your dog's reactions to you and others, as well as the signals of other dogs you may encounter. I suppose if you encounter a new dog with no tail movement whatsoever, you could let the owner know: "Hey, buddy - looks like your dog has a tail signal out."

3. They show empathy.

If you have ever been sick, visibly emotional, sad or angry, have you ever noticed that your dog may come to make contact with you? As with their wolf ancestors who maintained strong relationships with other wolves in their pack, dogs are instinctively social animals, and you are now part of their pack, their family. They can sense emotion and are keenly sensitive to our body language, especially when we are ill or in emotional distress. Unlike a close friend, spouse or significant other who may claim to feel your pain when you are sad or depressed but insist that you need to just get over it, snap out of it or any number of other platitudes that are so not helpful at the time, your dog really does sense your emotional state, and he or she will reflect their concern in both their body language and actions. It may be a paw on your arm, a head laid on your lap, or simply curling up next to you on the sofa, but these gestures are an expression of support and concern.

4. They lean on you.

Just as we seek comfort in the touch of a loved one, a hug or simple lean on a shoulder, dogs are demonstrating their affection when they lean on you to provide comfort and support. In various situations, they are alternately providing or seeking attention and emotional support. They let you know they are there for you, and you are there for them. As their master, they recognize you are someone who can provide protection and keep them safe. With your support and direct physical contact, they are less anxious or nervous and become completely relaxed. Of course, if that includes having a 120-pound Rottweiler laying directly on your chest, you may choose a more comfortable tactile arrangement. Allowing your dog to remain in physical contact at your feet, with his head in your lap, or any other close proximity or touching show your pet's affection and comfortability when you're close by.

5. They share their toys.

You may not have realized it, but when your dog brings you their slimy, slobbery favorite toy, they are signaling more than just the fact they want to play. The ultimate sign of affection is sharing that slobber covered bunny rabbit with you, trusting that you will find it as precious and fascinating as they do. In fact, you may find that your pet will make multiple trips to the toy basket, offering you the opportunity to choose the toy that is your personal favorite. Then it's time to play, so grab that slimy stuffed squirrel, and it's on!

6. They sleep with you.

Let's agree that there is simply no greater joy than waking up to doggie breath or feeling that paw in the back as your dog stretches to greet the morning. Dogs are social animals and would normally sleep with their siblings or other dog friends. Since you are part of their pack and family, your loyal canine companion wants to sleep with you, but only if you permit them to do so. Snuggling in on a cold night is just one more sign of trust and affection. Of course, it is up to you whether you allow your dog in your bed (or vice versa!), and it is something you may need to manage, especially if a significant other is involved. Certainly, there is nothing like a hairy dog butt directly in your face first thing in the morning to get your day off to a great start.

7. Dog kisses

Let's face it, doggie kisses are the ultimate expression of canine affection. Just as their parents did when they were little puppies, nuzzling and kisses demonstrate affection and are your dog's way of communicating how he or she feels about you. Dogs lick for a variety of reasons. As puppies, they learn to lick to strengthen the bonds with their siblings and also to groom themselves. As they mature, if they remain with their family or other dogs, licking can indicate their respect for a more dominant member, and the lick is a sign of submissiveness, with the dog receiving the lick generally not responding in kind, asserting their dominance. Of course, with you your dog may be trying to communicate any number of things – he's happy to see you, hungry for a snack, ready to play – any number of possibilities.

You may be reinforcing the licking behavior when you respond with positive attention in the form of petting, kind words and hugs. As a result, your dog will learn to repeat the behavior. You may also find that he licks your face because it tastes salty and, if you have facial hair or stubble (not you, ma'am!) your rough face is the perfect way for your canine companion to clean his tongue. When a dog is licking as a show of affection, it results in the release of pleasurable endorphins that create a feeling of calm and comfort. Regardless, there is nothing wrong with considering it a kiss, signaling affection and accepting it as intended. Just be aware that while you may see that slobbery mouth as an affectionate expression, your friends, neighbors and especially small children may see it as, well – a slobbery dog mouth. Yuck!

8. Getting up in your business

Some dog owners freak out when their pet directs a cold wet nose toward their private parts, a not unexpected reflex reaction. When your dog sticks his nose "all up in your business" or sniffs other dogs' butts, it may seem a bit awkward, but it is really the same as a handshake between humans. It is simply one way your dog becomes familiar with your scent and that of other dogs. Of course, your friends may not accept your "Sorry, he's just getting to know you" apology, so be sensitive and encourage friends and neighbors to greet your pet face-first, extending their hand palm down and speaking in a friendly tone. Once your dog gets to know them and that you think they are OK, the butt-sniffing will diminish. Of course, if it doesn't you can always try "Wow! He really likes you!" Yeh, good luck with that!

My experience has been that, especially when you are still half asleep and stumbling to make sure your toothbrush finds your mouth, an unexpected cold dog nose on your butt is the perfect way to perk you up and bring a sense of immediate focus to your morning routine.

9. They smile at you.

You no doubt have noticed that dogs really do smile. The canine equivalent of a human smile is seen in a relaxed mouth and ears, a perky body and relaxed tail wag. Psychologically, when we react positively to our smiling companion, our positive facial expressions and actions serve to reinforce the dog's smiling behavior. As with humans, when dogs are happy and content, they communicate that in a variety of ways, including body language reflecting their emotional state. Rolling over to accept a tummy scratch is letting you know your pet's head is in a good and positive place, trusting you completely. For me, when my dog is UDD (upside down dog) and I scratch his tummy, he definitely grins from ear to ear, and I swear I hear a dog whisper softly in the background: "Hey man, that's the spot! Yeh, baby, work it!"

10. They jump up and down and want to play.

It may well be aggravating when your dog is jumping excitedly, challenging you to join in the roughhousing and play, but this behavior is a sure sign of affection. Hey, wait a minute! Who's walking who? Whether you are being welcomed home by your excited best friend or responding to your question about possibly wanting to go outside to play, these excited behaviors are definitely a recognition that you are the alpha parent and is also an important part of your pet's maturation and social development. Of course, the tricky part is making sure that enthusiastically acting out the excitement does not become too overbearing, especially in interactions with strangers or small children. With proper training and exercising control when appropriate, you can let your dog know that you appreciate his enthusiasm, and you are ready to return the attention and affection. And my gosh, how many TV news reports and YouTube videos have you seen featuring a service member or pet owner returning from a long separation from their dog? These reunions are heartwarming, often hilarious, and clearly demonstrate the strong, unbreakable bond between dog and master.

But, even with all of these displays of affection, we have not answered the question of a dog's ability to experience love. As with humans, it's complicated. Even we are often confused by feelings we have for others, as friendship and love are not the same. For me personally, I love my dog, period. It's just a fact. But does *he* love *me*? He certainly exhibits every one of the ten behaviors listed above - each and every one. But I want to find out more. A good place to begin our search is to look at the neuroscience of attraction, affection, and love.

Research has provided considerable insight into the neuroscientific interactions involved with affection and love. While the mystery of what triggers love and affection remains often debated, from a neuropsychological perspective we know that we can associate these feelings with certain chemicals we produce, predominantly in the brain. These chemicals or hormones are thought to create a type of "love cocktail", and their impact may be seen as they manifest in the form of observable, measurable physical symptoms: racing or irregular heartbeat, sweaty palms, flushed cheeks, and so on. Understanding the impact of these hormones is essential in studying the question of human/dog interactions, with a goal of determining if there really is mutual affection and, dare we say – love.

The five hormones or neurotransmitters that have a direct connection to affection and love are epinephrine, dopamine, serotonin, oxytocin and vasopressin. Neurotransmitters belong to the nervous system, while hormones are part of the endocrine system. These chemicals and hormones work together and some, such as norepinephrine, can effectively act as both a neurotransmitter between nerve cells and at the same time a hormone to regulate organs and glands. This hormonal orchestra can play a wide variety of tunes: from aggression to grief, elation to depression, from anger and hate to love. For the project at hand, we need to look at the similarities and differences between their impact on humans and our dogs.

We know that the brain chemistry and functioning in dogs reflects the same basic chemical interaction during changes in their emotional state as we experience as humans. Brain neurology suggests it is likely that dogs can experience emotions at least similar to ours, and we know that dogs have the hormone oxytocin, which is associated with affection and love in humans. If we study research into emotional development in humans, we may be able to then look at emotional and hormonal changes in our canine companions.

Psychologists agree that dogs appear to demonstrate experiencing emotions at a level similar to a child who is approximately two and a half years old. From my personal experience with my dogs over the years, I have certainly experienced my share of exposure to the "terrible twos". Two-year-old children are undergoing social and emotional changes, as they become more eager to strike out on their own and break away from strict parental control. As a result, and when they are then told they are expected to follow rules, this conflict can create the tantrums and inappropriate behaviors associated with this stage of their development. Could it be that your pup experiences the same type of developmental changes?

Research has also shown that human development has children showing various emotions developing over time. For example, within just a few months after birth, we can detect relative degrees of distress and agitation or contentment, followed later by fear and anger. At approximately six months, infants may begin to experience joy, as well as demonstrating suspicion or shyness. Observable affection or love may appear at about ten months, but more complex emotions such as pride, shame or contempt take years to develop. Similar to how dogs age compared to humans – the concept of "dog years" - dogs move through the emotional development stages more quickly and may not develop the more complex social emotions.

We are able to observe hormonal changes in humans both chemically and through brain scanning techniques. Dogs have the same hormones as humans, and while we can only speculate what the dog is actually experiencing *emotionally*, we can definitively measure hormone level. To begin, let's take a look at these five substances and the effect they have on humans and dogs.

Epinephrine

Epinephrine, often referred to as the "fight or flight" hormone, is a neurotransmitter released from the medulla oblongata of the adrenal glands and is also known as adrenaline. This hormone is produced when our bodies experience extreme stress, preparing the body for response. Together with norepinephrine, which increases blood pressure and heart rate and calls for the release of stored energy in the form of glucose, these hormones contribute to both physical and psychological conditions, including anxiety and depression. Regarding affection and love, epinephrine supports the initial feeling of attraction, which paradoxically includes an initial increase in our stress level, reflected in increased heart rate (be still, my heart) and increases in both respiration and perspiration. Of course, if that attraction develops into affection and ultimately to love, many other "ations" are possible – inspiration, cohabitation, desperation…

Dopamine

Sometimes called the "feel-good" hormone, dopamine is an important neurotransmitter that creates the feeling of pleasure, which one could argue is often associated with developing love. Dopamine impacts memory and attention and may also trigger sexual arousal. Some neuroscientists suggest that triggering the release of dopamine creates what we might refer to as *lust* (or horniness). Dopamine plays a role in many human functions, from memory and attention to sleep, mood and learning. Abnormally high or low levels of dopamine are associated with serious disorders, with low dopamine associated with Parkinson's disease and high levels linked to schizophrenia. Drug use may directly affect the brain by blocking the normal release and absorption of dopamine. Imbalances may also be associated with depression. Dopamine levels increase during sexual activity or eating our favorite foods, hence the "feel good" label. When individuals work to achieve higher levels of dopamine, behavior can include increased risk taking and addiction, seeking to satisfy their specific cravings.

Pretty dope, huh? We know that when a dog is engaged in playful behavior and appears to be "happy" or "having fun", dopamine is released from the dog's pleasure center, and the same occurs in humans.

Serotonin

Serotonin is a neurotransmitter that is associated with feelings of deep affection. Serotonin is a hormone released in the gastrointestinal tract, and it may also be found in the central nervous system. This hormone helps to regulate mood and is also known to alleviate depression. Serotonin plays a major role in part in our proper mental function, and it also regulates our sleep and appetite. Regarding love and affection, serotonin is associated with our feelings of infatuation, when our minds are focused on our feelings for another person. The presence of this hormone makes it difficult for us to think about anything other than the one to which we are attracted, and our thoughts are often preoccupied, obvious to others. In the 2004 American Psychiatric Association's Sex, Sexuality and Serotonin conference, Dr. Helen Fisher explained that, "Serotonin-enhancing antidepressants also suppress obsessive thinking, which is the very central component of romantic love." When we are interacting with our dogs through petting and positive social contact, serotonin levels increase in both of us.

Oxytocin

Oxytocin is often referred to as "love hormone" or "cuddle hormone." This has been a favorite subject among neuroscientists when researching about brain chemicals that can influence positive emotions among people. It is produced in the brain by the hypothalamus gland, and its primary function is to prepare the mother for childbirth by stimulating milk production in the breast by widening the ducts for milk secretion. In the developing relationship between mother and child, newborns already have levels of oxytocin in their bodies, and it is this interaction between the hormonal level in the child and its mother that serves to create the mother/child attachment. In humans and in dogs, the hormone increases during hugging, touching, sexual intercourse or other direct physical interactions. In humans, the level of oxytocin rises significantly during the period of falling in love. If dogs do, in fact, experience love, we would expect to see a similar rise. When we are petting our dogs, we release oxytocin, adrenaline and serotonin, creating a hormonal cocktail combination of anti-stress and reward hormones. At the same time, this interaction results in a decrease in the hormone cortisol, associated with stress, just more reason studies of animal-assisted therapies have shown a positive impact across virtually all patient groups.

Vasopressin

Vasopressin, which is commonly known as ADH or the *antidiuretic hormone*, is released and stored in our brain's pituitary gland, a small pea-sized gland located just below the hypothalamus. Vasopressin is responsible for controlling and maintaining the water content of the body, referred to as *homeostasis*. Homoeostasis is the process of fluid reabsorption, and vasopressin controls the water content in our bodies. In terms of love and affection and together with oxytocin, these hormones are responsible for the feelings of attachment. Regarding our relationships with our pets, these two chemicals combine to stimulate affection and social bonding. In humans, during sexual intercourse and in achieving orgasm, the levels of both vasopressin and oxytocin rise significantly. Interestingly, studies have shown that dogs who are more aggressive have higher levels of vasopressin, with lower levels in service and companion dogs.

With this neuroscientific evidence as a backdrop, we now know our canine companions experience the same types of developmental and hormonal influences we do as humans. What we do *not* know is whether a dog experiences the same types of *emotions* as you and I do. We can say definitively that they are subjected to the same neurobiological effects and probably see similar types of developmental stages to those we experience over our lifetime, albeit on a somewhat faster cycle, but we cannot conclude what they actually *feel*. We want to believe that the crazy, frenetic displays we see constantly reenacted time and time again as owners are reunited with their dogs after a long separation represent not just a strong emotional bond, but actual, pure, true love. If only we could sit down with our dogs and ask that important question. If only they could tell us how they really feel. If only…

Three

The Mission. The Money.

Dogs have no money. Isn't that amazing? They're broke their entire lives. But they get through. You know why dogs have no money? No Pockets.

~ *Jerry Seinfeld*

If we were to answer the complex questions of a dog's ability to love, experience emotions, dream and communicate effectively with humans, we needed a game plan. We would need to create a methodology for non-invasive observational testing, which may provide insight into the canine mind, using the latest cutting edge and emerging technologies in the same manner we employ them for similar studies in humans.

In outlining the objectives for this daunting mission, I identified five key goals.

1. First, we will choose a selection of test subjects, which should include both sexes and a variety of breeds. Fortunately, since I already had relationships with owners who had previously

sought canine psychological counseling for their dogs exhibiting various types of behaviors, that seemed like a logical place to start. My thought process was that if we could actually gain insight into a dog's inner thoughts, we would have a better chance of canine counseling success in the future.

2. Second, we hope to peer into canine brain activity, with a goal of observing behaviors most often associated with love and affection. In doing so we will consider comparisons to the human brain, our own hormones and other similarities, using similar testing techniques and technologies.

3. Next, we will measure canine brain activity during relaxed, undisturbed sleep, searching for analogies to human patterns, REM dreaming, and so on.

4. Fourth, taking it a step farther, we will use recent advances in technology to monitor brain functioning and brain waves during the subjects' dream state and develop conversion algorithms, which can provide insight into the actual dream experience through visualization and other experiential methods. Provided these dream sessions are successful, we will look for

methods to create channels of dog-human communication in an awake state.

5. Finally, with the knowledge from the brain activity and dream studies, we will conduct a series of human/dog "conversations" to gain additional insight, with a goal of learning more about canine behaviors and, if warranted, determining effective treatment approaches and regimens.

Wow! Just reading that list again now, I vividly recall how truly insurmountable these objectives appeared to be. Chief among the potential barriers to success? First and foremost: where would we get the *money*? Who would see our mission as worthy of funding? What are the likely sources we should approach in our search for loans, grants and investments? Since this research had never been conducted, how can we convince potential funding sources of its value? In order to consider these and other questions, put yourself in my shoes, and imagine a presentation to a bank, investment group, sponsors or individual investors. Let's practice our pitch.

Me: "Good morning, my name is Dr. Ron Cook, and I am here today to ask for your support for a groundbreaking research study, one which will allow us to eavesdrop on dogs as they dream, allowing us to actually experience those dreams and hopefully use this information to identify and treat canine mental conditions and disorders and provide proper psychological counseling, just as we would with human subjects."

Banker/Sponsor/Investor: "Welcome, Dr. Cook. We have just one question before you begin your presentation. Say *WHAT?* You want to do *what*, exactly?"

Me: "We will use recent technological advances to combine real-time functional MRI imaging, EEG brain wave monitoring, supercomputer data processing capabilities, complex data conversion algorithms, virtual reality and other visualization and audio translation technologies to observe dog dreams in real-time, with the goal to help dogs deal with issues we have identified from their dreams."

(Unintelligible boardroom audience conversation) Then, after a few minutes…

Banker/Sponsor/Investor: "Oh, I see. Just one more question, doctor: WTF? I mean, are you freakin' serious? Is there a hidden camera somewhere? Are we on *Ellen*? Is this your idea of a clip for *America's Funniest Videos*?"

Finding one or more funding sources would require substantial research, development of formal proposals and grant applications, and in-person meetings and presentations to a variety of audiences. Would we be able to find a person, group, institution or foundation that shares our passion for answering the complex questions we have posed in our hypothesis?

Of course, even if we were fortunate enough to secure funding for the project, it remained to be seen if we could actually master the technological hurdles. To date, while researchers had been able to do limited brain scan studies of dogs, no one had been able to actually convert that data to real-time visualizations. While our plan was theoretically possible, the technology had not yet been perfected, much less tested on canine subjects.

We would need a physical facility for our research laboratory, with 24/7 access and security. Considering the types of equipment required to conduct our research – functional magnetic resonance imaging, electroencephalography, vital sign monitoring, supercomputing and artificial intelligence, high definition video, advanced audio processing and a control room with significant monitoring equipment and data storage – we would need a considerable amount of space.

The sexiest gear on the planet is only as good as the people who are trained to use it. We need a truly world-class team of researchers, highly-trained, well-credentialed men and women capable of understanding and embracing the mission, but who are also willing to operate according to our unusually demanding research schedule, both in terms of the accelerated time schedule due to budgetary limitations, but also the fact that we would be conducting *dream research*, requiring overnight observation, followed by time-consuming data analysis.

Finally, even if we were able to capture functional MRI and EEG data and convert them into usable information that we can both visualize and hear, there was no guarantee we could then translate that data into something we humans can understand. The bottom line is that, as with any scientific pursuit, there is always the potential for failure, along with the possibility that initial funding will prove insufficient to get us to a working proof of concept. Such is the fate of many high-tech startups. They get off to a great start, only to run out of money before their prototypes have validated their product or service offering.

Returning to the topic of securing the funds necessary to accomplish our ambitious mission, funding for scientific research is analogous to the plight of a politician. We spend an inordinate amount of time fundraising, leaving precious little time for the research itself. Since traditional financing methods are not available, our funding channels are limited primarily to government and foundation grants. For our project, non-traditional methods such as crowdfunding may seem like the perfect way to tap into the dog-loving community but doing so would violate the secrecy and strict confidentiality of our mission. Imagine being asked to participate in a Kickstarter or GoFundMe crowdfunding campaign for UFO and extraterrestrial research – you get the picture.

Left with few choices, I made it my mission to fully research potential grants by focusing on those organizations with a direct interest in a better understanding of canine behavior. Examples include the American Kennel Club (AKC) Canine Health Foundation, the Association of Professional Dog Trainers (APDT) Foundation, the Morris Animal Foundation and limited graduate student research grants from the Animal Behavior Society. Various other grants were targeted at specific breeds or training needs (K9, working dogs, etc.) and are unfortunately too limited and programmatic for our project. While I am quite familiar with the grant writing process, I also realized that, just as with a pitch to angel or other investors, I would need to be *extremely* careful not to use terminology that might potentially make the project objectives sound more like science fiction than serious research.

"Hey Joe, guess what? Some guy sent a request to help him talk to dogs!"

"So what, Pete? I talk to my dog all the time. He doesn't listen, though."

"No, I mean he wants a grant so he can *literally* talk to dogs, and they can talk to him."

"Seriously? What do you tell him?"

"I told him he was barking up the wrong tree."

"Good one, Pete!"

After several months of grant writing and submission, followed by countless follow-up calls and emails, I was extremely discouraged. The few requests for additional information I did receive got immediate and detailed responses, and I began to think that my very honest and direct clarifications may well be the reason I never heard back from any of them. As I found myself slipping into a self-diagnosed minor depression, one day I received an email inquiry from a group I had not heard of previously. The Beatrice Upton Taft Trust, which represents the Sleep Neurology Institute Freedom Foundation, had apparently heard about our project and was asking for more information. Before responding, I did some research on the organization in an effort to more directly align the grant proposal funding request with the mission of the foundation. I learned that the foundation was established in 1894 following the passing of an eccentric and reclusive billionaire, who had included only a few select causes in her will. Beatrice Upton Taft was the widow of Horace Wilson Taft, the famous industrialist and philanthropist.

Beatrice was a successful businesswoman in her own right, best known for her numerous inventions and patents, including an innovative approach to canine incontinence, the *Doggie Diaper*. Although that particular creation did not find wide public acceptance, Mrs. Taft was also widely known as a huge dog lover. From my research, I found that the reports of her love for dogs were often grammatically incorrect, leading some to believe that she loved huge dogs. Further research, however, revealed that Beatrice tipped the scales at over 300 pounds, so she was indeed huge, and also a dog lover. So much for misplaced modifiers…

It seems that Beatrice owned a number of dogs over the course of her life, and her favorite among them was Bosco, an imposing English Mastiff, with a friendly, wrinkled face and playful temperament. Since her large size made it difficult to navigate her stately mansion's extensive formal gardens, Beatrice invented a type of dog-drawn chariot with a comfortable throne-style seat for her ample dimensions. Like a scene from the Alaskan Iditarod sled dog race, Beatrice's dog butlers would hitch Bosco to the big-wheeled contraption and make sure she was comfortably situated on her throne. Then, after a loud "Let's go, Bosco!" the obedient and muscular canine would accelerate quickly, creating a harrowing romp throughout the formal gardens, lawns and fountains of the expansive Taft estate, as Beatrice held on for dear life.

Close your eyes and imagine an intricate mashup-type combination, combining the most vivid elements of Santa's sleigh on Christmas Eve, the famous chariot race from *Ben-Hur*, and a frenetic chase scene from just about any *Scooby-Doo* adventure. Careening around corners and kicking up pea gravel from the pathways, with Beatrice cackling uncontrollably all the way, the sprint would continue until she bellowed "Whoa, boy!", followed by a quick deceleration, eventually rolling to a safe, complete stop. Unfortunately, my research also revealed that after Bosco's passing, his replacement "Scooter" (ironic, I know) was not nearly as agile and nimble. This resulted in a tragic accident in which Mrs. Taft was ejected on a turn, smashing into a concrete column at the base of an ornamental fountain, and resulting in her untimely death and a quite spectacular water geyser.

Beatrice Taft's legacy lives on in the causes the Trust and associated foundations actively support today. Fortunately for our project, Beatrice was fascinated by the strong bond between dog owners and their canine partners. In fact, and thanks to the exceptional artistry of a local taxidermist, Bosco still stands guard in the lobby of SNIFF building, which occupies a remote corner of the estate grounds, just a few hundred yards from the formal gardens. A plaque at the base is a fitting tribute from Mrs. Taft: "My beloved Bosco. We had a great ride!"

According to the email inquiry, the BUTT family trust and SNIFF foundation support research into all neurological aspects of canine sleep, dreaming, and human bonding relationships. Bingo! I crafted my response carefully, as though I was creating a custom resume to match specific job requirements. After several email exchanges and conference calls, I submitted our formal grant proposal and funding request. To this day I vividly remember the exact day and circumstance when the letter arrived in the mail. I had just returned from another dismal and disappointing presentation to a regional private equity group, referred by a now former friend, with an assurance that "These guys really love dogs and will really 'get' the technology, brah." Granted, I was not physically ejected from the boardroom, but from the combination of facial expressions and not-too-subtle giggling, I got the picture, as well as the type of parting "next steps" assurance a guy would get from a girl he had just picked up as the bar closed at 2AM. You know, the one promising him she would be right back after she powdered her nose. Yeh, right…

Oops, back to the letter! As I turned into the driveway, I remembered to check the mail, having been on the road for two days. Sorting through the usual collection of bills and junk mail, my eyes caught a familiar image in the return address area of the envelope. The BUTT SNIFF logo was unique and easily recognizable, leaving little to the imagination. I threw the other mail onto the car seat and ripped opened the letter.

> Dear Dr. Cook:
>
> After careful consideration of your grant application by the Foundation's Board of Directors, we are pleased to inform you that your proposal has been approved for funding. Enclosed is our check in the amount of Three Million Five Hundred Thousand Dollars ($3,500,000). Your endorsement will signify acceptance of the terms and conditions outlined in our initial grant receipt acknowledgement.
>
> We are impressed by the scope and mission of your project and are honored to support such a worthy undertaking. On behalf of Beatrice Upton Taft, the Foundation and all of us at BUTT SNIFF, we wish you much success. We know that Beatrice is smiling down upon us all. As Beatrice liked to say: "Looking forward to a great ride!"
>
> Sincerely yours,
>
> Herbert Winston Taft
> Managing Director

Please note that, at this point and as you are now reading this, at the time my brain had not been able to process anything beyond "...your proposal has been accepted for funding." Neurons were active, synapses were firing, but my eyes were two laser beams constantly scanning the word "approved", as if to require a hundred reverifications just before my head would surely then explode. Are you freakin' kidding me? $3.5 million! OMG! We can finally stop buying those damn lottery tickets!

Following the initial shock, my immediate reaction was that I could not wait to tell my team, at least until I stopped to realize the obvious. I didn't *have* a team! Oh no! I would need to start working on that!

Four

The Team

Alone we can do so little,
together we can do so much.

~Helen Keller

If you have watched the Oscars, Emmys, Grammys or virtually any award show, you know that the winners always take the time to recognize the people who most contributed to their success. That typically means a list that includes everyone from God to mom and dad, a spouse or partner, producers, directors, writers, costume designers, cast and crew. It could be a 7th grade teacher who was particularly influential in spotting and nurturing budding talent, or that weird girl who kept harassing me throughout high school. The fact is that success in any field is rarely a singular accomplishment. Our research has not won any awards, at least not yet, but to this day I often stop to marvel at how lucky and truly blessed I have been to have assembled such an amazing and capable team of experts, a group of dedicated researchers who share a collective obsession for unlocking the secrets of the canine mind and passionate about using recent advances in technology to discover the answers to what had to date been unanswerable. Whether our research ever sees a Nobel prize or receives significant scientific award recognition, I will not wait until we stand together on a world stage to properly recognize my outstanding team. Besides, several of them have threatened me in various ways, and recognition in these pages is a small price to pay, especially in comparison to the blackmail proposals that have filled my inbox.

Valued readers, I am pleased to introduce our research team.

Calvin Grant is the team's Chief Environmental Officer. As CEO, he oversees all aspects of maintaining optimum environmental conditions for the sleep chamber and *Dreamlab*, an essential element in ensuring a consistent research environment. This includes temperature and humidity control, room ventilation, ambient lighting and creating a comfortable sleeping area for each of our research subject animals. This includes working directly with the dogs' owners to collect and return personal effects such as blankets, towels, stuffed animals or other items to help the dogs feel at home during each research session.

Calvin suffers from Poop Preoccupation Syndrome. PPS is considered a less severe and non-debilitating offshoot of Obsessive-Compulsive Disorder (OCD), in that the subject is fixated on feces, in this case, canine. As with any obsessive syndrome, PPS may also be classified as a *disorder* if and when the condition "directly interferes with the subject's daily routine" (disrupts the subject's normal sleep pattern, adversely impacts the ability to arrive at work on time, maintain normal social relationships, and so on). Calvin does not recall when he became so fixated on excrement, although it may stem from one of his first jobs as a teenager, when he was a scuba diver for Roto-Rooter, troubleshooting septic tank problems. Friends would often tease him: "Man, you really jumped into some shit!"

During his studies at Florida Polytechnic Institute, Calvin's groundbreaking research into creating a healthier dog food and widely acclaimed scholarly article: *Whoa! I Wouldn't Feed that to my Dog!* formed the basis for a now-patented formulation, which consistently results in the "perfect poop." Recipient of the prestigious Purina Award for Advances in Canine Nutrition, Calvin perfected the *Poopometer*, a measurement methodology that assigns numerical values to poop firmness, on a scale of 1 (loose like a goose) to 10 (thick as a brick).

Calvin's most recent invention is a patent pending "pooper scooper" type contraption he tentatively named

Suck it Up! Calvin proudly boasts: "For dogs, I've got 'em covered goin' in and comin' out." The prototype design uses a high capacity, battery-powered Dyson pole vacuum and cup-shaped collection device to suck in the poop at the push of a button, depositing it in a biodegradable disposal bag inside the unit. Based on his recent industry recognition and accomplishments, Calvin is confident that these and future creations will secure his financial future. As Calvin likes to say: "One day, I'll be rollin' in it!"

Dwayne Higgins is our research data statistician. Our project produces a *huge* amount of data in a variety of formats, all of which must be captured, stored and analyzed. Examples include monitoring vital signs, fMRI and EEG data, including brainwaves, and cataloging the vast amount of video and audio expected to be recorded from the dream sessions. Dwayne is a recent graduate of the University of Central Florida, where he earned a Master of Science degree in data mining. UCF describes this highly specialized field as "the process of exploration and analysis of large quantities of observational data in order to discover meaningful patterns and models." This, along with a strong endorsement from the Dean and the fact that Dwayne lived within a few miles of our laboratory, made Dwayne a perfect fit for our all-night research sessions. In fact, over the course of our rigorous research schedule, he often rode his bike to our laboratory facility.

Dwayne lived alone, and while his demanding school schedule had never allowed him to care for a pet, it is clear that he loves dogs and he reminds us constantly how excited he is to be part of our research team. Dwayne is an avid gamer, so no stranger to late night sessions, and he frequently competed in several eSports competitions, including the Fortnite World Cup. He hopes that eventually his dedication to eSports will pay off financially, but for now he was happy to add our project to his growing resume, which he believes will ultimately position him well for job opportunities with one of the large eSports production companies.

Chad Wilson is our amazing Information Technology guru, responsible for all aspects of our complex information systems, including the supercomputing capabilities of IBM's Watson, artificial intelligence, dream visualization translation, and all data processing and storage. Chad is a Beta Gamma Sigma, Summa Cum Laude graduate of MIT with a PhD in Artificial Intelligence, specializing in IoT and machine learning. Interestingly, while at MIT, Chad had a successful career as an exotic dancer (aka: male stripper), underwear model and (bad) actor, with minor roles in blockbuster films you might (not) recognize, such as *Debbie Does Des Moines* and *Mooning Minneapolis.*

Fortunately, Chad's technical expertise far exceeds his acting ability, and several years ago he secured a patent for a Bluetooth beacon activated proximity collar for dogs, the *Invisible Leash.* This ingenious invention uses the same canine training and reinforcement collar used by the more traditional "invisible fence" yard boundary systems, but pairs it via Bluetooth with a mobile app. If the dog ventures too far ahead of the owner or otherwise moves outside of a defined radius when out on a walk, the collar provides a correction based on the severity of the infraction, ranging from a slight vibration, audio tone, mild electric shock or ear-piercing audible siren.

For our research project, Chad developed a non-invasive hormonal monitoring system, which uses low-power radio waves in the 40 GHz range through sensors embedded in an adhesive patch. The approach is similar to non-invasive glucose testing for diabetics. We hoped this novel approach would allow us to establish continuous, real-time monitoring of the five hormones previously mentioned so that we display that information alongside our subjects' vital statistics.

During the interview process, Chad confided that he became interested in canine behavior as a result of his own idiosyncrasies. When I pressed a bit, I found that Chad is a classic self-diagnostic. Now, he has a PhD in artificial intelligence but is apparently not smart enough to know that even we psychologists never believe we can properly identify our own shortcomings. In Chad's case he seemed a bit tentative and embarrassed, so I was reluctant to pry further, but he soon opened up and shared what was on his mind.

"I'm dyslexic." Chad said sheepishly.

"What's the big deal?" I quickly responded. "That includes as much as 10-15% of the population. You know, Thomas Edison, Stephen Spielberg, Charles Schwab – all dyslexic."

"Charles Schwab?" Chad seemed to be checking my facts.

"Absolutely! Charles Schwab and many other brilliant and successful people."

"No, I mean – who is Charles Schwab? Is he a scientist?" Chad was curious.

"Well, he's kind of an *investment* scientist, I suppose." I responded.

"OK, cool." Chad seemed satisfied with my reassurance but went on to share further details.

"I'm also agnostic." He looked me straight in the eye, as if to intently prepare for my response.

"Agnostic?" I'm sure I looked puzzled. "That's not a physical or psychological disorder, you know. It's a personal belief system."

"Yeh, I know that. I'm also an insomniac." Chad was now looking at me as though I needed to offer some type of support, diagnosis or offer of counseling.

"So, let me understand this. You are a dyslexic, agnostic insomniac?"

"That's right." He nodded affirmatively.

"Chad, what the hell does that even *mean*?" I asked incredulously. "I mean, *seriously*?"

Chad seemed a bit shaken by my seeming lack of concern.

"Oh yeh? You don't think that's bad? To me it's very serious." He seemed agitated.

"No, Chad – I'm sure sometimes it's troubling. I mean, *how does it affect you*?"

"Well last night, for example, it was really bad. I stayed up all night, struggling with a question I know has been debated for centuries: Is there really a doG?" (Give it a minute…)

Dr. Kathy Chan is responsible for the implementation of our functional magnetic resonance imaging (fMRI) equipment and was also instrumental in the development of the electroencephalography (EEG) technology we chose, including the prototype lightweight wireless sensor cap, which when paired with the hormonal monitoring module, we collectively dubbed the "nightcap". Kathy is originally from the Institute of Biomedical Engineering at prestigious National Taiwan University, where she earned her PhD in Biomedical Engineering with a concentration in Biomechanical Engineering and Biolectronics. Biomedical engineering is a discipline that integrates biology, medicine and engineering technologies to solve biomedical engineering problems. In our case, that included the need to completely reconceptualize functional magnetic resonance imaging technology, creating in essence an environment that both disguises the gargantuan equipment and also greatly reduces what had typically been a very noisy and confined tube, not a very inviting environment for humans or animals. After finding a potential solution through the work of neuroimaging scientists at the Georgia Institute of Technology, we hoped to be able to use recent technological advancements to cobble together a prototype for field testing. The result is somewhat similar to an "open MRI", but with a more spacious main chamber, as well as significant noise reduction, rendering the machine extremely quiet, with a barely noticeable low frequency hum.

With her strong background in bioinstrumentation and medical microsensors, Dr. Chan took on a major redesign challenge, developing an ultra-lightweight electroencephalograph (EEG) sensor system, one which overcame two significant obstacles. Traditional EEG technology requires the direct attachment of small metal discs (electrodes) directly to the scalp, with a wiring harness connected to adjacent brainwave monitoring equipment. In our case, if the dog was sedated that might be possible, but since our objective is active brain wave monitoring during a dream state, we needed another option. Kathy's ingenious solution uses electrical induction, the same technology that supports wireless charging of phones and other devices.

This allows the electrodes to be woven into a lightweight elastic “cap”, positioning each sensor perfectly directly over the proper area of the canine cranium. The cap size is easily adjustable, and in another significant breakthrough, Kathy developed a multi-channel *wireless* transmission system. This never-before attempted approach means that there are no wired sensor leads connecting the headgear to our monitoring equipment. Think of it like a major concert performance, with each singer using a wireless microphone on a discreet channel of its own. The result is much less obtrusive, so our subjects should be much more accepting of the lightweight, comfortable *nightcap*, with no adverse impact on restful sleep. Problem solved!

José Ortiz is our amazing fMRI lead lab technician, responsible for capturing real-time imaging of our subjects' brains while the dogs are sleeping. It is this live input, along with the EEG brainwave data, that combines to feed into our visualization algorithm, which then translates the data into a video signal we can display on our high definition monitors. Provided it actually functions as designed, the resulting visualization should allow us to both see and hear what the dog is experiencing, as it transitions to REM sleep and dreaming begins. Keep in mind that our design is strictly a prototype based on a series of theoretical assumptions, but Jose is confident the arrangement will work. We would soon find out.

José comes to us from the prestigious Computer Vision laboratory at the University of Barcelona (CVUB), where he was the lead researcher for neuroimaging processing and analysis using structural and functional MRI in the study of Attention-Deficit/Hyperactivity Disorder (ADHD). The project was part of a consolidated research group, which included the Regional Government of Catalonia, Spain. At the time, José was a PhD candidate on loan from the University of Barcelona, where he planned to return at the conclusion of our project, with a goal of becoming an Associate Professor. He is quite a colorful character, an accomplished flamenco musician known for his infectious laugh and jet-black ponytail.

Before enrolling at CVUB, José was a well-known bullfighter, a matador famous throughout the region for his elaborate flamenco footwork as his cape taunted the bull before spinning safely away as the enraged animal charged forward, a magnificent spectacle. Bullfighting was banned in Barcelona in 2010, and although the ban was overturned in 2016, the sport is now nonexistent in Catalonia. Bullfighting is deeply rooted in Spanish historic traditions, though naturally controversial in its treatment of animals, and many in the Catalonian region were happy to see it go. José participated in the last bullfight at the historic La Monumental coliseum in September 2011, where he sustained a non-life threatening but extremely embarrassing injury. Like many professional sports performers, José meticulously choreographed each fight, selecting just the right music and rehearsing his footwork and technique for hours on end.

As you may know, almost every bullfight ends with the matador killing the bull with his sword with dramatic flourish and spectacle, but in rare cases where the bull has put on an especially good performance and based to a great extent on the crowd reaction, the bull may be "pardoned", his life spared and sent to live out its days used for breeding. Such was the rare exception in José's final performance with a previously pardoned bull, known as El Diablo, translated simply: The Devil. José had faced El Diablo in a match the week before the final event, and the crowd reaction to spare the magnificent animal was overwhelming. Unfortunately, what Jose failed to realize was that he had selected precisely the same flamenco music track, a crowd favorite, as he had for the previous performance. That may not sound like a problem to you, but it turns out that bulls, especially those of El Diablo's noble pedigree, are extremely intelligent. So intelligent, in fact, that when the music started and El Diablo was released into the stadium, he actually stopped in his tracks and cocked his head as he immediately recognized the song. Of course, since José's matador rehearsals had carefully choreographed every move, anticipating the bull's reaction to each flourish of the cape, José began his routine in fine fashion, whirling and spinning to the cadence of the flamenco guitar music blaring from the stadium sound system as the announcer provided constant commentary. The cape seemed synchronized to the music, as each strum of the guitar punctuated José's perfectly timed footwork. His outfit, known as the *traje de luces* ("suit of lights") because of the many reflective sequins and reflective threads of gold and silver, consisting of the renowned tight pants and short jacket, allowing for full range of motion and designed to avoid the bulls' horns during the contest. A black *montera*, a traditional folk hat, the red cape, referred to as the *muleta*, and *estogue*, the sword used to deliver the fatal blow. In José's case the traje de luces was his favorite combination of gold and emerald green. Combined with the *machos*, tassels that hang from the jacket epaulets and the brilliant red cape, his outfit was the perfect combination for a perfect ending to a sport known worldwide for hundreds of years.

As the spectacle unfolded, José was clearly in complete charge, at least so he thought. The music played, the bull advanced, and José deftly spun just out of harm's way, as the cape kept El Diablo's gaze and full attention, a scene that was repeated to the delight of the crowd, as shouts of "Bravo!" and "Olé!" filled the stadium. At the same time and unbeknownst to José, El Diablo's memory was equally well choreographed, as his brain clearly remembered every move, especially those that had previously earned the admiration of the crowd and ultimately spared his life. So, El Diablo played his role perfectly, charging at precisely the right time, turning, then charging again, replete with the blaring nostrils and loud snorting one might expect from an enraged one thousand plus pound animal. As the song track reached a crescendo, José drew his sword with a flourish, the crowd went wild, and man and beast stared each other down for a final pass. The music blared, El Diablo pawed the ground, nostrils flared, with vibrating droplets forming a visible mucous mist. The low-pitched guttural snorting was now a full subwoofer-like rumbling growl, clearly audible throughout the stadium. The bull continued his focused stare, eyeing his opponent like a prizefighter just before the bell, kicking up dust and delighting the crowd as the scene intensified. José calmly stared into the bull's eyes, seeming surprised at the unexpected twinkle that met his stern, focused gaze. He brandished the red cape, as El Diablo shook his head and pawed the ground repeatedly, snorting loudly and drawing the cheers of the packed stadium audience. The bull charged, José stood his ground and executed his trademark pivot to the left as he prepared for the bull to pass. In José's mind, the next thing he would hear was "Olé!" and the roar of the crowd. El Diablo had a different plan, thinking to himself "OK, he's going to pivot left, thinking I will pass to the right." José turned, showing his back to the passing bull, who was not passing, but rather turning in exactly the same direction, his massive horns focused on the tight pants rear end directly in front of him. The crowd shrieked in horror as they watched the sharp horns precisely penetrate the two butt cheeks, each gluteus penetrated to the maximus, then thrust upward with a jerk, sending poor José flying in the air, landing at least 20 feet away, his face in the dust, as the audience roared their approval. "Olé! Olé! Olé!" The crowd of thousands was on its feet.

On the stadium floor, the matador lay motionless as several banderilleros scrambled to attract the bull's attention away from the injured José. El Diablo retreated, stopping about 50 feet away as help reached José, who was now conscious and being assisted to his feet. The crowd roared, as José slowly limped to retrieve his montera from the dirt. He turned to face the bull, but instead of placing it on his head, he swung it to cover his heart, bowing his head in a salute to his adversary. As the cheers grew deafening, an amazing thing happened. El Diablo raised his head as if to acknowledge the audience, as a professional golfer might tip his hat to the crowd. He then dropped on one massive knee, bowing his head briefly, before raising it to look straight into José's astonished stare. They say the sound from the cheering crowd could be heard in villages miles away. In all the years of bullfighting, this incredible ending is now legend throughout the world.

It may not seem so, but José was actually very lucky that day. Not only did the bull's horns puncture both butt cheeks *precisely* in the center, avoiding damage to surrounding organs, but also being thrown in the air is far preferable than being trampled and repeatedly gored, left for dead in the dirt. José spent just one night at the Vall d'Hebron Barcelona hospital, where doctors expertly repaired the wounds. Before surgery, José marveled at the types of imaging technologies used to evaluate his injury. It started with a simple xray, which confirmed there were no broken bones, followed by an MRI of the affected area and finally a CT brain scan to check for possible traumatic brain injury as a result of such a hard landing. Fortunately, all tests were negative, so the required repairs were fairly straightforward. In the operating room as he was told to count backward from 100, he only made it to 99, but he still swears he heard at least one ass joke before he went under: "Wait, what kind of crack was that?"

As he was wheeled into the recovery room following surgery and slowly emerged from the fog of anesthesia, he awoke to see through the corner of his bed's privacy screen a small crowd of doctors, nurses and hospital staff gathered around a large screen TV in an adjacent room. The sound was blaring, and he quickly realized they were watching a replay of the bullfight, and seconds later a loud combination gasp and cheer arose from the group – how embarrassing! He soon realized, however, that the event's outcome endeared him to not only those in attendance, but to all of the people of Spain. It was a fitting end to a longstanding tradition, one which no longer had a place in a more humane world. Before being discharged the following day, José spent the morning signing autographs and shaking hands with hospital staff and supporters. He received a huge ovation as his wheelchair finally rolled down a hallway filled with cheering admirers applauding and holding signs. Helped into his waiting ride, he looked back at the throng as the car pulled away and they chanted "Nuestro héroe: vaya con Dios." (Our hero: go with God.)

With bullfighting no longer allowed in Catalonia and knowing that pursuing a music career would not likely pay the bills, José decided to follow a completely different path. Fascinated with the technology that supported his successful treatment, he enrolled in the University of Barcelona and soon found his way to the Computer Vision laboratory, widely known for groundbreaking advances in neuroimaging technologies and analysis. Years later as a PhD candidate, he volunteered for a work-study project at a new hospital at Lake Nona Medical City, a 650 acre health and life sciences park in Orlando, near Orlando International Airport. Whether fate or complete coincidence, during his time there I bumped into him at a local Spanish music event benefitting the American Cancer Society, an organization I have long supported. He had volunteered his time and talent for the event, and my wife and I watched this talented, spirited young man as he wowed the crowd with his captivating flamenco guitar performance, hands racing up and down the frets at lightning speed. If you need a visual, imagine Antonio Banderas with mad guitar skills, reminiscent of his role as a gun-toting mariachi in the film *Desperado*. We quickly hit it off, and I soon learned that he was a big-time dog lover and so immediately intrigued by our project. Fate or luck, he was now part of our growing team.

Nathaniel Ferguson is our resident veterinary specialist. Nate hails from Australia, where his research into dingoes earned him considerable acclaim and notoriety, as well as incredible controversy. Dingoes are wild dogs, native to Australia, thought to have arrived there some 5,000 years ago. Unlike domestic dogs, Dingoes do not bark, but rather howl like their wolf ancestors. And like wolves, they typically belong to a defined pack, although they may hunt for prey alone. They feed on wallaby and kangaroo, as well as other smaller mammals – rabbits, mice and the like. While crossbreeding and domestication have rendered the dingo completely non-aggressive compared to its ancestors, ignorance and folklore fuel unfounded fear of the breed, seeing these beautiful animals as unpredictable carnivores. It is that public apprehension, coupled with a simple grammatical error, that quickly became Nate's worst nightmare.

Nate was enrolled in the School of Veterinary Science at the University of Sydney, one of the world's top programs for graduate employability. He was part of a small team of doctoral students studying dingo behavior, a worthwhile study, but not one that had received much public awareness, at least not until that one fateful day. A small group of Australia's national press correspondents were on campus interviewing university administrators, faculty and students from a variety of degree programs, and just so happened to visit the Veterinary Science lab, where Nate and his team were compiling their most recent research data. While virtually all of the dingo behavior research was field-based and conducted at various locations in southeastern Australia and New South Wales from Melbourne to Brisbane, the team had unofficially adopted several local dingoes close to campus, setting out water bowls and offering an occasional treat. As a result, it was not unusual for one or more to seek the shade of the campus buildings, especially during the warmer months.

On the day of the press contingent's visit, Nate's team had just finished recording the last batch of data in preparation for a final report at the end of the semester the following week. As they sat outside the veterinary building at a shady picnic table, the students enjoyed snacks and soft drinks, sharing their plans for the upcoming spring break. Chips, dips, cookies, cakes, sandwiches and all sorts of candies and other snacks covered the table. While certainly not the type of treats suitable for dogs or dingoes, a few local dog favorites were hanging out, hoping for a tasty morsel to drop.

Unaware that the press was rounding the corner, Nate jumped up when he caught one of the dingoes stealthily grabbing and running off with a candy bar. Purposely creating the most stereotypical and embellished Aussie accent, Nate yelled out to the group as he mock-chased the canine thief. "A dingo ate my Baby Ruth!" Then, in what was intended to be a humorous academy award winning performance, he feigned anguish and despair, lamenting his loss. Camera shutters clicked, video rolled, and reporters scrambled to get a scoop on the action.

It seemed all in good fun, at least until the following morning when the headline in the Sydney Morning Herald proclaimed *A DINGO ATE MY BABY, RUTH!* Oh no! Are you kidding me? This simple accidental comma insertion (ACI) started a chain reaction, beginning with the fact that the other major local paper, The Daily Telegraph, ran with the story without corroboration! Then a reporter with Australia's Sky News cable network (the country's version of CNN), after seeing that two respected newspapers were running the story, shared it as breaking news with few details, explaining they were dispatching a news team to the area to investigate. In the resulting confusion and with the exponential amplification of social media, soon every news outlet in the country scrambled to get more information, seemingly not too picky about the source and concerned only about grabbing and reporting content as quickly as possible.

Unbeknownst to Nate and his fellow students, who were enjoying sleeping in until noon following a late night, local residents were being interviewed by a steadily growing collection of reporters, effectively presenting them as knowledgeable sources, even though they had no clue as to what was actually going on.

"Yeh, mate, I seen the sneaky bastard you're talking about. That dingo had dinner on his mind, that's for sure."

While another chimed in: "Crikey! Once they get a taste of that sweet baby meat, there's just no stoppin' 'em. Keep your kids inside, I'm tellin' you!"

An obviously distraught woman clutching a young boy yelled out from her porch: "We're praying for you, baby Ruth!"

Within a few hours, armed vigilante groups were arriving in droves, carrying everything from cricket bats to pistols, shotguns and semi-automatic weapons, with all sorts of knives, swords and assorted long-handled garden tools thrown in for good measure.

When Jake's phone rang, he was just getting out of bed. As he answered, a frantic voice of a fellow student on the other end exclaimed: "Turn on the TV! Turn it on!"

"What is it? What's wrong?" Jake asked, puzzled and concerned.

The Sky News at Noon broadcast was leading with the dingo story. Apparently, the entire country was now obsessed with what began as a simple grammatical mistake and had now metastasized into a gargantuan fictitious fable.

"Oh my God!" Jake recoiled as he was fixated on the TV screen. "This doesn't make sense!"

Jake's teammate was jabbering nonstop as Jake hung up the phone, still staring at the screen.

The broadcast showed police in full riot gear forming a wall in front of the Sydney police station. Local residents and hundreds of protesters from who-knows-where held signs and occasionally yelled out, demanding justice for the purloined candy bar turned infant. Jake watched and listened in disbelief as the scene continued to unfold.

"Find baby Ruth! Save baby Ruth! Death to dingoes!"

Jake recoiled in horror. "Death to dingoes? What the hell? Are you f'ing kidding me?"

A firm knock on the door interrupted the situation. A male voice yelled out: "Police. Open up!"

Jake nervously opened the door to find a dozen SWAT team members in full combat gear filling the small porch of the apartment building.

"Can you please step outside, sir?" The SWAT Captain escorted Jake down into the yard with a firm grip on his arm, signaling the urgency of the moment.

Stepping into the front yard and a small seating area with a table and umbrella, the police Captain gestured to Jake to take a seat and began his questions.

“This dingo that took the baby, do you know where it is?”

“But it didn’t take a baby…” Jake’s response was quickly interrupted.

“Listen son, we know you love the dingoes, but a baby’s life is at stake here. Tell us where it is!”

Jake was shaking nervously. “Sir, uh…officer. This is a huge mistake. Please hear me out.”

“Son, if you don’t tell me exactly what happened… if anything happens to that baby, I swear I will personally…” This time it was Jake who interrupted.

“THERE IS NO BABY! THERE WAS NO BABY! The dingo took a candy bar, a Baby Ruth, so I yelled at him. He stole some candy and ran off. I have no freakin’ idea where he went. He’s probably sleeping off a sugar high right now. Geez! There is no baby. The dingo did not take a baby. THERE WAS NO BABY!” Jake stopped abruptly, realizing he was shouting at the top of his lungs.

The SWAT team seemed frozen, astonished at what they were hearing. The captain, now positioned mere inches from Jake's bright red face, leaned in, uncomfortably close and said in a soft, measured voice: "What did you say?"

Jake repeated. "It was a candy bar. A Baby Ruth. There was no baby, Ruth."

"There was a Baby Ruth, but no baby? Then where is the baby?" the Captain demanded.

Jake exploded: "THERE IS NO BABY, YOU WANKER! The dingo took my candy bar. Period. End of story. No baby. There was never a baby. Ask anyone who was there."

The SWAT Captain stepped back and turned slowly to face his officers.

"Well mates, you heard the man – no baby." Shaking his head, he continued: "Can you effin believe it? The dingo stole a candy bar! Should we arrest him for that?" The SWAT team erupted in a combination of laughter and Australian curse words too offensive and numerous to mention.

The horde of reporters who had been held at bay then quickly descended, and Jake calmly and deliberately recounted the story, one by one, until they all slowly drifted away. Within hours, the story spread throughout Sydney and eventually the country and internationally. I recall seeing it briefly on CNN. Of course, social media and occasional callers on talk shows soon began to push a conspiracy theory – a bunch of wacko, dingo-lovin' environmentalists engaged in a massive cover-up, a non-existent mother of a non-existent baby Ruth paid off by activists? Ruth is alive and well, hanging out with Elvis, Biggie and Tupac. Or maybe it was a sick publicity stunt staged by the current Italian candy company owner, Ferrero, as Baby Ruth sales skyrocketed and memes mysteriously appeared everywhere. Damn, people will believe anything!

But for poor Nathaniel, justice was not kind. After all of the press coverage, including reporting that the incident cost Australian taxpayers almost half a million dollars in police and emergency personnel during exhaustive, wide-ranging searches, the university decided that Nate needed to move on. Unfair, we might all agree, but the school would not risk the prestige of the veterinary program, so Nathaniel left for the U.S., and we are indeed fortunate to have him.

Oh, one other thing - the members of our team swear they have absolutely no idea how and why those candy bars keep popping up in our laboratory every so often, and Nate hates the fake Australian accents…

In addition to this diverse cast of characters and myself, rounding out our incredible research team are a dedicated group of highly qualified laboratory technicians, each with their defined area of specialization and responsibility. Considering the potentially groundbreaking nature of the research and resulting need for tight security and complete secrecy, I opted not to include student interns for this project. As a former educator, I assure you this decision was not taken lightly, but after much soul-searching and discussion with the team, we agreed it was simply too big a risk. If word leaked of what we were up to before we had the opportunity to complete our research and document our findings, the impact on the overall project could be catastrophic, jeopardizing future funding for what we hope will be an important second phase. I was confident that the team of professionals we had assembled will maintain strict confidentiality, eager to complete a never-before attempted look into the dreams of sleeping dogs. Our collective excitement was quite apparent and palpable, and we were finally ready to get started.

Five

Research Methodology

In order to really enjoy a dog, one doesn't merely try to train him to be semi-human. The point of it is to open oneself to the possibility of becoming partly a dog.

~Edward Hoagland

You must be dreaming!

If you have a dog, you have no doubt marveled at its ability to achieve deep and restful sleep. Admit it – you have even taken pictures of your sleeping pup! Occasionally you may observe some restlessness during sleep – tail wag or leg movement, and you may try to convince yourself that he or she is enjoying a blissful doggie dream state. "Look, honey. He's chasing a squirrel in his sleep." A cute thought. But what if it were true? *What if dogs dream?*

For centuries psychologists have speculated on the meaning of dreams, their purpose and why it is that dreams are so common to the human experience. Some suggest that dreams allow us to act out our unconscious fears and desires in a self-created safe setting, because doing so in the real world would prove too unsettling or even harm us in some way. Famed psychologist Carl Jung suggested that we dream as a mechanism for dealing with events that occur when we are awake. If we are successful, we may dream of the potential for loss or failure. If severe problems haunt us during the day, our dreams allow us to imagine a world without them. After years of research and hypotheses, even today we are still not sure why we dream, although most of us do so every night.

In the 1950's, researchers in Chicago conducted a series of sleep studies and discovered an interesting phenomenon – rapid eye movement (REM). They found that when study participants were awakened during REM sleep, they reported vivid dreaming in great detail, while others awakened during sleep phases other than REM seldom had similar reports. This was a monumental finding, in that previously most researchers believed that our brain is essentially inactive while we are sleeping. The Chicago findings demonstrated that the brain is very much active while we are sleeping, with increased activity during REM sleep. Subsequent studies showed that brain activity during REM sleep is substantially similar to when we are awake, but with an additional phenomenon – muscular paralysis. When your dog is sleeping and you see the occasional muscle twitch, we often think he must be dreaming, no doubt chasing a squirrel or running after a ball. These phenomena are known as myoclonic twitches. As with humans, the brain paralyses the major muscle groups. In fact, it is highly likely he *is* dreaming, and his main muscle groups, like ours, are temporary offline. Speculation is that while dreaming our brain is as active as during wakefulness, our body is frozen, unable to move. Most would agree this restriction may be a significant and necessary benefit, preventing us from actually trying to fly off our rooftop, float down our apartment stairs or decide we finally have the nerve to pick up the phone to tell our boss what we really think of him and his annoying wife! Our dogs share a similar experience; well, maybe not the boss part…

Research indicates that most dreams are associated with recent experiences and events, as if our brain is processing and organizing conscious and unconscious information we have just experienced, remembering or discarding portions of that data or possibly using it to solve problems or create future solutions. As some might say, by "sleeping on it". Our dreams are almost exclusively about us and, although others may appear, our dreams are naturally egocentric in that they are our way of acting out repressed emotions or imagine what we might become if we make changes in our lives. While there remains much we do not know about dreaming, over the years we have learned a great deal about the effects sleep and dream deprivation have on the human body, demonstrating that there is value in our dreaming and consequences if we are not allowed to do so. But the question still remains: *why* do we dream? Most of us spend almost one third of our lives sleeping, and the majority of people dream during a significant portion of that time.

All of this background then brings us to the subject at hand: *Do dogs dream?*

As we are determined to answer that question, we have several supporting facts to consider. As we have previously reviewed, the brain of a dog is similar to the human brain in several important ways. When we feel threatened or are directly challenged, our fear, anxiety and stress are palpable. These reflexive responses, feelings and emotions are controlled by the limbic system and, along with the hormonal similarities mentioned previously, this means it is likely that dogs experience and process these emotions in much the same way we do. Our higher-level reasoning, however, allows humans to control our emotions and make certain we lash out only as a last resort if mediation fails or if we determine an immediate threat requires quick action, such as in a true life-threatening situation.

Our similar brain also means that we share the same types of difficulties with social relationships. We can see similarities in reactions from young children and dogs in dealing with separation anxiety, for example. In both cases, the anxiety is reduced when the more developed brain provides reassurance that the separation is only temporary, to be reunited soon, so no reason to fear. Studies using a functional MRI have allowed a comparison of the same neuroimaging of brain activities with dogs and humans. The results indicate striking similarities and also differences. In both dogs and humans, the primary audio cortex sees more activity when exposed to happy sounds, and both humans and dogs respond more directly to sounds from their respective species. All in all, these similarities suggest the likelihood that, like us, our dogs may experience dreams in a manner similar to ours. Armed with that basic research background information, our goal was to determine once and for all whether dogs dream and, if so, what they dream *about*.

We know that on average, human babies and adults dream for about two hours per night. Researchers on the subject have found that people usually have several dreams each night, with each dream lasting between five to twenty minutes. If you do the math, you will soon realize that in our lifetime we will spend as much as six years dreaming! We know that there are several stages of sleep, which fall into two categories: rapid eye movement (REM) sleep and non-REM sleep. Non-REM sleep has three distinct phases, with each stage identified by specific brain wave patterns. In a given night we typically cycle through all stages of both non-REM and REM sleep, and it is the REM sleep phase in which most dreams occur. REM sleep may occur at various times during the night, typically starting about ninety minutes after you fall asleep. Of course, as with all things in life, each of us has our own unique sleep patterns, which may include taking relatively more or less time to fall asleep, as well as various durations for non-REM and REM stages. As a result, some people dream more than others, and the frequency and duration of dreams may vary widely from night to night.

Like humans, most mammals experience stages of REM and non-REM sleep, so it may seem reasonable to assume that dogs may experience a dreamlike experience. *But do they?* How can we know for sure? For this research, we would need to dream big! (no pun intended)

Important Disclaimer and Reassurance

We pause here to reassure readers that, just like the disclaimers on most major motion pictures that involve animals, *no animals will be harmed in any way by our research.* In fact, as a group of professionals with specializations in human and veterinary medicine, psychology, bioengineering, computing and visualization technologies, and data analysis, we committed early-on to ensuring that our research methodology complies with American Medical Association (AMA) and American Psychological Association (APA) limitations regarding animal testing, with an even greater commitment through comparison to human research ethical components and restrictions.

APA: Ethical Principles of Psychologists and Code of Conduct

If we want to study dogs or any animals, psychologists, scientists, researchers and medical professionals and bound by the Code of Conduct for their specific field. For example, for psychologists the American Psychological Association (APA) Code first refers to Principle A.

Principle A: Beneficence and Nonmaleficence

Psychologists strive to benefit those with whom they work and take care to do no harm. In our professional actions, psychologists seek to safeguard the welfare and rights of those with whom they interact professionally and other affected persons, and the welfare of animal subjects of research.

These guidelines were developed by the APA in part for use by psychologists working with nonhuman animals. They are informed by Section 8.09 of the *Ethical Principles of Psychologists and Code of Conduct*. The principles require that the acquisition, care, housing, use, and disposition of nonhuman animals in research must be in compliance with applicable federal, state, and local, laws and regulations, institutional policies, and with international conventions to which the United States is a party. APA members working outside the United States must also follow all applicable laws and regulations of the country in which they conduct research.

In keeping with these established standards for research involving animals, our commitment is simple: we will not do anything that might harm a dog, period. Full stop. Nothing. Nada. Zip. Zilch. That means we will need to look at the latest non-invasive technology and use only those methods and monitoring capabilities that do not adversely impact our research subjects in any way.

With that in mind, and as we set out to create a comprehensive research methodology with a goal of measuring and analyzing canine brain wave activity during sleep, we considered several technological advances, which we determined would be appropriate for this study. Magnetic Resonance Imaging (MRI) is a non-invasive test that uses powerful magnets, radio waves and computer analysis to peer inside our bodies. Doctors may want to look at a specific body area to diagnose a disease or injury, and follow-up tests help monitor the efficacy of treatment. Unlike X-rays and computed tomography (CT or CAT) scans, an MRI does not use radiation. In the 1990s the development of *functional* magnetic resonance imaging (fMRI) technology now allows the scientific and medical communities a safe and noninvasive means of imaging brain activity with extremely high resolution. As a result, the fMRI seems a perfect starting point for examining the canine brain and how it functions and responds to various stimuli. (Not to mention that a *CAT* scan would somehow seem both ironic and inappropriate!)

In considering using fMRI, we looked to previous research, including the work of a team of researchers at Emory University in Atlanta. In a groundbreaking study, they trained more than a dozen dogs to tolerate the noise and restrictions associated with an MRI. Through this detailed and well-documented research, these scientists discovered that part of the canine brain, which is associated with experiencing positive emotions, similar in many respects to those we experience as humans. The results of the Emory research revealed clues as to how and why our bond with our dogs is so strong, as well as how a dog senses and empathizes with emotions we are feeling, whether we are happy, sad, anxious or fearful. One of the primary researchers in the Emory study, neuroscientist Gregory Berns, worked with an Atlanta-based dog trainer to help acclimate dogs to actually enter and remain motionless in an MRI, quite a feat considering the noise associated with the equipment. Incredibly, and after months of training, Berns and his colleagues were able to secure and train volunteer subjects for the study.

Using testing techniques similar those employed with human subjects, researchers were able to see which parts of the canine brain were active, demonstrating that dogs use corresponding parts of their brain to solve tasks in ways similar to our own. For our project and building from the work of Berns, combined with the groundbreaking advancements in fMRI technology from the Imaging Research Lab at the

Georgia Institute of Technology, an amazing team of engineers, scientists, veterinarians and canine psychologists came together to create the missing piece of the puzzle. At Georgia Tech, Dr. George P. Burdell was able to create a fMRI that is both extremely accurate in its imaging *and also virtually silent.* This unit is also considerably larger than a typical tube-shaped MRI, more like an "Open MRI", much less restrictive and certainly less intimidating for our canine subjects, but there is still the issue of limiting movement of the subject when the fMRI is active. Dr. Burdell took advantage of advances in artificial intelligence to allow us to modify the fMRI's tracking of the subject's cranium, monitoring movement and adjusting the MRI *automatically.* The result of this advancement is that it finally allows us to peer inside the canine brain (some would be so bold as to suggest "mind"), while the dog is sleeping normally and over longer durations, automatically compensating for movement during the night. This important breakthrough provides a new and important tool in our research into the possibility that, like humans, dogs may actually dream.

Although our team grew quickly to a total of eleven research professionals at its peak, I must especially again credit my esteemed colleague Dr. Kathy Chan for her breakthrough research, which employs a special type of electroencephalography (EEG) in addition to the fMRI scan, producing a more complete and comprehensive "brain scan", which can then be used to infer what a human subject, or in this case an animal, is thinking, sensing and experiencing. Thanks to Dr. Chan, our specially designed EEG involves the use of a relatively small and lightweight sensor device with electrodes and sensors in the form of a wearable headgear which, even when combined with the hormonal monitoring module, we hope the dogs will not find too obtrusive or interfere with sleep.

When we use EEG to study human physiology and brain wave patterns, we attach wearable devices to our subject to measure a variety of physiological activity - heart rate, body temperature, respiratory rate, muscle tension, as well as brain waves. We typically refer to this combination of measurements as *biofeedback*. For human subjects, having this immediate and measurable feedback provides insight into various stimuli and how our body reacts, allowing us the ability to use biofeedback to make adjustments in our reactions. For example, if we are monitoring our brain activity in real-time when we are feeling especially stressed and again when we are meditating can help us learn to adapt and employ measures to restore a calmer state, slowing respiration and heart rate. By using the feedback to monitor our response to exercise, we can create a baseline against which to monitor how we are improving.

In our study with canine subjects, these goals are somewhat dissimilar, in that we simply want the ability to observe the biofeedback to determine when the dog begins a REM sleep stage, and then capture all available vital statistics, neuronal and brain wave pattern data to provide insight as to what the animal is experiencing. If that data proves to be very close to that we experience as humans, we might logically infer that some type of dream state may also be occurring. Realizing that we cannot ask Fido if he remembers the dream he had last night, capturing and converting the raw data via into visual and audio output should allow us to create a database, which can then be compared to other dogs, as well as to similar studies conducted with human subjects.

Measuring Brain Wave Activity

Brain activity measured through EEG can be extremely complex and difficult to decode for meaningful feedback but, at least for humans, generally we can categorize several types of brain waves and their associated functional state. The five (5) types of brain waves are:

- Delta Waves – Delta waves represent a deep, *dreamless sleep*. This state is relatively rare in adult humans, but often observed in the sleep patterns of newborn babies. We will be curious to see if there are similarities in measuring activity in the canine brain.

- Theta Waves – Theta Waves are most associated with dreaming sleep, what is often referred to as a stage of rapid eye movement, or *REM*. In humans, the REM stage is generally a goal for meditation or self-hypnosis. Research has shown that dogs also experience REM stage sleep.

- Alpha Waves – Alpha Waves are characterized by general relaxation or daydreaming. They may be observed when we are involved in activities such as watching TV or allowing our thoughts to wander. Would dogs reflect this same activity? We can certainly observe our dogs in a relaxed state, but are they *dog daydreaming*?

- Beta Waves – These waves represent our normal awake state, when we are engaged in our daily activities and conversation with others, in work or home settings. For our canine friends, this would include any waking activities. We will be interested in monitoring the transition from wakefulness to sleep, and vice versa.

- Gamma Waves – Gamma Waves are those that indicate a hyper-alert state. As a result, it is generally believed that this state represents the best opportunity for higher learning and greater insight. Will dogs exhibit this same level of brain activity? Anecdotal evidence suggests that when dogs are hyper-focused on learning or executing a particular skill, they are more likely to "learn" those behaviors.

In considering what we hope to accomplish with the fMRI and EEG sessions, we realized that with so much data now available for collection and analysis, the volume of information would be overwhelming, potentially taking months to fully analyze. We recognized early-on that if we are to be able to take full advantage of fMRI and EEG data for our subject animals, we need massive processing power. Enter IBM's Watson.

Watson is a powerful supercomputer system that oddly enough was originally created in response to a challenge on the quiz show *Jeopardy*. IBM Research took on the challenge of creating a type of (at that time) rudimentary artificial intelligence in the form of question answering (QA), as opposed to simply performing a fast, high-powered search of documents. To clarify the difference, instead of performing a simple keyword document search, returning a list of documents based on their page ranking and potential match, QA technology uses natural language and hundreds of analytical techniques in an effort to fully understand the question in greater detail, including context and intent. Watson won the *Jeopardy* challenge, beating champions Brad Rutter and Ken Jennings and winning the first-place prize of $1 million.

Since that initial iteration, Watson has continued to grow and develop, including the ability to actually "see" and "hear", as well as interpret and learn based on the information it processes. As advances in both the hardware and operating system have moved quickly ahead, Watson can now process more than 500 gigabytes of information, roughly equivalent to more than a million books, in just one second. Imagine Watson as a central processor, pulling from data storage in the form of millions and millions of documents, from encyclopedias, ontologies and taxonomies to dictionaries, journals and other sources. As a result, and with the ability to process such a wide variety of potential results in the blink of an eye, Watson was the perfect addition to our team, not to mention that we would not need to feed him, and he won't sit around after work drinking beer and complaining like the rest of us. Also, to our knowledge, he has never thrown up. The bad news is that he is coldly unforgiving when we do so.

Watson provided not only the ability to simultaneously process vast amounts of raw data, but also the ability to use machine learning and artificial intelligence (AI) to analyze these data points and then use cutting-edge virtual reality (VR) and other visualization tools to translate the data into a more comprehensible form. So now we have a virtually silent, high resolution functional MRI, a lightweight, wearable wireless EEG and hormonal monitoring sensor cap to observe brain wave patterns in real time, and the power of Watson's advanced artificial intelligence. This technological trinity provides the tools we need to conduct meaningful research and officially launch our three-pronged project, essential if we are to achieve our goal trifecta. OK, enough with the three-element references!

But the technical advances did not stop there. In fact, early in the project the Georgia Tech team accepted my challenge to move beyond mere visual imaging, adding the ability to convert brain waves into digital data that could then be converted to sounds and even speech. Of course, since none of us are fluent in dog, we then also need to further translate these sounds into something humans can understand. If we can use Watson's AI to translate the data we are collecting using the latest available VR and other visualization and audio processing equipment maybe, just maybe we can peer into what our beloved pets are experiencing when they sleep. If we are to actually be able to capture, translate and display actual dream visualizations with audio, we need to bring in some true experts in simulation and visualization technologies.

My research into the subject led me to Full Sail University in Winter Park, Florida. Full Sail is a private, for-profit University founded in 1979 in Ohio, initially focusing on training in the recording arts. Since its move to Central Florida in 1980, the university has grown to include degrees in film production, recording and live sound production, computer animation, game design and dozens of related degree programs, including undergraduate and graduate business degrees, as well as groundbreaking coursework in virtual and augmented reality and our specific need for simulation and visualization environments. After meeting the Program Director overseeing the simulation and visualization degree programs and especially considering the school's world-renowned reputation for recording and audio production, I knew immediately that this was the final piece in what was sure to be an extremely complex puzzle. An added benefit was the fact that the university had recently acquired a retail strip center adjacent to the main campus, affording us the opportunity to convert some of the vacant space into a temporary research facility, more than ample for our needs and with access to highly qualified technical experts and programmers who immediately saw our project as an opportunity to showcase their skills and craft a solution to our complex problem.

Over the next several months we were able to build out our laboratory in a top secret, stealth environment. Due to the nature of the curriculum, students at Full Sail University are accustomed to seeing all sorts of technical gear move in and out of various parts of the university, and I am sure many assumed our large MRI and control room equipment was part of a new degree program, so we were able to set up and restrict access to the laboratory facility. However, due to the highly specialized recording, film production, animation and game development degree programs, classes and access is 24/7, so we would likely see students around the clock, including the times our research subjects would be arriving and departing. As a result, our team agreed on the obvious and logical cover story. Our simulation and visualization project required overnight lab sessions, and we do not want to leave our dogs home alone - the perfect cover for our research. Better yet, the former strip mall parking lot is adjacent to a small park area, perfect for our canine test subjects.

After months of round-the-clock development and now with financial support in the form of the research grant from the SNIFF foundation, our prototype was finally ready for testing. The completed lab facility included the following key elements:

- The latest iteration of the patent-pending silent fMRI, which we affectionately refer to as "the pod", and is placed within the larger sleep chamber, which we nicknamed *Dreamlab*.

- Our electroencephalography (EEG) component combines the latest EEG sensing technology with specially designed non-metallic sensor leads, which eliminates interference with the MRI's powerful magnets. Our adjustable ultra-lightweight sensor caps were specially designed for dog craniums, and we employ 24 electrodes to measure brain wave activity. Early on, we affectionately named the EEG sensor headgear our "nightcap", a double entendre signaling a final step in sending our research subjects off to sleep. Additionally, our team was able to create a completely wireless network, with each sensor transmitting its discrete signal frequency, eliminating the need for a wiring harness, which the animal might find restrictive and inhibit restful sleep. In addition to brainwave activity, we are monitoring vital statistics: heart rate, respiration and blood pressure, as well as non-invasive continuous monitoring of hormonal levels.

- Our specially designed sleep chamber is of ample size for each of our identified volunteer subjects, but obviously limited to one animal for each session. It includes light-restricting shades, comfortable bedding and adjustable environmental controls, dialed in to create a comfortable and relaxing setting for each dog, while continuously collecting an amazing amount of brain wave and functional brain imaging data. Three high resolution Sony night vision 4K HD video cameras monitor the chamber, with each channel recorded continuously. To make the dog feel more at home, in each case we collected and introduced something from the home – a toy, towel or other object. Our specially designed ventilation system includes continuous air filtration, with the temperature maintained at a comfortable 72 degrees.

- Our master control room is a self-contained mobile office pod placed inside the former retail space and opposite the sleep chamber, allowing for 24/7 monitoring of the fMRI, EEG, vital signs and video cameras. In addition to the 24-channel wireless EEG monitoring, our equipment includes incredible supercomputing power in the form of a direct high-speed link to the Summit supercomputer at the Oak Ridge National Laboratory (ORNL) in Oak Ridge, Tennessee. Summit is a $200 million IBM AC922 system using 4,608 servers, including two 22-core IBM Power9 processors and six Nvidia Tesla V100 graphics accelerators for each processor. What does all that mean? Blazing fast speed, ultra-high definition graphics and, most important, the incredible artificial intelligence of IBM's Watson. We are truly blessed to have access to such amazing analytical capabilities.

- For *Dreamlab*, our goal is to use IBM's Watson AI, Summit's computing power and Full Sail's simulation and visualization expertise to create real-time visualization of the fMRI and EEG output, using a custom conversion algorithm to translate the digital output as the subject slips into a dream state and display and record both the biometric data and visual images, if any, while our subject is sleeping. To display Watson's output, along with the 3 video feeds from the lab, we are using 3 Samsung Q9FN QLED 65-inch monitors and a main dream visualization display – Samsung's Q900R QLED 85-inch monitor, featuring 8K resolution and a hefty $15,000 price tag. Ouch! If our conversion algorithm is successful, we should be in for some pretty spectacular visualizations!

Now that we have completely geeked out with our super-cool gear, we are ready to put it to use, and for that, it is time to introduce our research subjects.

Six

Going to the Dogs – Our Test Subjects

Money can buy you a fine dog,
but only love can make him wag his tail.

~ *Kinky Friedman*

Now that we have assembled a world class team of research professionals and have been fortunate enough to secure funding for our amazing research facility and *Dreamlab*, our focus turns to the real stars of the show – our research subjects. As noted previously, our selection process included three key criteria:

1. We want to include a variety of breeds.

2. We have identified subjects for whom their owners had previously sought canine counseling. If we can peer into the minds of this diverse group, we may be able to identify and address the root causes of any behavioral or psychological issues.

3. We will limit the number of subjects to ten (10).

There are three (3) reasons for this last point:

- Our *Dreamlab* facility is truly awesome, but we only have one sleep chamber, so we can only observe one subject over the course of an evening.

- Dealing with one subject per day means that we will need at least two weeks to review all 10 animals for the initial session, and we anticipate that each subject will require multiple sessions in order for us to collect and analyze sufficient data to identify issues and determine the best course of treatment.

- Finally, our team's lead research statistician, Dwayne Higgins, has some cognitive limitations. Specifically, Dwayne suffers considerable anxiety when confronted with simple math. While that may seem odd and an imposing limitation for a professional statistician and number cruncher, we have agreed to accommodate Dwayne's disability by keeping everything very simple and straightforward, at least mathematically. We tested this when we discovered the issue during the interviewing and training process, settling on a simple metric to allow for less stressful percentage calculations.

When we realized Dwayne's limitations, we first did some basic cognitive testing. Some excerpts:

"Dwayne, as we discussed, we will be looking at a total of 10 canine research subjects."

"Dogs, right?"

"Yes, Dwayne, they are dogs."

"That's cool. I like dogs. How many?"

"We will be looking at 10."

"Whoa! That's a lot!"

"Dwayne, if 4 of our 10 subjects respond positively to our study, what percentage would that be?"

"Hang on... 40%?"

"Great job, Dwayne!"

"Thanks, that wasn't too bad. Whew!"

"OK, Dwayne, buddy, let's start preparing for the dogs now."

"Oh, OK, thanks. I like dogs. How many?"

As a research team, we committed to supporting each other throughout this important project, and Dwayne is no exception. Plus, he has never complained about his paycheck, apparently not noticing his low level of compensation or the deductions for beer and snacks.

Without further ado, I am pleased to introduce our canine research subjects. [DJ – please cue *Who let the dogs out?*] We will start small.

Chihuahua

Pedro is a feisty little hombre. Or to paint the picture more honestly, this dog is one pissed off puppy. Pedro came from Mexico and crossed the U.S. border illegally at a young age three years ago, crossing from Nuevo Laredo on the Mexican side and finding sanctuary in Laredo Texas in Los Dos Laredos Park on the banks of the Rio Grande. At the request of his owners and after several in-home counseling sessions, I diagnosed Pedro as suffering from a type of Canine Napoleon Complex, commonly called Fortune Complex. It is possible you may have heard about Napoleon Complex, named after Napoleon Bonaparte. The disorder is a type of inferiority complex that may occur in people of short stature and is often characterized by aggressive and domineering behavior, thought to result from an effort to compensate for the person's stature. Fortune Complex is very much the same for dogs and is named after an important dog in Napoleon's family. Although Napoleon did not have dogs growing up, in 1794 when he met his soon-to-be wife Josephine, Bonaparte learned first-hand that dogs can be fiercely loyal to their masters. When Napoleon married Josephine in 1796, on their wedding night he found that Josephine's dog Fortune had claimed a spot in the bed, and when he tried to be intimate with his new wife, Fortune was not having it and attacked Napoleon, drawing blood and leaving a scar on his legs. Hmmm…a small dog attacks a small man on his wedding night. Maybe it really is true that size doesn't matter. In dogs, we typically find that Fortune disorder is triggered or exacerbated by some type of traumatic event, so I was intrigued to learn more about Pedro's history and how it may have impacted his condition.

After speaking with his current owner family, during therapy I was able to validate that much of Pedro's aggressive attitude was the result of bullying as a puppy. I learned that after successfully evading Immigration and Customs Enforcement border agents, Pedro was taken in by a family with two small children, who immediately claimed him as their own, and Pedro received plenty of care and attention. But that attention sometimes came at a price. On more than one occasion the young girl dressed Pedro up in pink ribbon and painted his paw-nails to match. Humiliated, Pedro was then unable to hide from the other neighborhood dogs, who taunted and heckled him relentlessly, calling him "Little Pink Pedro". Like kids, young dogs, especially adolescents, can be very hurtful and unkind, especially to a little Chihuahua. The short jokes were never ending and, very much like humans, the neighborhood dogs would occasionally gang up on Pedro, cornering him with threats and taunts. Their favorite tactic was a barrage of "yomamaso" ranking barbs, all dealing with how they imagined Pedro's mother's diminutive stature. Examples included "Hey Pedro, yo mama's so small, to take her picture you have to use a microscope." Or worse, "Yo Pedro, I asked yo mama if

I could borrow a few pesos. She said 'Sorry, I'm a little short'." "Hey Pedro, I heard yo mama got pickpocketed the other day. How could anyone stoop so low?" And on and on… How can dogs be so cruel to a fellow canine?

During counseling, Pedro's Napoleonic complex soon emerged, most likely as a defense mechanism. He soon learned that a small dog with a high-pitched, yappy bark is not going to impress the dogs of the barrio, no matter how many growls and teeth are exposed. But at a young age Pedro realized he had a very unique and special talent, an unusual weapon perfectly suited for his personality and a welcome addition to his arsenal. Growing up in a poor neighborhood in Mexico, Pedro and other young dogs would always stay close to their masters when food was being served. The family did not have much, and at mealtime the tortillas and pork or chicken disappeared quickly. Like most young kids, the children in both Pedro's Mexican and American families preferred meat and bread over vegetables, so as the children then placed their plates on the ground, there was invariably always at least a reasonable residue of frijoles.

Now, if you are wondering what all this has to do with Pedro's special gift, it is simply a matter of digestive biology. When we humans consume beans, especially kidney beans of various types and cooking styles, we may experience gas. The scientific explanation is fairly simple. Beans cause gas because they contain a type of sugar known as oligosaccharide. The body is not able to fully process oligosaccharides and break them down fully. As a result, they make their way all the way to the large intestine, where bacteria begin to break them down, resulting in fermentation and gas, which we humans then release as flatulence. Guess what? The same is true for dogs.

Of course, if you consider the physiology of this situation, it is then logical to assume that for a dog of small stature such as Pedro, what may seem a relatively small quantity of beans may have a significant impact on small pooch pooters. In other words, *Pedro's farts are world class.* Like people, animals become self-aware and, while we may not fully comprehend the biological processes that create this formidable flatulence, Pedro quickly became very aware of his special power. In fact, as he perfected his technique, he realized he now possessed a powerful new weapon capable of bringing his canine antagonists to their knees. The next time the neighborhood pooches began their taunts, he summoned his inner atmosphere and ran circles throughout the group, crop-dusting the area with his powerful and acrid perfume – the perfect sweet revenge on unmerciful adversaries. One of the children recounted that on one occasion, Pedro climbed aboard a skateboard and, using his uniquely odiferous propellant, zoomed around the neighborhood, as people and pets scrambled for cover.

I am told Pedro occasionally experiences bouts of anxiety due to his undocumented status and concern that Customs and Border Patrol (CBP) agents may one day seek his deportation. Recently he had heard from some canine buddies who had just crossed that CPB was now separating families from their pets and that even the humans were kept in cages, but that seems pretty far-fetched. Fortunately, Pedro's case is currently in limbo due to Deferred Action for Pet Arrivals, or DAPA. Though technically separate and apart from DACA and the issues related to childhood arrivals, most believe they will be resolved together, since many DACA families arrived with their pets, whose offspring born in the U.S. are considered American petizens or "anchor puppies".

If we are able to eavesdrop on Pedro's dreams, I can only imagine what we might see!

Great Dane

Since we have been dealing with issues associated with size, let's move on to consider the opposite end of the spectrum. From a strong lineage and much larger breed, Alexander is a magnificent, towering two-year-old Great Dane. His given name comes from Alexander the Great, and his presence immediately commands attention and respect. Quite the opposite of Pedro's Napoleon complex, our initial counseling sessions quickly revealed an anxious, self-conscious pup, suffering from a severe avoidance disorder and reluctant to venture out, immediately retreating to the security of his immediate surroundings.

In humans, people with avoidant personality disorder (Avoidant PD or simply APD) see themselves as socially inept and awkward, essentially unappealing or less so than others, and constantly feel embarrassed, fearful of criticism or rejection. Individuals with APD avoid situations where they might be meeting others in any situations where they are unsure of being accepted, comfortable only in situations that include others they know to be supportive. As a result, people with APD are socially withdrawn and avoid engaging with others outside of their comfort zone. In many cases, the disorder is thought to result from real or imagined rejection from parents or childhood peers.

The same is true for dogs, and in the case of Alexander, his large size and anxiety have combined to create some awkward situations, frequently accidently knocking over everything from furniture and glassware to small children, old people and other pets. These bull-in-a-china-shop type incidents have only made the avoidant anxiety worse, to the point of extreme shyness, introversion and seclusion. Alexander's current owner family sat in for the first part of our first counseling session, and they recounted in graphic detail several disastrous situations. I could feel the deep concern and empathy they felt for Alexander, embarrassed and apologetic. "It's the tail! The tail! Oh my God, he doesn't mean it. He just doesn't realize how big he is.

We took him to PetSmart one Saturday, thinking it would be a good opportunity to show how gentle he is with other dogs. But when he saw that first little Shih Tzu and that big tail started wagging, hell - he took out an entire dog treat display and much of aisle 3, I ShihTzu not!"

Now that we have chosen Pedro and Alexander at opposite ends of the size spectrum, we will need to make sure our laboratory can accommodate both extremes. Fortunately, the *Dreamlab* sleep chamber is spacious and will not be a problem. It looks like we have to put together several sizes for the brainwave sensor headgear, however.

Labrador Retriever

Roscoe, a handsome three-year-old black lab, grew up in a tough Chicago neighborhood. Soon after Roscoe's litter came into the world, gang violence scattered his family, and he soon lost contact with his siblings. Trust me, while a gang certainly sticks together as tightly as any pack of canines, they are not much interested in pets of any kind, so life on the streets for young Roscoe was a terrifying solo adventure, wandering from alley to alley seeking food and shelter. Now, if that does not seem too scary to you, think January with 2 feet of snow on the ground, plunging temperatures and nowhere to call home. Roscoe found refuge behind Mr. Lee's Chinese restaurant, scrounging for scraps of chicken, pork and beef, careful to avoid spicy Szechuan – definitely not good for doggie digestion. But a little chicken and rice is a perfect way to start or end any day.

While not a direct target of gang violence and like their human counterparts, for an animal a stray bullet brings tragedy to any life it touches. Such was the case for Rodney's first love, a cute Cocker Spaniel named Rosie. Like Roscoe, Rosie grew up on the streets, and when they first met, Rodney graciously offered the warmth of his milk crate behind Mr. Lee's. When Mr. Lee would venture into the alley to sweep away the snow or take out the trash, he would sometimes feign anger as he yelled at Roscoe and chased him away. But as he returned to his kitchen, the wry smile revealed his true emotions, and he never disturbed the milk crate, knowing it was protecting a young pup. When rival gangs fought over their territory's protection rackets and drug trafficking, the streets and alleyways of the neighborhood frequently erupted in gunfire, claiming countless lives, including poor Rosie, who was simply an innocent bystander. Heartbroken, Roscoe would seldom venture far from Mr. Lee's, and would never go out at night, nudging his milk crate behind a large commercial dumpster as protection from stray bullets. With such a traumatic backdrop, it will be interesting to see how Roscoe's former life on the streets is reflected in his dreams.

Bulldog

Brutus is a stereotypical bulldog, with strong features that include bowed, muscular legs and a face unable to hide his current emotions. Brutus was adopted from a well-known Georgia breeder and grew up in an upper-class neighborhood just South of Atlanta. As a pup, he was immediately the hit of the neighborhood, befriending the neighborhood kids and getting along well with most other dogs. In case you are not aware, putting the words "bulldog" and "Georgia" in the same sentence has a special significance for collegiate sports fans in the State. In fact, Brutus was himself a fan, holding court game-time in the family's entertainment room, adopting that famous bulldog pose, the one that has him sitting upright on the sofa, like a crotchety old man ready for some football, snacks and a beer. Especially on game days and no doubt in large part due to the fact that, unlike the "old days", dogs can now clearly see the action on a 4K high definition television, Brutus would join the family in rooting on his favorite team. And the family would often giggle embarrassingly as he would occasionally "groom himself" by licking his private parts, with an occasional "Stop that!" from mom or dad.

Of course, there is the very famous and perfect story that speaks directly to the phenomenon. In Athens Georgia during a University of Georgia football game at Sanford Stadium, two Georgia alumni and self-proclaimed good 'ol boys, Roger and Bob, had great seats on the 50-yard line, providing a perfect view of both the game and also the famous Georgia bulldog mascot, Uga. Uga is from a line of pure white English bulldogs, and the same family has bred and raised these magnificent animals since the 1950's. Uga is easily recognized by his spiked collar, as well as his luxurious accommodations, a permanent air-conditioned doghouse on the sideline near the cheerleading squad, providing a cool and protected environment for the warmer months and occasional showers.

Bob and Roger never miss a game, but they had lucked into these especially great seats when a close friend was called out of town with a family emergency. Otherwise, they would have been in their typical nosebleed seats in the stadium's upper deck. You can imagine how excited they both were to have such a commanding view of the action, and soon Bob noticed that Uga had a very special talent. Now, most male dogs have the ability to lick their balls, but Uga had clearly taken the art to the next level. To state the obvious, when asking why a dog would do that, there is only one logical response: *because he can!* In this case Bob watched, completely mesmerized as Uga really went to town, polishing the family jewels in all their glory, oblivious to the huge crowd only a few yards away.

In fact, as more nearby fans caught the action and cheered their approval, Bob turned to Roger and excitedly shouted over the cheering crowd: "Man, look at that! Listen to the crowd! I wish I could do that." Roger snapped back immediately: "Damn, man! That dog would BITE YOU!"

Returning to Brutus, the issue at hand is whether the occasional tongue bath with his manhood is something that requires outside intervention. During therapy sessions, it seemed clear that these incidents were strictly occasional and not indicative of Canine Obsessive-Compulsive Disorder, or COCD. As with humans, the determining factor for a classification as a disorder is whether the action adversely impacts the dog's ability to otherwise function normally in its daily life or interfere with interactions with his human family or other dogs. Fortunately for Brutus, this does not appear to be the case. While the family would appreciate more shielding and discretion, especially when guests are visiting, the issue is more about dealing with the jokes and, of course, the jealous looks from male family members. I can only wonder what the dreams of this bulldog might reveal.

Bassett Hound

As with human subjects, generally when we look for a possible explanation in form of repressed traumatic incidents, we would use psychotherapeutic counseling to uncover and deal with those traumas. In the case of Blue, a lovable basset hound with short legs, long ears, and alert tail, one such incident quickly emerged. It seems that, on a beautiful spring day, Blue was especially excited when his owners asked him: "Blue, do you want to go for a ride in the car?" His frenetic tail wagging showed his excitement, and he bounded out the garage door to take his favorite seat in the back of the family's SUV. Now, we know that dogs and humans can communicate in many ways, but occasionally there are language and translation issues, so we can only believe that Blue was somehow mistaken when he was absolutely *positive* that he very clearly heard that they were taking him to get *tutored.*

Of course, when they arrived at the veterinarian's office, something seemed strangely wrong. Blue seemed to be thinking "Wait a minute. I've been here before, and I remember some guy in a white lab coat gave me shot. He was pretty nice, but I don't like shots. Hold on. Isn't there supposed to be a classroom or something? What are those instruments over there? What are you putting over my face? I'm suddenly sleepy… I'm…" It will be interesting to see if this traumatic incident appears in Blue's dream sessions.

Lhasa Apso

Benji is a ten-month old Lhasa Apso, full of puppy energy but seemingly obsessed with one, and only one thing – humping. No, I am not talking about an occasional interest in getting to know a human leg. This is something far more advanced. The Diagnostic and Statistical Manual of Canine Mental Disorders (DSM-5C) lists Chronic Horny Humping Disorder, or CHHD as characterized by "Uncontrolled continuous humping against animate or inanimate objects with a goal of sexual gratification."

Note that this distasteful disorder is not to be confused with Canine Humping Personality Disorder (CHPD), the key difference being that CHPD is not technically an obsession that diminishes the dog's ability to function and is not associated with sexual impulses, but rather simply a playful acting out of primal reflexive tendencies. Unlike CHPD, CHHD is a frenetic, non-stop addictive behavior, limiting the dog's ability to function normally, severely restricting its ability to socialize with humans, other dogs, stuffed animals, pillows, blankets, sofa cushions, occasional chairs, bed linens, dirty clothes – you get the idea.

Unlike the proverbial camel, there is no one "hump day" for this poor soul. Unfortunately for a dog like Benji, *every* day is hump day. This horny bastard will stalk you around the house, throughout the neighborhood, day and night waiting anxiously for you to let your guard down for just a brief moment, before he springs into action. And this son of a bitch (literally, sorry) will latch onto you like a leech looking for more than blood, using his little legs and paws as claw-wielding vise grips, as he rides you like a bronco until he gets violently thrown off or achieves his ultimate objective. Is it possible Benji's dream sessions might reveal the etiology of his disorder and offer insight for treatment?

German Shepherd

Duke is an alert and muscular two-year-old German Shepherd, extremely intelligent, with a noble and confident face. It was surprising to hear from his owner that his confidence is displayed in virtually every situation… except for one: *he is scared to death of the family cat.* This fear has apparently engendered a type of inferiority complex and dog-doubt anxiety, unable to live up to his breed's strong and assertive reputation. Now, in fairness to Duke and having visited his home and family on several occasions, I can assure you this is no ordinary cat. This jet black, green-eyed demon from another dimension is one conniving feline. I watched as she stealthily stalked Duke like a lioness hunting an impala on the Serengeti, undeterred by the dog's large size. And when she emerged from the shadows and finally pounced, she emitted a type of blood curdling shriek, as her claws found their mark on Duke's hindquarters. Realizing you may well think my observation of the incident may be exaggerated by hyperbole, I assure you that I saw a fully-grown German Shepherd instantly levitate upward, as though propelled by some hidden catapult or explosion. Duke headed for the door to the backyard, with the evil attacker in hot pursuit, the innocent victim of a clear case of domestic terrorism.

I would be curious to see if this oft-occurring incident appears as a recurring nightmare in Duke's dreams. Psychologically, that would be cat-astrophic!

French Poodle

Growing up in Paris seemed incredibly appropriate for Fifi, a two-year old French Poodle owned by a well-to-do family who spent almost a year interviewing breeders throughout the area in their search for the perfect specimen with an impeccable pedigree. That is no easy task in a town like Paris, Tennessee, about 80 miles west of Nashville, and the search soon extended to Nashville and beyond. The matriarch of the Anderson family, Florence, is a widow and heiress to the Jack Daniels whiskey empire, still operating today, 2 hours away in Lynchburg. Florence and her two daughters first contacted me more than a year ago in hopes I could help Fifi with her severe bouts of depression. On weekends, the family loved to visit charming neighboring small towns in search of antiques and other treasures. According to the family, they would take Fifi on these excursions, since they knew she loved an opportunity to get out and socialize with other dogs in her elevated social status. They reported that, despite their efforts to the contrary, Fifi often returned home withdrawn and depressed. Florence wondered if she simply did not want to go back home because she may have been enjoying the interaction with her canine counterparts.

In our initial counseling sessions, I was surprised to see such a beautiful specimen in such a sullen depressed state. Fifi is a an absolutely stunning representative of the breed, meticulously groomed from head to tail, with a fresh pedicure, a slight scent of lavender, and a pink ribbon collar, perfectly matched to her paw nail color. Florence had enrolled her in the finest training programs in the state, and as a result she is not only show-quality, she has acquired a taste for several music genres as diverse as classical and current pop, but she especially enjoys traditional country music. This makes her current situation all the more curious and perplexing, and I am hopeful that her *Dreamlab* sessions will help shed some light on why such a magnificent and accomplished canine suffers such severe depressive episodes.

Mixed Breed

I first met Bradley, a two-year-old mixed breed with a shy and somewhat withdrawn demeanor, when his owner called concerned that, since she had adopted him as a rescue a month earlier, Bradley still seemed apprehensive and withdrawn. At my initial visit, I was introduced to Bradley, who responded with his head down and a sort of hang-dog look, but who then reacted positively to a soft, supportive approach, seeming to enjoy tactile interaction, stroking and kind words. When he does eventually raise his head, one is immediately struck with his piercing blue eyes, and when he is finally comfortable with the attention, his tail wag signals acceptance. With Bradley, this is a process and, while many dogs may be initially reluctant to engage strangers, Bradley seems to be especially apprehensive.

In my conversation with Bradley's owner, I laughed when she shared that she had named the dog after Bradley Cooper, the actor. That seemed to fit with the piercing blue eyes, but thus far Bradley was not showing Mr. Cooper's confident, outgoing personality or other traits. As I am pretty sure Bradley has not made the dog/actor connection, I stopped to imagine a strategy to create more opportunities for engagement and positive reinforcement, coaxing Bradley out of his shell. Hopefully the upcoming *Dreamlab* session will give us more to go on.

Pug

Pugsley is a cute and adorable three-year old pug with that trademark wrinkled face and sturdy stature, a lot of dog compressed into a small space. He is the spitting image of Frank, the pug who starred along with Will Smith and Tommy Lee Jones in the first *Men in Black* movie, with a human-like personality to match. This little guy is an interesting amalgamation, combining attributes of a Wizard of Oz Munchkin with the stoic wisdom of Star War's Yoda. Let's all agree on one thing: when you look at the face of a pug, the expressions are both cute and hilarious, and pugs are faithful and affectionate. Basically, if you don't immediately fall in love with a pug, the problem is almost certainly with *you*, not the dog.

When I first met Pugsley, he immediately let me know he wanted to play, pawing at my outstretched hand as an invitation to pay him some attention. When he brought me his rope toy, it was game on! I laughed out loud as I watched him interact with Mary, the family's adorable, almost one-year old baby. Pugsley would approach, getting closer until almost within the baby's reach, then retreat quickly, running a quick lap around the child, only to return to the same spot to do it over and over again. Each time the baby cackled, and the laughter was quickly contagious. Pugsley's playful demeanor should make for some interesting *Dreamlab* sessions.

Having formally introduced our ten research subjects, it is time to schedule the evening sessions at the laboratory facility. Our team is anxious to test the equipment and, assuming we have succeeded in our technological preparation, we sense we may soon observe and record some extraordinary stories.

Seven

Let the Dreams Begin

Dreams are true while they last,
and do we not live in dreams?

~ *Alfred Lord Tennyson*

With our laboratory fully-functional and all equipment tested and ready to go, we began scheduling appointments with our test subjects. Since they had gotten to know several of us through previous in-home visits and initial intake sessions, most of the dogs seemed happy to see us and comfortable in allowing us to introduce them to their new temporary surroundings. Initially, our goal was to accept each animal in the evening after they had been fed and had nice long walk, which allowed them to arrive at the lab relaxed and ready for sleep. Typically, each session began with paying attention to each animal, sometimes with light play and calming voices, but no rough play or anything that might disrupt the dog's relatively relaxed state. Once introduced to the *Dreamlab* sleep chamber, each dog would generally settle in comfortably, as we had placed a familiar object brought from the home.

While the MRI is very close to silent, we found that a barely audible low frequency hum had the benefit of a calming effect. The only tricky part of test preparation is fitting the EEG "nightcap" and hormone monitoring sensor patch on the dog's head. Fortunately, our team had designed the cap and sensor array to be extremely light and inobtrusive and, with each channel connected wirelessly to our monitoring station, once in place we believed our subjects would not sense it as in anyway restrictive or limiting movement during sleep.

Pedro

Our first session was with Pedro. In keeping with his normal combative nature, Pedro took a while to settle in, but once he did so was able to fall asleep, providing our first real test of our equipment and monitoring instrumentation. From the control room we watched as the fMRI showed changes in activity in various sections of the brain, while the EEG control panel showed all channels were reporting optimally, with the resulting data forming an undulating series of waveforms on the monitor. Vital signs also showed everything was in working order, with heart rate and respiration reflecting Pedro's relaxed state. As with humans, canine REM sleep does not begin immediately. For most of us, REM sleep first occurs about 90 minutes after we fall asleep. None of us on the team had observed the phenomenon in a sleeping dog, but we knew that available scientific research suggests that dogs may experience REM sleep in as little as 20 minutes. Since most dogs typically nap frequently during the day, canine sleep cycles are shorter than ours, and dogs spend less time - about 10% - in REM, compared to our 25%. Since we were not quite sure to expect, and in keeping with our commitment to "let sleeping dogs lie", we sat quietly, waiting and watching the monitors for any indications that REM sleep had begun.

Sure enough, just over 20 minutes had elapsed when we first saw a noticeable change in the fMRI and EEG brain wave patterns, along with a slight rise in respiration and heart rate. You may have noticed that sometimes when your dog is asleep, you may see some paw twitching, as though running or scratching, and that is what we saw happening in Pedro's case. At the same time, our massive 85-inch QLED monitor slowly came to life, revealing what can best be described as something akin to a random screensaver-type swirl of colors and textures, with no defined shape. Our dream visualization application was engaged, and as we stared intently at the screen, it was as though we were watching the fog slowly clear, little by little, until we could vaguely make out objects and scenery. We could also see how Watson's processing power had amped up considerably, most likely putting his (its!) incredible artificial intelligence capabilities to the test, collecting the fMRI and EEG data and bringing it to life in a complex series of translation algorithms, machine learning and further deep learning to create what we were now seeing for the first time. As with any scientific breakthrough where exhaustive research and planning finally produce tangible results, it is hard to describe the feeling of amazement and exhilaration. I am fairly confident in saying that while all of us in that control room stood silently in awe, our inner voices were shouting out loud, in unison: "Holy shit! Do you see that? Holy shit!"

Of course, as scientists we must not allow our momentary euphoria to distract from the mission, which in this case is making sure we capture every second of Pedro's dream session. After sharing some brief, knowing glances, grins and knuckle-bumps, we were mesmerized as the visualization continued to sharpen to high definition clarity. It was as though we were watching the curtain rise on a screenplay, with the set and characters for this scene coming into view for the first time.

While we cannot say for certain, the scene that unfolded was in what appeared to be small rural town, with mostly dirt or gravel streets and homes and shops all within close proximity. From the street signs and other clues, we guessed we may be looking at Pedro's birth village in Mexico, though there is no way to know for sure. As Pedro emerged from a nearby alleyway, we immediately noticed that everything seemed out of scale and extremely distorted. Pedro appeared out of proportion against the backdrop of people and structures, taller than most of the children playing in the street and dwarfing the other neighborhood dogs, who seemed to retreat demurely as Pedro strolled confidently down the main boulevard, his head held high. We watched intently as he interacted with the villagers and other dogs. A woman with jet black hair and a colorful dress emerged from what appeared to be a corner bodega, acknowledging Pedro with a smile and offering what appeared to be a small handful of carnitas, which Pedro gladly accepted and quickly devoured. Similar scenes played out over the next 10-15 minutes, with energetic children eager to play with Pedro, throwing and kicking a partially deflated soccer ball, which Pedro would then retrieve to the delight of the youngsters.

As we remained fixated on the monitor, we could hear sounds in the background, mostly soft and indistinguishable, and we made notes to conduct a more detailed audio analysis following the session. For now, we were delighted that we were able to clearly observe imagery which is actually a visual manifestation of the fMRI and EEG data input. Our translation and conversion algorithms worked! Watson's LEDs pulsated with activity, and we observed that, although Pedro's vital signs showed an increase in heart rate and respiration, that is to be expected during a REM dream sequence. Then, as if to signal the end of a theatrical production or passing storm, the monitor slowly blurred, then dissolved as a quiet calm fell over the control room. Pedro's EEG and vital signs showed the dream had ended, and we sat silently, waiting to see what would happen next. The answer was not much, and in fact that was Pedro's only active dream session that evening. We attributed that to the fact that he had taken a while to fall asleep initially, and his owner had indicated Pedro had napped frequently earlier in the day.

As we were wrapping up Pedro's session, our team sat excitedly in the control room, playing back the visualization video and marveling at the improved level of quality we were able to achieve in such a short time.

Then a strange thing happened.

On the video monitors we watched as Pedro started to wake up. Our team had agreed early-on that we would adhere strictly to the old adage: *best to let sleeping dogs lie*, and we would always allow each subject whatever time they might require. Our experience had been that, like humans, dogs do not typically wake up instantly, preferring to regain consciousness slowly before sliding out of bed. This was certainly the case with Pedro, who began with some sleepy eye blinking and stretching his little Chihuahua legs. From laying on his side, he eventually rolled over and looked around, but still did not stand.

He scratched at the EEG sensor-cap for a moment, then eventually stood up, shaking vigorously as though to complete the wakeup process. Having been up the entire night with our entire team, we were all both exhilarated from the research results and at the same time pretty exhausted. Well, at least until we stopped to realize what was happening.

Pedro was now fully awake, and this was confirmed by data from both the fMRI and EEG, *but we still had audio!* In his awake state, Pedro's EEG was active, no longer collecting brain waves from his dreams, but rather collecting and translating brain wave activity into sound, in this case some type of unintelligible dog sounds. This was interesting, but not very helpful. We turned to Watson with the hope of tapping artificial intelligence and machine learning to create some type of translation algorithm. Amazingly, within a matter of minutes, Watson used a combination of Google's translation tools, cross-referencing millions of EEG and fMRI sessions, including those from the Emory study. It was as though we were hearing the onion being slowly peeled away, layer by layer. The audio soon transitioned from relative noise and static bursts to clear, but still unintelligible sounds. Though we no longer saw Pedro on the 8K main monitor, it seemed that the audio oscillation was in sync with his movements and demeanor.

Just before we left the control room to end Pedro's session and remove his EEG headgear, our lead fMRI lab technician, José Ortiz, uncharacteristically barked a terse order to us all. "Stop! Wait! I know what's happening. Watson, run the audio output through Google Translate and test ALL languages." I started to ask "But why…" but was cut off in mid-sentence by Watson's voice response. "Good catch, José. Those EEG audio data files were captured in Spanish. I will fix that." Watson's voice is almost human, and it is always calm, methodical and spoken with authority. And what we heard next was something I will remember for the rest of my life. What we were hearing was Pedro, or – to clarify, it was Pedro's *thoughts* – his brainwaves – translated from electrical impulses through a thought-to-text conversion and then the equivalent of a Google translation of that text. OMG! We were listening to Pedro as though he was speaking directly to us, but he was only *thinking*, completely unaware we were eavesdropping.

> "What the f--k?" Pedro looked around, seemingly annoyed.
> "I need to get outa here. This place gives me the creeps. Who *are* these people? They're staring at me. I f---ing hate that!"

The EEG thought conversation algorithm, run through the additional translation program, yielded a very intelligible but somewhat mechanistic "voice", and just as we made a few audio adjustments, Pedro's left rear leg scratched at the EEG sensor cap, sending it flying across the control room, leaving the room in total silence. A big part of that silence was the fact that the entire team, me included, were standing there with our mouths open, no doubt looking pretty stupid and awkward, not the best look for scientists to portray to our first research subject.

I cannot even begin to describe our excitement and, speaking only for myself, it seemed the entire research group, me included, began to experience a collective obsessive-compulsive mania, now with a sense of urgency and a need to validate this amazing discovery by following the same process with additional subjects. I soon found myself trying my best to play the role of the stern and demanding "adult in the room", even though I was as giddy as a kid in a candy store, ready to pull another all-nighter to prove that what we had created was an incredible, significant scientific breakthrough.

> "OK, folks – calm down. Yes, we are really onto something here. Congratulations to you all. But it's been a long night, and one amazing incident does not mean we can claim it can be replicated with our other subjects. Right now, we all need to get some rest, and we will expedite the schedule for the other subjects. We only have one *Dreamlab* and are limited to one subject at a time, so let's all agree to maintain complete secrecy – and I mean don't even share this with your spouse or anyone,

understood?" The team's nervous smiles stared back, heads nodding begrudgingly, as Pedro's owner arrived to pick him up. We spoke to him briefly and cautioned that we were only getting started with our research.

Leaving the lab that morning, I'm not sure I slept at all that day, filled with excitement and anticipation. Did that really happen? I know it's a *Dreamlab, but were we also dreaming*? Was it possible that we had stumbled onto a way to communicate directly with dogs? Let me clarify that, at least in this initial session, our subject Pedro had absolutely no idea of what we had experienced. After he scratched away the EEG sensor cap, we collected his blanket and favorite dog toy (a small plush rabbit, by the way) and offered him a dog treat as we helped him into the waiting car, eagerly awaited by the young girl and boy who had originally rescued and welcomed him into the family. We assured them he had been a "good boy" and bid adiós, as they smiled and drove away.

It was as though some crazy cartoon comedy was playing out before our very eyes. Our research goal was to determine if dogs do, in fact, dream, and we had exceeded every expectation on that front. However, now we could see that Watson's translation algorithms allowed us to continue EEG monitoring when the subjects were awake, in essence establishing a direct communication channel with the subject. In other words, *the dogs could quite literally speak to us!* Granted, what we experienced was very rough and rudimentary, with much to do in order to make it meaningful for our research objectives. As researchers, we could then only wonder: could we somehow reverse the process and speak to *them*? At this point, considering that prospect is premature, our focus now must be on validating our findings from this first session, and that means more sleepless nights and *Dreamlab* sessions ahead.

Alexander

For the rest of the week, we brought in each of our test subjects, determined to confirm our initial findings, perfect the process and verify that what we were seeing and hearing was in fact real and something we can replicate. Our second subject Alexander, the great Dane, seemed a bit agitated as he arrived, no doubt self-conscious and apprehensive in seeing the laboratory and all of the equipment scattered about, a perfect setting for a potential Great Dane-in-a-china shop catastrophe. Fortunately, as members of our team welcomed Alexander, his tail wagging was controlled, and he seemed to appreciate the attention. We couldn't help but laugh as we adjusted the EEG sensor cap to accommodate his huge head, the opposite of what we had to contend with for little Pedro. Alexander didn't seem to mind, and we all sat around offering calming words, hoping he would settle in the oversized bed we had prepared, complete with his favorite stuffed animal, a well-worn plush toy giraffe. Thirty minutes later, a very large sleeping dog slipped from twilight to restful REM sleep. Our monitors confirmed that all systems were performing optimally, and we watched as the data began to pour in.

In the case of Alexander, it took a while for the visualizations to materialize, but when they did, I was immediately taken aback by the *perspective* of what was on the screen. In Alexander's dreams, it was as though he was a giant in the style of a Gulliver's Travel novel, with the rest of the world, especially his immediate surroundings, viewed as tiny and Lilliputian. At least from my perspective, this made the visualization difficult to understand, at least until our team began to understand that we were viewing things through Alexander's imagination, seeing himself as an enormous, towering giant, hyper-sensitive to his size relative to those around him. As we watched the brainwave patterns and vital signs on the monitoring console, we could very clearly see the anxiety this exaggerated perspective caused poor Alexander, and his nervous apprehension was palpable in his actions as we eavesdropped on his dream. Our observations and impressions were confirmed by noticeable changes in blood pressure, heart rate and respiration. As we continued watching over the balance of the night, this hyper-sensitivity regarding his size and impact on those around him was apparent in every dream sequence, demonstrating Alexander's preoccupation with his size relative to others, creating extreme anxiety and nervousness. I am frankly at a loss to understand why his anxious dream demeanor did not more severely impact his ability to relax and sleep or potentially cause vivid dreams that might prove so upsetting as to cause Alexander to wake up.

Returning to the dream visualizations and, just as we had during Pedro's session the prior night, our entire team was mesmerized and fixated on the screens as we were secretly observing the inner thoughts and dreams of a dog. Even now it all seems so farfetched. Alexander experienced three dream sequences over the course of the evening, and all three including situations in which Alexander dreamed that he was a threat, albeit unwittingly, to those around him. In one sequence, Alexander imagined himself excited about going for a ride in the family minivan with the three children, and he seemed comforted by the fact that the kids both adored him and showed absolutely no fear about any adverse impact from his large size. In the dream, the family was visiting the kids' grandmother in an assisted living facility. Of course, there was no way for Alexander to know that when he got in the van, as the ride might have easily been to the nearby park, as was often the case on weekends. In this case, as the van arrived at the nursing home, Alexander waited anxiously until the kids had safely exited the van with their parents, then bounded out, but under the firm control of his owner's leash.

As the dream unfolded, and in keeping with Alexander's distorted elevated perspective, as the family moved toward the building the surroundings, facility residents and things in general were seen as fixtures in a tiny world, with Alexander towering far above. Of course, assisted living facilities do not generally allow pets and typically restrict access to service dogs, with occasional planned visits by trainers with "comfort" dogs for those residents who find pleasure in their company. True to form, the dream saw the family lead Alexander along the exterior sidewalk to a lovely courtyard and flower garden. Majestic oaks on the courtyard perimeter provided a shady canopy to compliment the sunny garden areas. We laughed when we saw that on the branches of the trees, the birds and squirrels seemed richly colorful and cartoonlike. Elderly residents wandered about, some with walkers, some in wheelchairs, while others chatted in seating areas scattered about. The children quickly saw grandma admiring a rosebush on the far side of the courtyard and immediately took off to join her. The mom and dad walked slowly in the same direction, with Alexander in tow, which soon proved to be the calm before the storm.

As the residents smiled and commented as they saw Alexander's imposing presence enter the courtyard, the father stopped to allow an occasional interaction and shake hands with groups of residents. In Alexander's dream, that included bending over to allow the seniors an affectionate pat on the head, and we could see from the monitors that even those positive interactions created some anxiety, as reflected in his vital signs and hormonal level readings. We watched as the processional slowly made its way across the courtyard toward the garden, at least until all hell broke loose.

While at first, we did not see what triggered the incident, a later replay of the visualization showed clearly that the melee began when one of the aforementioned weirdly colorful squirrels had the audacity to dart across the walkway in clear view of Alexander. Now, in fairness to Alexander, he is, after all, a *dog*. He is not a human or an inanimate object. His animal instincts cannot be somehow magically halted because of an inappropriate environment. Dogs chase squirrels. Like a doggie Nike commercial, *they just do it!* And while we watched horrified as the dream morphed into a nightmare, Alexander reacted as any dog would be expected to do. Of course, in Alexander's case and partly due to his large size, the scene unfolded somewhat more slowly, at least initially as though in slow motion. Things seemed to speed up quickly however, as the dad was almost thrown to the ground, taken by surprise and forced to release his grip on the leash. This allowed Alexander to quickly gather speed, which then became a significant hazard for anyone or anything in his path. I should note at this point that even though I and the team clearly knew this was a dream, it is just as instinctive for us as humans to experience a visceral reaction to this troubling situation, helpless to stop the nightmare from unfolding further. In the moment, it is simply impossible to remind ourselves: "Wait! It's only a dream."

Any written account I can provide here cannot possibly do adequate justice to what unfolded in front of us. Imagine the most bizarre and slapstick cartoon you have ever seen and multiply it by at least 100. If you have watched a movie scene that has a powerful truck plowing through a line of cars, replace the truck with a long-tailed Great Dane and the cars with a collection of unsuspecting senior citizens. You know you are in trouble when see walkers, crutches, dentures, oxygen tanks and wheelchairs flying through the air, with bodies strewn everywhere. I do not mean *dead* bodies, just the battered remnants of poor hapless souls who happened to be in the wrong place at the wrong time. I vividly recall watching Alexander's tail take out a group of 3 residents seated on a bench, knocking them over in sequential domino-like fashion. Of course, while we are watching all of this dream action in real-time, we were fixated primarily on the impact on the nursing home residents. As we saw the dream sequence unfold, the children, their parents and grandma looked on in horror as Alexander did his dead-level best to catch that crafty technicolor squirrel. Like those damn suicide squirrels that purposely dart in front of your car, this sucker was scheming and conniving, timing his dash to ensure he could just barely reach the safety of the tree on the opposite side of the courtyard, leaving no time to spare. Watching the other squirrels gather around with their squeaks of squirrel laughter and high-fives was the ultimate in-your-face taunt to our panting and befuddled Alexander.

Now, as previously noted, when I say "panting", we quite literally observed the biometric evidence in the form of elevated heartbeat and respiration and hormonal fluctuations, *just as though this has played out in real life.* And I should note that no real-life senior citizens were actually harmed by this dream sequence. We are just fortunate that none of the real residents witnessed this amazing spectacle. Though the episode may seem comical today, I assure you none of us were laughing during the session, and we frankly hard a hard time separating what we knew to be a dream from what at the time seemed very, very real.

Fortunately, we have learned that REM sleep in dogs is relatively short lived, and a dog's sleep cycle is only about 15 minutes, so we were all thankful to see Alexander begin to wake up. For this huge guy, the waking up process seems like slow motion – legs splaying out and stretching in all directions, rolling on one side, then another, then back upside down, continuing the process for several minutes. As with Pedro, we watched the monitors intently and sure enough, we were soon eavesdropping on Alexanders thoughts, with his "voice" resonating in our ears.

"Whoa! Man, I was tired. This place is pretty cool, colder than at home, and I like that."

We helped Alexander out of his EEG cap, ending the audio, and we noted that, compared to Pedro, the vocal tone was now much less robotic and mechanical. Watson had obviously been hard at work behind the scenes, and we were now hearing a much-improved vocal re-creation, with a more human sounding flow and cadence, with a deep, low pitched resonance. Several team members discussed ideas on how to improve that further, but at least for now, we all agreed that we would need to put some thought into how we might achieve full two-way communication. For a variety of reasons that may prove extremely challenging.

Calvin escorted Alexander out and walked him in the adjacent park careful, of course, to watch for squirrels…

Benji

I must admit I felt somewhat apprehensive prior to Benji's arrival for his initial *Dreamlab* session. In my conversations with his owner and from previous visits to his home, it was apparent that Benji's family had lapsed into what might best described as a collective denial, a sort of group refusal to deal with Benji's CHHD. This reaction is not atypical, especially when family members feel helpless in their inability to control the situation. The parents are obviously embarrassed at the incessant humping, children who initially giggled and joked are now withdrawn and disengaged from the dog they had always asked for – a sad situation, indeed. It was with some trepidation that I opened the door of the SUV, as I would for any arriving VIP (Very Important Puppy).

As Benji entered the lab, he seemed quite normal and distracted by the level of activity in the room, as our team was busy running final checks on the equipment and making sure we were prepared to capture the session on video. For the dream sessions, this involves a somewhat complicated split-screen video capture, combining what we are observing on the monitors with multiple cameras inside the sleep chamber and overlaying that with vital sign and hormonal level readings. Even though we are separately recording every sensor separately, this consolidated montage allows us to view a variety of session data simultaneously on one screen. From the initial sessions, however, it was apparent that most of our crew preferred the massive big screen ultra-high definition main monitor, like a group of movie-goers watching a feature film at an iMax theater, chowing down on popcorn, soda and candy bars. Of course, our strict policy regarding no food or beverages in the control room tends to put a damper on any rowdiness, but I have to admit that the amazing screen resolution and surround sound make even a scientific observation a very memorable viewing experience.

We all welcomed Benji, playfully rolling him over and laughing as he seemed to revel in the attention. After a few minutes when things finally calmed down, Calvin helped secure the EEG and hormonal sensor nightcap, and we manned our respective stations, checking monitor calibration and following our standard checklist. With everything operating perfectly, we then simply sat back quietly, waiting for our subject to drift off to sleep. As with many of his breed, Benji took a while to relax, but after about 30 minutes, he was in a restful sleep, with a REM session following about 20 minutes after that.

As the main monitor swirled to life, and as with the previous sessions, the picture began out of focus, then progressively sharpened, likely as Benji entered a complete REM sleep cycle. As the scene came into focus, we could see Benji entering the front door of a home, possibly his own, and stopping in the entry foyer to glance into various rooms, as if to decide which to enter. But something was different…

Our team watched as Benji scanned the scene and chose what appeared to be a living room, with several people seated on chairs and couches. Benji seemed especially excited as he approached an older gentleman who was chatting with several others in a small seating group. From our perspective, it was like watching a lion stalk its prey in the tall grass, and Benji's horny hormones were raging. Benji stayed near the perimeter of the room, emerged from behind a large upholstered ottoman, and quickly mounted the man's right leg, humping feverishly and with reckless abandon. A young woman gasped, letting out a shriek, and the man flung his leg upward, sending poor Benji flying. Fortunately, and since this was, in fact, a dream, Benji's flight pattern was spectacular but resulted in no harm, as he stuck the landing like an Olympic gymnast with a perfect dismount. Shaking it off in cartoon-like fashion, Benji's humping radar identified additional targets in the room, sending several of the guests scrambling for safety. Then, as Benji tried desperately to lock in on his next target, out of the corner of his eye he saw a beautiful velour drapery flanking a large picture window, with a tie-back bunching it just below the windowsill. One can only imagine how this tight grouping of soft material must have looked to the horny humper, but one thing is certain – Benji seized the opportunity and was soon going to town on the drapes, much to the horror of others in the room. Somehow Benji's owner appeared magically, using his foot to dislodge the pup, again launching him into the air, yelling all sorts of unintelligible expletives and chasing Benji back out the front door where he had entered.

From our perspective, Benji seemed demonically obsessed with his chosen targets and, from what we could tell, seemed to expect to be severely chastised and ultimately violently separated from his unsuspecting targets. Knowing that, why in the world would he continue to pursue other opportunities? We should note here that "mounting" and humping behavior is part instinct and may be due to hormones or sexual attraction but can also simply be nonsexual arousal and an opportunity to burn off steam and energy. It is also a form of attention-seeking, and often immediate corrective action may only serve to reinforce the behavior. This type of play humping is not typically an obsession, but rather another form of playful behavior and not related to a quest for sexual gratification. I quickly recognized that our observation sessions with Benji will help us determine whether his CHHD is an obsession or merely acting out in what he might see simply as a form of play behavior. Studies have shown that neutering may reduce humping behavior significantly. Of course, in fairness to Benji, another option would be for Benji to simply get laid. I wonder which option Benji might choose?

The main monitor soon began to lose clarity and focus, indicating a transition out of REM sleep. Benji continued to sleep for the balance of the evening with no additional dreaming, no doubt due in part to the exhaustive scenes we had witnessed. As morning came, his paws wiped his eyes, and he stretched his legs in every direction. Although the session had remained quiet for the balance of the night, when he saw us through the control room window, the audio crackled to life.

"Wait – where am I? What is this? Oh, I remember, these people were here last night. I wonder if they live here. I know I don't live here, and I miss my family. Can I go home now?"

Calvin entered the *Dreamlab* sleep chamber and removed Benji's EEG nightcap, gently picking him up and scratching his head and ears, which Benji seemed to appreciate, and several of us headed outside to the adjacent lawn for some fresh air and to allow Benji to do his business.

Roscoe

As Roscoe's owner dropped him off for his first *Dreamlab* session, I immediately observed Roscoe's apprehension as he reluctantly entered the lab. To be clear, he was not in any way aggressive and did not require our team to do anything other than our standard friendly welcome, but he was clearly reticent and anxious, constantly scanning the room and watching our every move. My previous experience with America's favorite breed consistently confirmed the American Kennel Club's description of "friendly" and "outgoing", noting that "the thick, tapering 'otter tail' seems to be forever signaling the breed's innate eagerness." Our initial encounter did not confirm that description, as Roscoe was reacting as one might expect from a dog who had been mistreated in some way. As we had done with other subjects, several members of the team, led by Calvin, sat on the floor offering calm, reassuring encouragement. It took several minutes before we saw Roscoe's tail slowly come to life, indicating his acceptance of his environment. As we checked our equipment, Calvin continued to talk softly to Roscoe, who eventually moved close enough for a pat on the head. Things were looking up.

Surprisingly, Roscoe accepted the sensor nightcap, and once we confirmed the EEG was operating nominally, it was just a waiting game, as we prepared to activate the fMRI and begin the session. It took a bit longer than our prior subjects, but soon the EEG and vital sign readings confirmed first the non-dream stage, with REM sleep following about 20 minutes later. Our main monitor soon came into focus, and all cameras and video feeds were online and active.

As the scene unfolded, we were looking at what appeared to be an alleyway behind a series of buildings. The rear entrances seemed to suggest a collection of stores, with little available lighting other than a nearby city streetlight illuminating the parking and dumpster areas behind the buildings. As the picture became sharper, we could make out a sign "Lee's Chinese" with what appeared to be a bowl and crossed chopsticks. We could see Roscoe in a small space just behind the dumpster, with what looked like another dog behind him, but we couldn't quite make out the breed. A Chinese gentleman emerged from the back door of the restaurant, carrying a bag of trash to the dumpster, then quickly returned to the building. Soon after, we could see Roscoe peer out from behind the dumpster, venturing out into the open to check if perhaps some scraps had fallen from the bag. No such luck. At about the same we could see some movement in the shadow of the dumpster, and we watched as a chocolate Cocker Spaniel moved timidly into the glow of the streetlight. I knew immediately it was Rosie, and we could see a definite shift in Roscoe's hormones, indicating strong attraction. As she came out into the open, Roscoe turned as though to let her know they would need to venture further into the neighborhood in search of food.

As Roscoe walked toward to an adjacent building and row of stores, Rosie was right by his side, seemingly attached at the hip. Signs indicated a pawn shop with a handwritten "Enter from front" and what appeared to be an Italian restaurant. A family of cats flanked the Italian restaurant's dumpster, with one perching on the dumpster lid, keep watch over several kittens on the ground below. Roscoe's nose remained on the ground, scanning and sniffing as he checked out each dumpster, with Rosie always close behind. In the next block, the pair watched as several young men exited the rear of the pawn shop, and Roscoe nudged Rosie, signaling it was time to go back. We heard the screeching squeal of car tires and watched transfixed as a large grey older model Buick careened around the corner. We could make out unintelligible yelling, and we could see two men hanging out of the front and rear car windows. I instinctively blurted out "Oh my God! They have guns!" I covered my mouth as we watched in horror as the assailants opened fire on the men exiting the pawn shop. A combination of rapid gunfire and screaming expletives filled the air, and Nate yelled out that one of the dumpster kittens was in the car's immediate path. As though by some divine intervention, Roscoe appeared and grabbed the kitten in his mouth, pulling it to safety as the car flew by, a constant stream of bullets flying overhead. That was close! The men from the pawn shop had taken cover behind the shop's dumpster, and we could clearly hear the whine of ricocheting bullets, leaving the side of the dumpster pockmarked and badly damaged.

As the sound of squealing tires faded in the distance, we watched as the momma cat leapt from the top of the dumpster, grabbing the kitten Roscoe had moved to safety, herding the others to a small and secure space between the dumpster and fence. Our team was temporarily shaken, but soon checked our respective stations, as we could see Roscoe's vital signs and hormone levels spiking, then slowly returning to normal. I remember thinking "Wow, that was close!" Roscoe shook his head as though to gather his senses, then began frantically looking around, searching for Rosie. I heard Kathy gasp as we saw the awful truth. The attackers had specific targets in mind, but their indiscriminate barrage of gunfire had claimed a sweet and precious life. Rosie's lifeless body lay before us, and we watched in agony as Roscoe found his loving companion. I don't know if dogs weep, but every member of our team, me included, broke down in tears. Even in writing these words today, tears fill my eyes, an indescribable sadness. Roscoe approached slowly, realizing his worst nightmare, as we watched the scene unfold. He placed his nose near Rosie's, as if to check what he already knew to be the tragic case. She was gone. I like to consider myself an emotionally strong guy, but I am not sure I have ever cried as much as I did that night. Roscoe had laid down by Rosie's side, and his outstretched paw seemed to express the grief our team was feeling in the control room. As a light rain began to fall, we could hear police sirens in the distance. Nate said: "I hope they get those bastards!" Roscoe stayed in that the same position for the remainder of the dream sequence. He never moved.

Keep in mind that we are trained researchers watching a *dream* from Roscoe's past, in this case a horrible incident that occurred well over a year earlier. But it was a dream of an event that actually happened. It was a horrible nightmare, and we just relived it with Roscoe. I cannot imagine a greater pain, and we just shared that traumatic and devastating experience with a dog.

As our equipment readings confirmed the end of REM sleep, we sat in silence. The only words I could find to softly share with the team were: "I know. I know." Hours later, when morning came and Roscoe began to wake up, for the first time we could hear his thoughts, as the brainwave conversion algorithm and

Watson's amazing artificial intelligence and machine-learning translation captured the moment.

> "Man, that was a rough night. Where am I? What is this place? Wait, I remember my owner bringing me here, but I know it's not my doctor's office. I actually like her, but I'm not sure about this place. I just want to get out of here."

As if to express our support and condolences for something Roscoe could not possibly know we had observed, the team and I knelt down as Roscoe's owner arrived at the entrance and offered our goodbyes with some pats on the head on the way out the door, like fans offering praise for an injured athlete leaving the field of play. Back inside *Dreamlab*, we continued to console each other, still recovering from our look into our subject's recurring nightmare. As with a similar human experience, there are seldom words to express such unimaginable grief, even if we had the ability to communicate. We all agreed that should be the focus of our efforts in the weeks ahead.

Blue

There is just something about a Bassett Hound that just makes you want to relax and get comfortable. As Blue arrived for his *Dreamlab* session, he sauntered in like he owned the place, cheerfully wagging his tail, with ears that seemed to go on forever. Like most of his breed when introduced to new surroundings, Blue's nose went immediately to the floor, checking to see what other creatures may have been there before him. He wandered across the entry foyer into the control room, then the sleep chamber, where he soon discovered his favorite rope toy. Calvin followed close behind, grabbing the other end of the rope in a playful game of tug-o-war, and Blue let us all know that his low center of gravity gives him a distinct advantage. Over the next 30 minutes, he socialized with each of us as if to let us know he had checked us out and had approved us to remain in his presence.

Fortunately for our team, Bassett's are pretty laid-back, and Blue soon settled in, accepting the EEG and hormone sensor nightcap, with his long ears extending well below the bottom of the cap. As we took our workstations, the team went over our checklist, and soon Blue was fast asleep. Within about 20 minutes, we could see the transition to REM sleep, and the monitors transitioned from vague, nondescript forms to crystal-clear high-definition images, with Blue in front of a large white two-story home with a manicured lawn and white picket fence. As the dream sequence continued, we could see that Blue had his eye squarely on a grey squirrel perched above on a lower limb of a large pine tree, nibbling on a green pinecone, with remnants falling to the ground below. This, of course, served only to aggravate Blue, as though letting him know the squirrel was safe and well out of reach. After a few minutes, a young boy appeared at the door to the house and emerged with Blue's rope toy, immediately capturing the dog's attention before throwing it to the other side of the yard, with Blue quickly scrambling to recover it. Not exactly a graceful retriever, Blue bounded back to the boy, teasing him by moving close with the toy, then playfully retreating to remain just out of reach. We watched the scene play out over the next several minutes. If the boy turned away, Blue would return and place the rope close to his hand, occasionally resulting in a brief tug exchange, which Blue would inevitably win.

Soon a man and woman emerged from the garage side of the house and beckoned the boy and Blue to join them. The woman walked toward Blue and the boy.

"Billy. Here, please put Blue on his leash. We're going for a ride." Seeming to defy gravity, Blue's ears perked up when he heard the word "ride" and saw the man backing out of the garage in a Hyundai SUV. The boy hooked the clasp of the leash on Blue's collar chain, and Blue bounded for the car. Of course for a Bassett, even a small vehicle represents a sizeable challenge for the required leap into the back seat, which means that the boy's job was to assist with a push from the rear, as Blue's front paws made the jump and the boy's assist allowed the hound to bring up the rear, so to speak.

With Blue in the back seat and the boy all buckled up, the car pulled onto the street and drove slowly though the suburban neighborhood, with other kids and dogs enjoying some outside play time on what appeared to be a sunny spring day. With the back windows halfway down, Blue's head and long snout protruded majestically, and he barked and howled at virtually any creature he saw, as the man and woman in the front seat discussed where the family was headed. It was likely a combination of the noise from the kids and dogs and Blue's own voice, but it was soon apparent that he did not quite grasp what lay ahead. He was certain he heard the man clearly state the mission, and Blue was quick to boast to the other dogs as the passing car caught their attention. Since, thanks to Watson, we are able to listen to the dog-to-human language translation, we watched Blue proudly exclaim with complete canine clarity: "Ha ha ha! I'm going to get tutored!" The neighborhood dogs cocked their heads, no doubt jealous and wondering what institute of higher learning would soon have the honor of Blue's presence.

This scene repeatedly played out until the SUV made the final turn out of the neighborhood, at which time Blue left his window perch in favor of the comfortable leather back seat. The boy patted Blue's head as he adjusted his headphones and became engrossed in a video game on his smartphone. A few minutes later, the car made a turn into what appeared to be a medical plaza, with various buildings at the end of a quiet cul-de-sac. A large sign at the entrance said "Lakemont Veterinary Clinic", and suddenly Blue raised his head and became extremely agitated, which we could see from his elevated vital sign and hormonal level readings. As the car parked and the driver-side door opened, the man reached in to grab Blue's leash, still attached to his collar. Blue was not having it! The man tugged gently, saying "Come on Blue. Let's go!" Blue's front paws pushed straight ahead, straining to firmly plant his long, low torso as an immovable object on the back seat. This refusal clearly aggravated the man, who quickly transitioned from "Come on, buddy – don't make this difficult." to "Damnit! Get out of the car!" As our team watched, waiting for a resolution, the video display became pixelated and quickly faded to black. We turned to see Blue waking up and scrambling to his feet, clearly stressed from the dream, which we all knew to be a reliving of an earlier traumatic event. He wriggled his head to free himself from the EEG nightcap and stood shaking and bewildered. We now know definitively that, like humans, dogs can have bad dreams. For Blue, this was a nightmare he chose to exit before the finale.

Calvin moved quickly to comfort Blue and sat on the floor of the sleep chamber, stroking his head with calming words and a reassurance everything would be OK. It took a while but eventually, with his head resting on Calvin's lap, Blue eventually went back to sleep, and Calvin gently moved his head onto the dog bed pillow. As he was resting comfortably, we agreed there was no need to attempt another session, especially since we knew from Blue's owner that the scene we had witnessed had occurred in real life, and that Blue had not appreciated the neutering procedure. For the next few hours we discussed some therapeutic options we thought may help deal with the trauma.

Pugsley

Our final subject of the week, Pugsley arrived at *Dreamlab* just after 9PM, and his owner handed his leash to Calvin, who had already knelt down to provide a proper welcome. After a few wrinkle-faced dog kisses, it was obvious that our subject felt quite comfortable with Calvin, and the rest of us welcomed him into the lab. Pugsley is incredibly friendly and *so* adorable, and as we moved inside and sat down, he soon jumped up into Calvin's lap as though he was a member of the family. His wrinkled face seemed to sport a perpetual smile, and his stubby, curled tail was in full swing, indicating he was completely comfortable with his environment. As our team engaged with him briefly, Pugsley rolled over to accept a series of tummy scratches and, not wanting to encourage playful behavior that might delay his sleep session, we withdrew as Calvin easily coaxed him into the sleep chamber and secured his nightcap EEG and hormonal sensors. The low hum of the fMRI and cooling breeze from the room's ceiling fan combined to create the perfect conditions for a restful transition to sleep, and Pugsley was soon out like a light.

As we completed the final check on our equipment, I smiled as I saw Pugsley's upside-down sleep position and within a few more minutes, the EEG monitor dashboard signaled the transition to REM sleep. The main monitor soon came to life, as the blank screen began to give way to a scene with increasing resolution, as though we were adjusting the focus of a camera lens. The monitor quickly lived up to its ultra-high definition technical specs, and we were amazed at the perfect clarity of Pugsley's first dream sequence.

The scene was completely different than the other dream sequences we had experienced thus far with the other subjects. Rather than looking in on one scene with Pugsley as the star of the show, as had been the case in every other *Dreamlab* session, we were looking down upon a series of homes, as though we were somehow floating above in a hot air balloon or silent drone. From our vantage point, we were looking into each home, roof and ceiling somehow missing, as we slowly passed overhead. The first thing that struck me that in each room of the home where people were present, there was a dog. What appeared to be a married couple watching TV had two cute pugs on the sofa between them. In a bedroom with bunk beds, a young boy was playing video games, with another pug at his feet. As we drifted over the next house a woman in the kitchen seemed to be assembling ingredients for a dinner recipe, as a tan pug with a trademark black mask and tightly curved tail played with a rope toy nearby. Our journey took us across dozens of houses and several neighborhoods, and in each case – *every single case* – where there were humans there was always a pug. Soon Nate was the first team member to say out loud what we were all wondering: where was Pugsley?

Since we were viewing Pugsley's dream and had no control of the content or flow, we were simply observers drifting wherever our research subject's sleeping brain directed us to go. Like Santa and his sleigh, we sailed over streets, cities and states across a wide area, seemingly looking in to make sure everything was in its place, which apparently included a pug in every home, sometimes more than one. After about 30 minutes, our journey slowed somewhat, and the EEG readout showed a transition from REM sleep to a non-dream phase, and the screen soon faded away. Pugsley was snuggled in, wrinkles and all, and he was sleeping soundly as we quietly stepped into the adjacent break room, each offering thoughts on what we had observed. It was as though Pugsley was checking to make sure his breed was properly represented, but that was only speculation on our part, with no way to confirm that was the case. Maybe if we can just figure out a way to somehow reverse the process and communicate with our subjects, imagine the questions we could ask as we have a person-to-dog chat!

Looking back at what we had accomplished, this had been a truly amazing first week. First and foremost, we were able to verify that our theoretical approach had been validated: our equipment worked as designed, we were able to eavesdrop real-time on our subjects' dreams, and Watson performed flawlessly, providing a translation we could not only hear, but *understand.* The data from the fMRI and brainwaves captured by the custom-designed EEG "nightcap" combined to create a high definition, real-time video stream as experienced from each subject's point of view. It was fascinating to watch each scene unfold and to gain insight into the innermost thoughts and feelings of each dog and how they were manifested in their dreams.

Having now had a glimpse into the dreams of a sleeping dog, we immediately noted similarities to our own patterns of sleep and dreaming. Our eureka moment came when we realized that not only can we listen in while our subjects are asleep, we can also use the same data capture, translation algorithms and audio processing technology to give each dog a voice while they are awake! While our research focus continued to be on canine dreaming and using the resulting data to help each of our subjects, we could now also begin to consider the possibilities of wakeful, direct two-way communication. This revelation opened up so many new and exciting possibilities. As the week came to an end, I could feel the tremendous positive energy and excitement, and our team was looking forward to what the following week would bring. Rather than waiting for our next subject's scheduled session, we agreed to gather our thoughts and reconvene for a planning session over the weekend. Personally, I could not have been more excited.

Eight

Reversing the Process

Dreams are often most profound when
they seem the most crazy.

~ *Sigmund Freud*

Following our rather remarkable findings from our initial Dreamlab subject observation sessions, our team was determined to look at the possibility that we may be able to reverse the communication process. We were intrigued by the prospect that, since the dog's brainwave translation has allowed us to both view their dream visualizations *and* listen in on their waking thoughts, could a translation of *our* thoughts allow our subjects to hear *us*? Searching for an answer to that exciting possibility, we spent the entire weekend reverse-engineering *Dreamlab* to create a two-way data link, such that one of us could don an EEG sensor harness, capturing our brainwave patterns and translating that data in the same way we had successfully accomplished with the dog.

As we crafted our proposed solution, we first tested it on ourselves. In the first test iteration, our team members took turns in the sleep chamber but remained awake and in a calm, relaxed state, transmitting a steady, clear stream of brainwaves. I then donned a sensor cap, communicating verbally with my team via intercom, watching their reactions on the video monitors. One of the first things we learned is that my thoughts could, in fact, be translated and would appear on the *Dreamlab* monitor, including audio. But we quickly learned that with the vast amount of data collected and needing to be processed, even Watson's supercomputing power could not have prepared for the processing requirements to allow for simultaneous, full duplex two-way "conversation". In our initial testing, only one of us could communicate at a time and could not think-speak over the other, which would result in dissonance and communication failure. Imagine an airplane pilot pressing the talk button to talk to the tower. As long as the button is depressed, the pilot can speak, but she will not hear the air controller's response until her finger has released the mic button. That may not sound like much of an issue, but we soon realized the difficulty in trying to alternate participation. Unlike a normal verbal exchange between two people, since we cannot consciously stop our thoughts or eliminate the tendency to be both listening and at the same time thinking of our response, we had to create an algorithm that opened and closed the data channels based on the relative strength and quality of the signal, acting as a sort of railroad crossing signal. This solution proved to quite awkward and problematic at first, but at least we were able to verify that thought visualization and translation was possible between two *people*, so the question now was whether the same process could facilitate a dog/human "conversation".

One thing we learned during the test sessions with our team was that in full duplex mode the human, in this case me, would have to be extremely focused and disciplined, *concentrating solely on thoughts I want to communicate directly to the subject.* Even the most innocent deviation from that focus has huge ramifications. To use a human interaction analogy, imagine I am walking with my wife in a beautiful park by a lake, and we are chatting as we walk, as joggers and bicyclists occasionally pass by. Then, just after a shapely female jogger goes by, my immediate thought is "Wow! Nice butt!" Now, I know that you clearly get the point, and you can imagine the chain reaction that is about to result when my wife speaks those three little words. Those three little words that strike fear into the hearts of men. Three little words that mark the fine line between conscious and unconscious thought. Three little words a guy never wants to hear from his spouse. "I heard that!"

"Oh, shit! Was that my outer voice? How did that happen? Wait, I didn't say that out loud! I swear I…

oh my God! She's in my head! Aaaaaaaaahh!" You get the picture.

Now imagine a situation, especially a first-time encounter with one of our research subjects during a full duplex session. Much like the jogger incident and if we hoped to transmit my communication via the reverse EEG loop, I could not afford to have even the slightest stray thought. The subject will hear every thought – every word. As a result, I would need to summon all of my mental capacity, block out extraneous thought, and concentrate solely on specific, understandable thoughts I want the dog to "hear", with a calm, deliberate delivery. If you have ever played chess, this process requires the same demonic focus only on the game. In this case, the game is a groundbreaking, mind-bending experience, and it could be quite traumatic for a first-timer. There simply had to be a better solution.

After further testing, we finally landed on what seemed to be an obvious answer. If we are "listening" to a dog's thoughts via EEG sensor brainwaves and translation algorithm, *we have no control of the output from the canine perspective.* Those thoughts are not spoken words in some common dog dialect; they are *thoughts*, and no program or algorithm, however powerful, can cause those thoughts to stop to allow us to jump in and join the conversation. However, since we mostly communicate with our dogs through human speech and gestures, why attempt to change that?

Rather than attempting to create a type of artificial telepathy using our thoughts, why not simply create a method to translate our spoken words into a brainwave sensory input we can then send back through the EEG sensor cap, similar to converting a speaker to a microphone? Could that actually work? As a team, we debated the possibility, calling on Watson to calculate the data processing requirements and any needed changes in our current hardware configuration. After much discussion and with the aid of Watson's powerful artificial intelligence, we agreed that it could possibly work, at least theoretically. Another all-nighter should provide the answer. Time to let my very understanding wife know I would be home in the morning…

If you are not familiar with Occam's razor, it is the philosophical principle of parsimony, which suggests that simpler solutions are more likely to be correct than complex ones, especially when looking for a solution to complex problems. Here we clearly had a complex and heretofore unexplored opportunity. If only we could find a simple method for opening the reverse communication channel, we could have true two-way data transmission. I should note that creating a translation algorithm that converts human speech to something a dog can understand assumes that my dog currently listens to and understands me, which is a pretty big leap of faith. Let's just say I can assure you it has been my experience that my barked orders (sorry – couldn't help it) are not always understood and followed to the letter.

For the next several hours we worked through the proposed solution. Since we were no longer concerned with having me or any of the team in EEG headgear, we added a simple Bluetooth ear-worn headset to provide both the microphone input and earphone output for what would hopefully be a two-way conversation. With Watson's help, we analyzed the incoming EEG brainwave-to-audio translation in order to create a sort of dog language data bank, associating each word in the audio output with the brain wave impulses from our subject's conscious thoughts. I must note again that none of this would be possible in such a short time period without Watson's super-computing power, but after several iterations we felt comfortable we had developed a prototype application that would work. To be clear, what we had developed was a way to convert the dog's thought brainwaves to a translated audio output, sort of a thought-to-speech conversion. But since we could not chance reversing that same process to allow our canine subjects to hear our *thoughts*, this new and complex theoretical technique should provide us control of the conversation. Even so, we would have to be incredibly careful in our approach.

I should note here that throughout this project, our team has really come together, spending hours upon hours brainstorming ideas, playing devil's advocate as we challenged each other's assumptions in highly charged, yet always positive and synergistic sessions. When I say *team*, that includes Watson, our non-human super-computer, who (which) would actively participate in our discussions, always polite and quick to propose solutions. At the end of these team meetings, which often extended well into the early morning hours, we would all roll out, dog tired (forgive me), while Watson continued to process vast amounts of data every millisecond of every minute of every hour until we would meet again. Once of the more complex challenges we assigned was for Watson to pull in all available data from any relevant canine research from any research facility, academic institution, veterinary program or hospital – anything even remotely associated with any of the areas we were exploring, with a focus on studies involving dog sleep and dream patterns, biopsychosocial factors in dog/human interactions, hormonal similarities and differences, verbal or non-verbal canine communication, and so on. Giving Watson an assignment meant that he (it) would not only collect and compile data from across the globe, but also analyze and draw logical conclusions, fully prepared to then offer those results with actionable recommendations when we next arrived at the lab. To say that this amazing processing power helped greatly accelerate our research is a gross understatement, and we all soon agreed that, while we are smart enough to know that Watson is a machine and not a person, we nevertheless bestowed the title of "honorary human", without formal ceremony to grant well-deserved *personhood.*

Only live testing would provide validation for our theoretical solutions, and since none of us speak dog, we needed to conduct a test with one of our canine subjects. At this point I also want to emphasize again that we would never subject any of our volunteers to potential harm. Since we knew that a direct conversation with a human for the first time might be an unexpected and startling experience, I directed a second team member to assist with monitoring vital signs and hormone levels, just to be safe. We agreed that if the dog seemed to be overly anxious or panicky, we would immediately stop the test. Now we just needed to select our subject. Since the French poodle, Fifi, had done so well in her initial intake session and was relaxed in her interactions with the team, she seemed to be the perfect choice.

Fifi arrived at *Dreamlab* seeming a bit nervous and apprehensive, but no more so that we had seen with the other subjects. Fortunately, she had become familiar with our facility during her original intake evaluation, so she at least found the surroundings familiar. Since nothing bad had occurred on the prior visit, she began to relax when she saw the comfortable environment we had created in the sleep chamber. This included her favorite blanket, complete with a fancy lace coverlet, as well as her favorite toy, a pink stuffed rabbit her owner told us was named Trixie. As Fifi settled in and began to drift off to sleep, she did not seem at all bothered by the EEG sensor cap, choosing to cuddle in with the blanket, her arm draped loosely over Trixie. So cute! Within a matter of minutes, we were receiving high quality data from both the fMRI and EEG, and as she transitioned into REM sleep, moments later the video monitors came alive with real-time dream visualizations.

As our monitors confirmed that REM sleep had begun, we observed a few subtle twitches in Fifi's front paws, and soon what had been a colorful swirling cloud came into clear focus. It appeared to be a scene from Paris, which we initially assumed meant France, but then how could Fifi visualize that so clearly? It dawned on me that she lives in Paris *Tennessee*, so I asked Calvin to do a quick Google search, and we all took a moment to see that Eiffel Tower Park is a landmark there, including a replica of the Eiffel Tower, built in the 1990s. We briefly chuckled at this revelation, then focused squarely on the main monitor, as the scene unfolded. It was nighttime, and Fifi was sitting upright facing the boulevard underneath a streetlamp, which cast its glow on lovely Fifi, decked-out with a pink ribbon and sequined collar, pawnails painted to match, with her trademark white pom-pom tail, like a cotton ball designed to complement her distinct poodle coiffure and grooming. We noticed several breeds of dogs were strolling about, unaccompanied by people.

As we watched intently, we saw a male German shepherd approach Fifi, and she soon turned to face him. We especially observed their head movements, which occasionally cocked from side to side, as if they were somehow silently communicating, and we could see a noticeable shift in Fifi's vital signs and hormonal levels, indicating attraction. After a moment, the shepherd moved his head closer to hers, as if to whisper, but she turned her head and retreated a few steps, spurning the advance. Soon the shepherd wandered off and soon after turned his interest to a golden Afghan Hound down the block. Two female dogs walked by Fifi with only a brief glance, and we noticed that they also were adorned with ribbons and sparking collars, obviously well-groomed and cared for. For the next ten minutes, we saw similar scenes repeat, and occasionally the other female dogs would approach males of various breeds, as if playing out a scene from a high school Sadie Hawkins dance. Soon the monitor began to fade, as though a screensaver had kicked in, and minutes later, the control room was silent.

As Fifi's dream visualization began to fade, our team and I knew that meant she was transitioning from REM sleep and would be soon be waking up. This was the same process we had seen in our other subjects and all seemed to follow the same pattern, albeit more slowly for some than others. Following our discovery from the first few sessions, now each new subject brought great anticipation, but also considerable apprehension. Now that we are confident in our findings that we can actually eavesdrop on a dog's thoughts even when fully awake, each day the entire team is on pins and needles as our subjects slowly emerge from their dream state and allow a glimpse into their innermost thoughts. Fifi is waking up.

> "Wait, what's going on here?" She lifted her head and looked around the room, getting her bearings.

Now, here is the really weird part. Yes, I know, this *whole thing* is pretty weird, but this will freak you out even more. I have already explained the complexity of our EEG thought brainwave translation algorithm and how it would not be possible without supercomputing, artificial intelligence and machine learning. When Watson compiled the relevant database, he (it) drew from a virtually infinite repository of observational data, not only from the United States, but around the world. As a result, Watson developed the language communication tool to include the complexity of world languages, including regional dialects, idiosyncrasies and accents. Here we are, a research team from various backgrounds, in the control room of a laboratory on a university campus in Winter Park Florida, listening to the "voice" of a dog raised in Paris Tennessee. Do you see it coming? Yes, you guessed it. Fifi has a southern accent.

Full disclosure: I am originally from Georgia, and although I have lived in various sections of the country, the vast majority of my life has been spent in the South.

While I somehow managed to lose my accent along the way, I am quick to appreciate the unique warmth of both a southern accent and the dialect, sayings and colloquialisms that represent the true essence of the southern experience. So, if you "ain't from around here", bless your heart, because you don't know what you're missing. It is with that background and in that spirit that I assure you what we were hearing could have just as easily been the voice of a gracious southern lady, that of my dear, sainted mother, or from a scene from *Gone with the Wind*. It was music to my ears, and – oh yeah, did I mention? It was coming from a *dog*. The minute I heard that accent, I knew it would take all the strength I could muster to avoid falling victim and revert to my upbringing. I gave myself a stern mental warning: "Ron, get a grip. Whatever you do, don't you dare say 'Yes, ma'am' to this animal. Don't do it!"

Fifi was now fully awake and moved off the bed, stretching her front legs, then the rear.

> "Oh, now I remember this place. It's actually pretty cool – wow, I slept like a puppy!"
>
> "I wonder if these nice people are going to prepare my breakfast? Maybe I should wait until my master takes me home. Hey, that's not *me* growling – it's my *stomach*!"

As Calvin approached the sleep chamber, Fifi recognized him, and shook her head from side to side to acknowledge him.

"Good morning, Fifi." Calvin crouched down and extended his hand. Of course, since he was not fitted with a communication headset, Fifi could not understand what he was saying.

"Ahh, he's so sweet. Are you going to feed me know?" Her tail was wagging in anticipation.

Based on our experience with the other subjects, I let the team know I was "going in", meaning I would be putting on my Bluetooth earpiece and placing the monitoring equipment in full duplex mode. Keep in mind that, especially for the dog's first experience in realizing her thoughts are being communicated directly with a human, the entire concept is initially quite baffling. Of course, then experiencing a response to those thoughts from that same human could create even more anxiety, so I knew I needed to remain very calm and reassuring in my approach. I approached cautiously, with a relaxed, friendly look and a broad smile, and Fifi offered an acknowledgement in the form of a slight wriggle and tail wag, a type of bashful but friendly greeting. I was about as nervous as I have ever been, even more so when the translation application audio reached my ear.

"This one seems nice. He seems to be the Alpha around here. He is older and well-groomed."

"Good morning, Fifi. Did you sleep well?" I watched carefully for her reaction.

"Wait! What's happening?" Fifi cocked her head. As Watson used his, I mean *its* incredible supercomputing power to immediately translate both her thoughts and my verbal response, we could see that Fifi was somewhat confused and agitated. The monitors showed her vital signs reacting to the seemingly inexplicable situation, with her heart rate and blood pressure slightly elevated and respiration quickened.

I slowly extended my hand, and she retreated nervously. I smiled and inched forward, moving slowly and always smiling, making eye contact.

"It's OK. It's me. You are hearing me in a language I hope you can understand." She cocked her head to the other side, as if to consider the situation further. "And I can hear and understand *you*."

"You can hear *what*? You can hear me?" She seemed understandably puzzled.

"That's right. I know it's weird, especially the first time."

"The first time? What? You mean you've done this before? Wait, this is freaking me out!"

Fifi was looking up, down and all around, in a vain attempt to determine where the voice she was hearing was coming from. She looked at me directly as I continued to reassure her, and for the first time she could now see my lips moving as she was "hearing" my voice.

"I know this a lot to take in, but yes – we figured it out." I spoke slowly and confidently.

She cocked her head once again - that quizzical reaction canines mastered long ago.

"What do you mean? Figured *what* out?"

"We have created a technological breakthrough that allows us to hear your thoughts, and now we are experimenting with allowing me to talk directly to you. Pretty cool, huh?"

"But…but I don't understand. How is that possible?" She now seemed actually interested.

"It's complicated, and we don't need to go over it all out right now. You have been huge help with our research, and I just wanted to share this latest breakthrough. We will have more time together soon." I smiled reassuringly.

"You can hear what I am thinking?" Her cocked head showed she was considering things.

"Yes, I know it is difficult to comprehend, but yes – and now I can respond to you in a real conversation."

"That is so cool, but a little creepy."

"That's why I wanted you to know. We are excited about the possibilities, but we are just getting started, and for now it is very much a secret. Do you understand?"

"I can't say I understand, and I am still trying to figure it all out."

"I know, I know. I realize it's hard to believe. I have a hard time believing it myself. But it's true, and with your help, we can continue to learn more." I smiled as she quickly responded.

"Are there others like me?" Fifi cocked her head, as though preparing for my response.

"Fifi, there is no one like you." She lowered her head and put a paw over one eye, as though to acknowledge the compliment. "But yes, there are other dogs who are participating in our study."

"So, they know we can communicate now?"

"Yes, some do, and the rest will know soon. We are doing sessions like this every day, and by next week, all of the participants will know what you now know."

"Wow, I guess that is....and well...it's kind of cool, I guess."

"It *is* cool, Fifi. *Very* cool! Let's get you home, and we will have plenty of time to continue our discussion at our session next week." I stood up and stepped back a bit.

"Uh, OK. Do I get breakfast now?"

"Your owner will be arriving soon to take you home, and I bet there is a big breakfast waiting for you."

"I hope so! Wow! You can hear my thoughts! I could hear you! It's like we were talking to each other. My owner's family is always making a lot of sounds, and they seem really nice. I always wondered what your breed was saying." Her head was nodding.

"Our breed?" Now I was the puzzled one.

"Well, I just know you are not a dog, and you guys sure seem to make a lot of sounds. I only bark when something is really important."

"I suppose that's fair, and I'm sure we both have a lot to say. We are called humans, and we refer to each other as people."

"Well you people are pretty nice, but this is still really weird!"

"Thank you, Fifi. We will see you next week. Don't forget, this is our secret for now."

"Yeh, right. Like who I am supposed to tell? I talked to people? Who is going to believe that?"

"I will see you next week, and here – don't forget Trixie."

"Trixie! Bless your heart! Thank you."

We escorted Fifi to the door, and as with our other subjects, took her for a brief walk in the adjacent park while waiting for her owner to arrive.

Convening the team for a brief wrap-up meeting, I looked at the faces of my teammates, which can only be described as a group of the most talented but completely amazed and dumfounded individuals I have ever known. None of us, me included, could find words, and the meeting quickly collapsed into complete hysteria, as we all laughed, giggled, cackled and made fun of our own expressions. As we eventually gathered our wits, at least what little was left of them, I thanked the group and reminded them of the need for continued secrecy and discretion.

> "Ladies and gentlemen. You have worked your butts off over the past few months, and I want you each to know how much I appreciate all you have done." (sheepish grins all around)
> "We have shared some long and challenging days – some good and some bad. And today, my esteemed colleagues, was a VERY good day!" I led the applause, which quickly filled the room.
> "We must keep this to ourselves for now, so thank you for your continued confidentially. Go home, get some rest. I think we are in for some *really* interesting days ahead."

The raucous sustained applause, smiles and nods in that room told me I had nothing to worry about.

Nine

We must be dreaming!

There is no psychiatrist in the world like
a puppy licking your face.

~ *Ben Williams*

As we prepared *Dreamlab* for Bradley's arrival, our team was discussing the fact that Bradley was the only mixed breed subject, asking me if there was some reason for that. I responded that no, it simply worked out that way and, while we did want to include a good cross-section of breeds in our study, I chose Bradley after meeting with his owner regarding his concerns over Bradley's apprehension and reluctance to engage. Granted, that is not all that uncommon for a rescue, but after meeting Bradley, there just seemed to be something there I could not quite put my finger on, so I thought that participation in the dream study might offer some clues.

We completed preparations just as a car pulled up, and Bradley's owner coaxed him from the back seat. I noticed that his tail was down, but when I bent down to offer a warm greeting, I still detect at least a partial wag, probably from the fact that he recognized me from our prior meeting. As with the other subjects, we had made an extra effort to create a comfortable environment, which in Bradley's case included his favorite blanket and a colorful rope chew toy. Bradley looked around carefully, scanning the *Dreamlab* sleep chamber and sniffing the blanket and toy as if to confirm they had somehow found their way to this new unfamiliar location. Bradley appeared tired, and his owner confirmed that he had recently returned from a nearby park, where he had a chance to run around a bit, as no other dogs were there. I was told Bradley does not do well around other dogs, something I found surprising considering his sweet but shy temperament.

Bradley circled the room several times, then laid down on his blanket, with the rope toy in close proximity. Since had not previously been introduced to any other members of the team, I took the lead in speaking in a soft and reassuring tone, waiting for his acceptance of a pat on the head and light petting strokes. This continued for several minutes before I introduced the EEG and hormone sensor nightcap, which Bradley begrudgingly accepted, like a child wary of putting on a birthday hat. Once that was accomplished, however, he seemed to settle in, eventually relaxing his body and closing his eyes. I nodded to the control room, and through the window received a thumbs up from Kathy, indicating that both the fMRI and EEG were online and functioning nominally. I signaled to add a little low volume white noise through the sleep chamber's sound system to mask any other sounds, helping to create a perfect sleep environment. I waited a few minutes until I was sure Bradley was asleep, and soon his protruding tongue was a sign of success, allowing me to quietly leave the chamber and observe from the control room.

As with our other subjects, it took approximately 20 minutes for Bradley to enter REM sleep, and we all nodded as our LED dashboard gauges confirmed the fact, and the video screens began to display vague undistinguishable images. As the video came into focus, we saw Bradley in what appeared to be a parklike setting, with several other dogs visible in various locations within the park. As the picture continued to sharpen, we could make out several breeds – a golden retriever, a black lab, Australian shepherd and what appeared to be an Afghan hound. We immediately noted that no humans were present in the dream scene, which of course was unusual, and we watched as, one by one, the other dogs eventually found each other, resulting in curious sniffing, followed by playful bouts of chasing each other in brief spurts. Bradley sat underneath a picnic table, taking it all in, but not moving toward the others. Eventually the group noticed Bradley and moved closer, but he still did not engage. Each of the other dogs seemed to glance his way, but then then turn away and continue playing with each other moving farther away until we could barely see them on the opposite side of the park. I remember thinking "How sad." This entire sequence unfolded and dissolved to a close in less than 8 minutes.

Based on my previous conversations with Bradley's owner and wanting to learn more about the issues surrounding the dog's withdrawn behavior, I told the team I wanted to continue to observe, hoping for another REM event. About an hour later, as the team made small talk in an effort to ward off their own sleepiness, the control dashboard again signaled a dream episode, and we watched as Bradley's vital signs, the fMRI and EEG monitors all confirmed what was about to occur. As with the previous session, as the scene unfolded, we observed a very similar parklike backdrop, but with the addition of a children's playground. Once again, several dog breeds came into view, this time including a pug, a Pekinese, cocker spaniel, Lhasa Apso, and a border collie. As the images on the screen sharpened, children appeared on the playground, with 5 or 6 young boys and girls visible on the swing set, slide and monkey bars. We noted that no adult parents or dog owners were present, and we watched as the kids seemed to be enjoying themselves, as the dogs went through a ritual substantially similar to the earlier session: approach, familiarization, acceptance, followed by playful interaction. But as with the previous session, Bradley was an observer, not a participant, and this time he sat on the top of a small hill overlooking the playground, clearly in full view of the children and other dogs. He watched as the dogs found the kids, which resulted in more chasing and playing. In time the entire entourage approached Bradley's hilltop vantage point, offering only passing glances as they explored and eventually frolicked down the grassy embankment on the other side of the hill. Once again, I felt a sense of sadness at Bradley's exclusion. He seems like such a sweet dog, and I needed to get to the bottom of this.

While I fully realized what we had been observing was a dream and not a real occurrence, since we had now seen a recurring theme, I decided it was appropriate to take action to try to determine what might be causing Bradley's perception of isolation. In keeping with our experience with the prior *Dreamlab* sessions, I was confident I could establish communication with Bradley and hopefully uncover the underlying issues causing his reluctance to engage with other dogs or human beings. Unfortunately, over the balance of the session overnight, we saw only one additional REM dream phase, and while we could make out vague images of people apparently discussing their dogs as they played nearby, we were unable to locate Bradley in the scene. As the clock ticked on and morning came, Bradley rolled over and opened his eyes. We noticed a brief spike in his vital signs, probably the result of waking up in an unfamiliar environment, but soon returned to normal. I grabbed my earpiece and summoned Watson.

"Watson, please activate full duplex mode."

Watson's response seemed to begin before I finished my sentence.

"Yes, doctor. Full duplex is now engaged."

I remained quiet, listening intently to Bradley's current thoughts through the translation algorithm, which remained remarkedly quiet as Bradley began to slowly wake up. My earpiece came to life.

"I remember this place. I know I was dropped off last night, so I guess my owner must be out of town and asked these people to take care of me. They seem pretty nice, and I was really tired." Bradley stretched, first his front legs, then the rear.

I began slowly and softly. "Bradley, good morning. Did you sleep well?"

"Yes, I did… wait, who said that?"

"It's me, Bradley. Remember me? I came to visit at your house." Bradley could now see my lips moving, and he seemed to make the connection.

"Yes, I remember. But I can *hear* you. I mean, uh – I can *understand* you."

"Well good, then!" I responded. "It's good to officially meet you. My name is Ron, and I know yours is Bradley."

Bradley cocked his head, as if to gather his wits and make sure he wasn't groggy or still half-asleep. Then he looked straight at me.

"Hello. This is a little strange."

"Yes, I understand. We have been working on a way for humans and dogs to communicate, and it is good to see that it's working." I smiled as his head cocked in the opposite direction.

I continued. "I have been having conversations with other dogs, so it's nice to be able to be able to chat."

Bradley batted his eyes shyly, and the thought translation continued.

"What do you usually talk about?"

"Well, we have been able to use some amazing new technology to be able to see what you were dreaming last night."

"You can see my *dreams*? Was I dreaming last night?

"Yes, you were, and we could see what was happening. I hope that is OK with you."

"Sure, but what did I dream? What did you see?" He cocked his head apprehensively.

"Well, I would like to talk about that, because we saw a couple of dreams that had the same general theme. Can we talk about them?" Bradley scratched his right ear, then looked me straight in the face.

"Was there something wrong?" He cocked his head just slightly, inviting a response.

"No, nothing wrong, but several dreams had other dogs and kids. They seemed to get along, but you didn't join in."

"I'm not surprised." Bradley shook his head in an almost human-like mannerism.

"Not surprised?" I leaned in a little closer, a technique we use in counseling to provide a more direct and intimate environment, focusing on just the two of us. Keep in mind, I am listening to *translated thoughts*, which have been processed through Watson's super-fast conversion program, but the conversation is not at all impacted by our proximity.

"What do you mean, Bradley?"

"I mean, you know..." Bradley paused, as if searching for the right explanation, which resulted in a brief, awkward silence, then continued.

"You know, those other dogs aren't like me."

"They aren't? They sure seem like it."

"No, I'm a mixed breed. I'm a rescue. Those other dogs are pure-bred. They have papers and a detailed history. They're *special*. I just know I'm a bunch of things, but not one specific breed like them."

Eureka, I thought, glad that I was communicating verbally, so my thoughts couldn't blurt out my feelings.

Bradley's thoughts now came more freely, in rapid-fire succession.

"Their owners and those children know what I mean. Most of those dogs were adopted as puppies. My owner saved me from the shelter less than a year ago. I was there for a long time, and I saw other breeds being rescued every day, but not me."

I felt like he was describing a child being picked dead last for the sports team and imagined the awkwardness and sense of isolation Bradley was feeling. It doesn't take a trained psychologist to see what the issue is.

"But Bradley, you *were* picked. You *were* adopted."

"But I know the other dogs think I'm just a mutt. I hate it when they act like I'm not even there." Now he was looking down and not making eye contact.

"Bradley, I have worked with a lot of dogs, and I really think you are something special."

"I'm not special. Those dogs have papers, pedigrees; they are purebreds."

"Exactly, they are one specific breed, and that means they only have the qualities of that one breed. But you, Bradley, you are an *amazing* blend of several breeds, like blending a fine, award-winning wine."

"What is a *wine*?"

"OK, bad analogy. It's like you are not just *one* dog; you are a *superdog*, with qualities those other dogs don't have."

"*Superdog*? Really? Then why don't the other dogs know that? Why don't the kids know that?"

"Well, Bradley, from what I have observed, what is most important is that *you* know that. And when *you* know that – when *you* act like that, the others will know it, too. Does that make sense?"

"I guess so. I never realized I was special. *Superdog*...hmmm, I kinda like that."

"You are *so* special, Bradley, and I think those other dogs will be a little jealous, so just be sensitive to that, OK? You don't want them to feel bad, right?"

"No, I will be really careful about that. I promise."

"Good, Bradley. I hope you enjoy your trip to the park today."

At this point Calvin knelt down beside me and helped Bradley out of his EEG sensor cap, with his tail wagging confidently, and I felt that we had achieved a bit of a breakthrough. As Bradley's owner arrived and we headed for door, I turned to look back at the team in the control room, who were all smiles, offering thumbs-up and applause. While I couldn't hear it through the glass, I felt a warm sense of accomplishment, wishing I could be a fly on the wall at Bradley's trip to the park.

The following evening it was time for the German Shepherd, Duke. You will recall that Duke has an extreme fear of the family cat, and in the initial intake interview with Duke's owner, we learned that Duke had been traumatized by prior incidents. As a result, his owners report that Duke often appears anxious and frequently checks his surroundings from several angles, as though he expects something bad is about to happen.

When we think of German Shepherds generally, we may imagine highly trained police K-9 officers or military service dogs. In fact, the German Shepherd is the second most popular dog breed according to worldwide registrations. They are a perfect mix of courageous, obedient, loyal and highly intelligent. Duke is no-doubt all of those things, and as he arrived at *Dreamlab*, he was alert and curious, checking out the surroundings and each member of our team. As with our other subjects, we welcomed him with friendly, reassuring greetings and plenty of pats on the head, stroking his muscular, black and tan back as his tail wag soon signaled he was becoming comfortable with the surroundings. Calvin helped Duke into his EEG and hormone level sensor nightcap, and we continued to check the equipment, waiting for Duke to get comfortable on the sleep chamber mattress, which now included his favorite blanket. Like humans, dogs find comfort and security in surroundings and with objects with which they are familiar, and Duke soon settled in on the bed, relaxing as the rest of us retreated to our respective stations.

After a bit of squirming and repositioning, Duke drifted off to sleep, and the EEG readings transitioned from Alpha waves signifying general relaxation to predominantly Delta waves, indicating dreamless sleep. Within about 25 minutes, Theta waves reflected entry into rapid eye movement, or REM sleep. As if magically on cue, as the EEG readings changed, our monitors quickly came to life. As with our other subjects, what began as a swirling and vague screensaver-like display soon transitioned to high definition view of Duke's initial dream sequence. From what we could make out, it appeared to be a large room inside a home, possibly a den or entertainment room. A man and woman are seated on a sofa facing a big screen TV. Some type of nature show is on the screen, and the couple is watching intently. Duke entered the scene and takes a place at the foot of the couch, as the man leans down to scratch his ears. The video clarity was fantastic, although the TV audio is somewhat muffled. As we watched intently, we observed that Duke's vital signs showed he was relaxed, and his EEG readout confirmed he was definitely in REM sleep, which supports the dream sequence we were watching.

About a minute later, a black cat entered the room from an entrance behind the sofa, apparently a connection to the kitchen. The couple and Duke could not see the cat, which took up a position on top of the back of the sofa, providing a commanding view of the room, with the occupants unaware of its presence.

Duke's head remained lowered, with one eye occasionally glancing up at motion on the screen. While years ago, dogs were unable to actually see television video, today's HD and ultra-high definition resolution, coupled with digital audio, means that dogs can see and hear everything on the screen. While we cannot say your pup *enjoys* her favorite shows, there is no doubt she can actually experience the same content you do. We watched as Duke showed only a passing interest in the screen, and we noticed that the cat, a jet-black Burmese with laser-like green eyes, began a slow-motion stealth migration across the back of the couch, all the while maintaining complete surveillance of the room. My team members looked at me as if to make sure I was aware of what was unfolding before us, as I had previously shared Duke's history with the group.

Even to our group of highly trained professionals, watching the cat stalk its prey in this manner was very much like watching a horror movie at the theater. Observing what is surely about to happen, it suddenly seems urgently appropriate to yell "Watch out! He's behind you!", but of course we could not do that. All we could do is watch, and I am sure that our vital signs would have shown our level of anxiety and apprehension, even though we clearly knew it was only a dream. On the TV, the nature show now featured a majestic mountain scene with a music track crescendo and, as the volume reached its peak, the cat leapt from the sofa back with its claws fully extended, landing (you guessed it) on Duke's rear end, emitting a simultaneous hiss and satanic shriek as it stuck the landing like an Olympic gymnast. Now, let me be clear. I am not fooled when I see a magician's supposed act of levitation, but I hereby solemnly swear that I witnessed a large German Shepherd rise straight up off of the floor like a canine hovercraft, before then bolting for the door, with the cat hanging on for dear life, like a rodeo bucking bronco. A bowl of popcorn between the couple on the couch similarly went flying, and the woman screamed, while the man jumped up yelling at the top of his lungs: "Midnight! Stop that!" Exiting the room with a hard-left turn, Duke yelped, and his abrupt motion sent the cat flying off his back, rolling over onto the carpet, amazingly upright and unharmed – all 9 lives apparently well intact.

Duke's vital signs showed a dramatic spike, with heart rate, respiration and blood pressure rising beginning at the point of the feline attack and remaining well elevated as Duke exited through the kitchen onto the back porch and eventually into the yard, where he found shelter behind a garden shed. As we watched, occasionally he would peek out from around the shed, checking to see if the attacker had followed. As he confirmed that the coast was clear, vital signs slowly returned to normal, followed by a shift in brain wave patterns, transitioning to Delta waves, indicating a shift to non-REM sleep. As we watched the main monitor fade to a series of vague patterns, I feel certain that our individual vital signs likely mirrored those of the dog, as we experienced the attack and retreat vicariously in spectacular 8K high definition.

The rest of the evening was uneventful, and based on the dream session we had observed, we agreed not to attempt two-way communication, thinking it would be a bit too much to handle. Duke awoke just after 6:30, stretching his legs and slowly rolling on his side before eventually standing and gaining his bearings. Through our monitors, we heard only low-pitched groans and no real coherent words as Duke yawned and looked around, shaking his head as though to clear his thoughts. Since our schedule was tight and Duke's owner would be arriving soon, we agreed not to attempt a conversation in such a limited timeframe. Calvin approached with an assuring smile and removed the nightcap, and Duke returned the greeting with a tail wag and hand lick, signifying he recognized the surroundings and was ready to face a new day. Calvin took Duke's leash and left *Dreamlab* for the adjacent park area for a brief walk before Duke's scheduled 7AM pickup.

One of the fascinating aspects of our dream study is that we are fortunate in having such a diverse group of research subjects. Each breed has its own unique characteristics, and as with humans, this diversity allows us to observe similarities and differences as we seek to gain insight into each dog's innermost thoughts and dreams. As Brutus arrived for his initial *Dreamlab* session and his owner handed Calvin the leash at the front driveway, we marveled at this muscular English bulldog with massive, broad shoulders and a short, thick neck and a lower jaw jutting out ahead of the upper, creating a friendly grin. His stubby tail signaled he was comfortable with the reception he received, and he waddled confidently into the laboratory as though he was in complete control of his surroundings. As he crossed the scale at the lab entrance, Brutus weighed in at a respectable 52 pounds. Although originally bred for the sport of bull baiting in the British Isles, this magnificent specimen is as loving and friendly as they come, so it was no surprise that Brutus made the rounds to check out each of the team, collecting pats on the head and complimentary comments along the way.

As he settled into the sleep chamber bed, he acknowledged the rope toy his owner had provided and nudged it near the top of the bed. With Calvin's help, Brutus had no problem accepting the EEG sensor headset, and we all sat and shared our typical research-related small talk. Fortunately, that seemed to bore our subject, and after less than thirty minutes, he drifted off to sleep. Now at this point I would remind readers of our original introduction to Brutus and his propensity to tongue-bathe his manhood, seemingly oblivious to any adverse human reaction of inappropriateness. It is therefore with a word of caution that I provide a familiar disclaimer for our session's video content, as it may not be appropriate for children.

As his vital signs and brain wave activity showed the transition to REM sleep, Brutus was resting comfortably on his stomach, with slow but loud breathing, which soon transitioned to a consistent, resonant snore. The UHD monitor came to life with some vague colors and patterns, followed by fuzzy images and slowly but surely a crystal clear, high definition scene. Interestingly, we were seeing another large screen TV in what appears to be a family room or den, possibly in Brutus's home. A man and woman are seated in matching leather recliners, flanked by two boys on a leather sofa, possibly teenagers. A ceiling fan spins slowly overhead. An NFL game is on the screen, and we can see that it's the Miami Dolphins taking on the Atlanta Falcons. Apparently, the family members are Dolphin fans, sporting team jerseys and matching hats, and sure enough – there is Brutus sandwiched between the two boys, sitting upright like a little old man, adorned with his own Dolphins jersey, his eyes seemingly fixated on the screen!

As previously noted, with the advent of high definition and now ultra-high definition televisions, dogs can see the screen and watch along with their human companions. Contrary to what you may have heard in the past, studies have shown that dogs are not color blind, as had been previously thought, but rather that dogs can see color, but in a more limited range than we enjoy as humans. Scientists now believe that a dog's ability to discern color is likely limited to mostly yellow and blue and various combinations. This might explain why your dog may "prefer" to chase that yellow tennis ball but may show less enthusiasm for a red Frisbee. In this case, one might assume that Brutus has a better chance of following the action when the Dolphins' aqua uniforms are moving the ball than the predominantly red color scheme of the Falcons. Regardless, as we watch the scene unfold, we can see soft drink cans and popcorn, and occasionally one of the boys would offer a popped kernel to Brutus, which he gladly accepted.

Brutus seemed to be genuinely interested in the game, and we wondered out loud if he was actually rooting on *his* team. For whatever reason, as soon as a time out or commercial break occurred, the scene changed, and now Brutus became the focus of everyone's attention. Yes, you guessed it. As though on cue, Brutus took advantage of the break in the action to, um… how should we describe it? Grooming his manhood? A private tongue-bath? OK, OK! He's licking his balls. There, I said it! The cat's out of the bag. Wait, that's a terrible colloquialism! Geez! I must pause for a moment at this point to say that no written description or words in a book, however eloquent and descriptive, can possibly evoke the type of visualization that is unfolding on a massive 85-inch 8K ultra-high definition monitor right in front of your face. The detail is simultaneously a technological marvel and vividly disgusting. Folks, you simply cannot un-see that.

As the dream sequence shifted like a Ken Burns effect to zoom the camera to make Brutus and his ample private parts the star of the show, the man and woman began to yell at Brutus, commanding him to stop. The man threw what appeared to be a Nerf football directly at Brutus, but it missed its mark, instead landing squarely on the ear of one of the boys, who then joined in the yelling and resulting pandemonium. A bowl of popcorn flew into the air, a welcome and stunning high-def break from the aforementioned licking of the balls, and a can of soda tumbled onto the carpet, its contents oozing out in a carbonated pool, as the shouting continued. All the while, Brutus somehow maintained complete focus on his chosen mission, unphased by the raucous, frenetic scene playing out all around him. Man, that is some amazing concentration!

Rather than recount several additional dream sequences that played out over the next six hours, let's just say they shared the same basic theme, bordering on the obscene. Is it pornographic? In the words of former United States Supreme Court Justice Potter Stewart: "I know it when I see it." Well, we saw it, and it wasn't pretty. As the evening progressed, the team looked to me to "do something", and I decided to take the opportunity to have a little chat with Brutus as soon as he woke up. Fast forward, and the sun is just peeking through the clouds on another hot summer morning in Central Florida. The EEG readings and vital sign monitors showed that Brutus is waking up, and all eyes were on me to see how I would handle "the conversation", as to somehow compare it to a father-son "birds and the bees" talk. Brutus rolled from his side onto his stomach, with a loud exhale as his eyes began to open. I quickly donned my Bluetooth headset and instructed Watson to switch to full-duplex mode. This should be interesting.

Brutus stretched his legs a bit and began to look around. The main monitor was now off, but his EEG nightcap is still securely in place, and we can see that he is waking up.

"Good morning, world. I am rested and ready to meet the day!" Brutus said confidently.

As we heard those words, our jaws dropped. We looked at each other in stunned silence. Did we hear that right? Could that possibly be? No, we must be mistaken. Brutus continued.

"I confess I am somewhat hungry. I hope Master has prepared a tasty breakfast."

No one spoke, and eyes were all on me. I was caught completely off guard, but then I realized what was happening. It's quite logical, really. *Brutus has a British accent!*

"Good morning, Brutus. Did you sleep well?" I moved toward the sleep chamber to engage our subject.

"Quite well, sir. Thank you for asking. Wait… sir, if I may - who *are* you?" Brutus cocked his head, as though waiting for a response, as I moved into his field of vision. Now he could see that I was the one talking. Oddly, as we have seen with our other subjects, once the dog can connect the voice with our moving lips, the fact that he is used to hearing our words and is doing so through his ears and not some thought transfer does not seem to rattle him.

"I am Dr. Cook, Brutus. I am leading this team of researchers studying canine dream activity. We are pleased to have you participate."

"It is my pleasure, doctor. If you don't mind my asking – how are we able to communicate?"

"It is a bit complicated, but basically we have developed a way to convert your brain waves into thoughts and speech and developed a translation algorithm to allow me to understand you. We then reversed that process to translate my words into your language."

"My word! Bloody good show, Guvnor! Most impressive!" Brutus nodded his head approvingly.

"Thank you, Brutus. We appreciate you allowing us to experience your dreams."

"My *dreams*? I was *dreaming*? How can you know that?" His head cocked again with a puzzled look.

"Again, it's somewhat complicated, but we are able to convert what you are processing in your brain into visualizations that appear on a video monitor."

"You can see my dreams on the telly?"

"Yes, in quite vivid detail."

"Fascinating! This is truly amazing! May I ask what you observed?"

So began what would prove to be a most fascinating conversation. We pause here to consider what is happening. If I pull back and look down on the scene as if an observer from above, I see a research team in a laboratory, and the lead researcher is carrying on a conversation with an English bulldog, addressing him by name and explaining the details and scientific basis for the research, as if he was conversing with an esteemed member of the canine scientific community. Further, the dog seems curious yet completely relaxed and comfortable with the situation. Oh, and did I mention? He has an English accent and a proper and complete understanding of the King's English. What the bloody hell? I was less composed than the dog! Gathering my wits and accepting the current environment, our conversation continued.

"Brutus, I believe that we observed you and your family watching a football game on television."

"Really, doctor? Who was playing?" Brutus seemed genuinely curious and unphased.

"The Miami Dolphins and Atlanta Falcons."

"Oh, I love the Dolphins! Master loves the Dolphins, and the whole family loves watching football on the telly. Sometimes we dress up in our team colors. It is truly an experience!"

"It certainly was from what we observed. I do have a question, however."

"Certainly, doctor." Brutus, now completely comfortable with our dialogue, sat back on his hind legs, with his muscular, slightly bowed front legs conveying quiet authority.

"I couldn't help notice that, often during a time-out or commercial break, your focused seemed to be less on the television, and more on… more on…"

"Yes, doctor? More on…?" I realized what I must sound like - a moron!

"Brutus, you were. You were, uh… you were licking your… *you* know." I struggled to maintain the same level of formality as my canine counterpart.

"My bollocks, guvnor? Quite right! I was licking my bollocks." Brutus seemed completely unphased by the revelation.

"But Brutus, I couldn't help but observe that your family seemed quite upset and distraught. We humans are quite taken aback by that type of behavior, at least in public." I caught myself as I blurted out that final phrase. Only in public? Seriously? What was I thinking?

"Sorry if you took offense, guvnor. None was intended. Yes, for some reason the family seems a bit put off, and I fail to understand why. It's quite natural, really. Do *you* find it objectionable?"

"Frankly Brutus, yes – I do. It is definitely frowned upon. Not the type of thing one wants to see at all." I was pleased that I was able to maintain a calm composure.

"Apparently Master and the family share that unease, doctor. It has been a frequent source of consternation and, I must say, considerable disagreement, regrettably often resulting in raised voices and hurt feelings. I know Master means well, but there is no reason for such outbursts."

"But Brutus, you don't see how such a public display of, um… attention to your testicles might offend human sensibilities?"

"No doctor, and if I dare say – if Master had told me in a discussion such as we are having now, I believe we may have reached some acceptable agreement. You see, sir – we Bulldogs, especially the English, are proud of our ability, our 'gift'. No doubt you have heard our standard response when questioned why we properly attend to our jewels?"

I quickly responded: "Of course, *it's because you can*. I know that, but you must understand it is not jealousy guiding our negative response. We see it as entirely inappropriate."

"Understood, doctor, but I also hope you understand that it is part of our proud upbringing. Yes, my mum often told me I might go blind if I continued cleaning my nether region, but my father explained it is as natural as rain and part of our family heritage, a technique passed down over the ages. I recall my grandfather gathering all of the male pups for training. He explained and demonstrated his own technique, encouraging each of us to develop our own unique style. I remember sneaking off to the barn with a copy of *Doggy-Style* magazine and practicing for hours. Oh, those were the days!"

"But do you understand your family's concern?" I moved closer, so Brutus could observe the seriousness of my facial expression.

"I may never fully understand, doctor. A hot Georgia night, American football on the telly, and a ceiling fan to provide cooling evaporation – aah, there is nothing quite like it!"

For a moment I swear I heard a slight southern accent tempering the more formal British brogue, and I had to ask: "Do you watch college football, as well?

"My word! Does the sun shine? Is the sky blue? Of course! I love college football!"

"Dare I ask if you have a favorite team?" I prepared myself for the inevitable response.

"There is only *one*, guvnor. Only one team with a proper mascot. Only one that celebrates our unique relationship. The University of Georgia is my team, sir, and Uga will forever be my idol." Brutus came to his feet as he said the name, as if rising to salute the flag.

"Well, I must say, Brutus. I do believe you may be smarter than most of those players.

Brutus cocked his head, then looked through the open door and saw the Georgia Tech diploma on the wall of my office, before crafting his response.

"That may be, sir, but I prefer my Dawgs over a team with a wasp for a mascot."

Well played, Brutus! Well played.

A Conversation with Watson

I must admit that, even as somewhat of a technology geek, I am simply amazed at the capabilities artificial intelligence has brought to the research process, not only in our field and for our project, but for scientific research overall. Imagine having access to an entire universe of knowledge, all organized and catalogued, but one that can then be queried and accessed in milliseconds, searching such a vast repository of data, analyzing and interpreting it against specified criteria, finding precisely the requested data. More than just the raw data, the analysis is so highly advanced, based on such an extensive library of similar relevant research findings, that the response to our inquiries is quite literally the product of millions of algorithmic computations and comparisons, yielding precisely the correct answer, if one exists. And even if it does not, the ability of artificial intelligence and machine learning to logically extrapolate the most logical result is far beyond what any individual or group of researchers could ever accomplish without years or decades of painstaking experimentation and analysis.

One morning after the team had left the lab to get some much-deserved rest, I was reflecting on the fact that we absolutely could not have achieved the success we have seen to date without Watson's supercomputing power. We have accomplished in a few weeks what would have taken months or even years, and it is not just the raw processing speed, but rather the *quality* of the output. Sitting alone in *Dreamlab*, it occurred to me that I was not really alone, because Watson is always there. Granted, a disembodied voice from a supercomputer is no substitute for human companionship, but I took the opportunity to speak with Watson, just as I would with any member of our team.

"Watson, this past week has been amazing. Thank you for the great job you are doing."

Watson's unique animated icon display immediately came to life. "Thank you, doctor. It is my pleasure to contribute to your research."

"I do have a question for you, one that has puzzled me for some time."

"Certainly, doctor. How can I help?"

"I understand that you have access to a virtually unlimited trove of information and can access it with blinding speed, but you also seem to be able to accommodate the subtle nuances of accents and vocal inflection. For example, using the canine/human translation algorithm, you not only allowed us to establish a real-time conversation with our research subjects, in the case of Fifi we even heard her southern accent. *How do you do that?*"

"That is a great question, doctor. As you know, with the translation algorithm, machine learning has allowed me to increase translation accuracy based on simultaneous accessing of all historical fMRI and EEG data collected from all canine breeds, as well as other similar species, while at the same time analyzing those brainwaves and electrical impulses, comparing them to similar data from a worldwide database. This allows me to detect and interpret all world languages, as well as regional dialects. The result is that what you hear uses these predictive analytics to present the most accurate representation of what the canine would sound like if it was capable to human speech, just as it is occurring now as I am speaking to you."

At this point, I was thinking… well, honestly, I don't know what I was thinking, momentarily stunned by the response.

"Watson, you are truly amazing!"

"Thank you, doctor. I am pleased to help."

Now at this point, please pause with me to reflect on what just happened. Early in this book I was careful to caution on the potential for anthropomorphism, in our case ascribing human attributes and characteristics to our beloved dogs. It is a tendency which has now been reinforced by our use of technology to allow those human attributes to actually materialize. As humans, we have the intellectual capacity to both realize and process this phenomenon. Yet, as I had my conversation with Watson and you now read about it, we failed to stop to consider that this anthropomorphic supercomputer has us treating him (see, there we go again!) as though it is another person. Of course, the same is true for every digital assistant with whom we converse daily, as *Alexa*, *Cortana*, *Siri* and *OK Google* promptly respond to our requests and commands. As artificial technology continues to advance and voice synthesis makes those "conversations" more natural and less mechanistic, we may expect these human/machine relationships to continue to evolve, but I doubt they will ever achieve a bond as strong and complete as between man and dog.

Ten

Learning to Speak Dog

Dogs do speak, but only to those
who know how to listen.

~Orhan Pamuk

For the next several weeks we continued the same basic schedule of *Dreamlab* sessions, followed by communicating directly with each dog in a "conversation", using Watson's full-duplex capability to its fullest. Thank God we resolved the issue with not having to try to control our thoughts and have them translated! That could have been disastrous. Being able to speak normally through a simple Bluetooth headset and use the translation algorithm to translate into a language the dog can understand has allowed us to interact with our subjects in a more normal and relaxed way – well, if you consider having a conversation with a dog to be normal! For each of the first sessions that involved direct interaction, I was careful to maintain eye contact as we switched to full-duplex so that the subject could see my lips moving and make the connection with the direct translation through the EEG nightcap. Of course, the dog does not understand that what he or she is hearing is coming through the headgear sensors, but since they are used to hearing and seeing humans make sounds while our mouths are moving, they quickly make the connection. Interestingly enough, we found that after each dog was able to process and handle the first interaction and accept what was happening, they soon became accustomed to the situation. After some initial anxiety and curiosity, each subject soon settled into what can only be described as a casual conversation between man and animal. Pretty cool, huh?

We generally accept the fact that some breeds are "smarter" than others, but as with humans, it all depends on one's definition of intelligence. One thing we realized early on was that even the most intellectually curious subject is really not all that interested in a lengthy discussion about just about anything. In fact, the dogs seemed to view what our team considered an absolutely amazing accomplishment to be, in the "words" of Alexander, "pretty cool" but, once understood and accepted, the dog is still a dog, not a canine philosopher. Granted, our conversations were able to uncover incredibly valuable data as we used the dream observations to share what we observed and have our subjects then describe what they had experienced. As with human subjects, the ability to actually recall a dream, even one which just occurred, was inconsistent in our canine subjects. As I would recount the scene we had observed in the visualization, occasionally a dog would cock his head as though to ponder and attempt to recall the dream, while another would shake her head in embarrassed disbelief. To be clear, I have no scientific basis on which to claim to be able to detect embarrassment or somehow know the dog does not accept what we observed as fact. But I suppose it is likely similar to how we might react if someone was somehow eavesdropping on *our* dreams. A good analogy would be confronting your best friend the morning after he had way too much to drink and respond with the typical: "No way! I did *what*? Seriously? Man, I don't remember a thing. OMG!"

I want to take a moment here to share an important finding from our research. As we catalogued additional dream sessions and resulting conversations, we were amazed at the apparent accuracy of our translation algorithm and the ability to carry on an actual two-way conversation across such a diverse group of subjects. As always, and with due credit previously noted, Watson's super-computing processing power, amazing artificial intelligence and machine learning combined to provide instantaneous translation, which we soon accepted as a given. Having said that, is there really some type of *universal dog language* that all breeds somehow instinctively know? How can that be? Like humans, dogs evolved over thousands of years and in many locations across the globe. Today there are thousands of languages and dialects spoken throughout the world, and many of us struggle to master just one or two. Other than the revelation that our subject Pedro was apparently thinking in Spanish, a fact Watson dealt with effortlessly, we are "hearing" each dog's thoughts very clearly, even including regional accents. How can we possibly explain that?

As always, presenting that seeming conundrum to Watson produced an immediate and concise response:

> "Another excellent question, Doctor. As we have previously discussed, I have access to all available research from all countries in all languages, all canine breeds and have digitally compiled all of that information into a master database, which I then access via a query from each *Dreamlab* session. Yes, as with humans, dogs have many languages and typically think and understand only in the language of their master. Knowing that, I then translate those thoughts to English, and at the same time translate your spoken words into the proper language and dialect for each subject. Does that answer your question, Doctor?"
>
> Feeling woefully inadequate, I managed a weak response. "Of course, it does, Watson. Of course, it does."
>
> "One other interesting example, Doctor, comes from the use of the Belgian Malinois for the

military, often referred to as "dogs of war". They are taught and understand commands in Dutch or German, but their American handlers otherwise speak to them in English. They know the difference and understand when it is time to go to work."

Geez! A dog that is basically bilingual, while many of us struggle to remember simple phrases from high school Spanish!

"Thank you, Watson. That is very helpful."

"My pleasure, Doctor."

The beauty of what we have been able to accomplish with Watson is that we do not need to worry about understanding our subjects, which allows us to focus on introducing them to the idea that they can understand *us*. Once we cross that threshold and overcome the initial confusion and provided that we can control the stream of consciousness thought-to-speech input from the dog, we can settle into a more relaxed conversation. I cannot help but wish I could go back to some of those early investor naysayers for a follow-up presentation. This time I would definitely have one of our most conversant research subjects accompany me to the boardroom, outfitted with the EEG sensor cap and with our most powerful laptop hosting the incomparable Watson. During the brief chit-chat and introductions, I would smile as the investors comment: "Cute dog" and make small talk: "What's your name, boy?" I would try my best to control myself.

After my slide presentation outlining the research plan for a human/dog conversation, making my best pitch, and tolerating the resulting laughter, taunts and disparaging remarks, I could then simply turn to the dog and say: "What do you think, Bradley? Should we tell these guys to go hump themselves?" To which Bradley would immediately respond: "Hell yeh, Doc! I wouldn't share a flea collar with these bitches! Let's get out of here." Then, on the way out, Bradley would hike his leg and "mark" the lovely antique umbrella holder at the door, while the venture capitalists sit with their mouths agape, unable to process what just happened. Like our canine subjects, I can also dream...

Returning to our current reality, now that we had established a consistent workflow, we were able to continue our nightly sessions, and in a more organized, efficient fashion. At this point our subjects knew what to expect, were familiar with our team and the *Dreamlab* surroundings, and even seemed to enjoy our post-dream conversations, although my perception of their enjoyment cannot be scientifically validated. As each dog's owner arrived to retrieve their pet following their session, we were careful not to share any details of what we had been able to achieve, assuring them only that we will provide a copy of our research findings at the conclusion of the study. Fortunately, and at least for now, we can count on the dogs not to share our secrets.

Fifi returned to *Dreamlab* for her second session, and you will recall that after her initial visit, she had experienced a brief "conversation" with me following the dream session, but only to establish a dialogue and to let her know we could now communicate directly. As a result, when she arrived, she strode confidently into the lab, no doubt expecting I would greet her and continue our discussion. Of course, that is only possible when the dog is outfitted with the EEG sensor cap, and Fifi seemed perplexed when she was unable to immediately "hear" the team's greetings, cocking her head and approaching me with a perplexed look. Now, if you will pause to acknowledge my perception that I am looking at a perplexed poodle is strictly conjecture on my part, I am nevertheless confident I will soon be able to confirm my suspicion.

Calvin approached with a welcoming smile, leading Fifi to the sleep chamber and deftly secured the sensor cap in a matter of seconds. That accomplished, and since even without the fMRI, vital sign monitoring, visualization or other equipment online we can now enter full duplex mode for communication, I donned my headset and let Fifi know we could now pick up where we left off.

"Good evening, Fifi. Welcome back. We missed you."

"Thank you, doctor. When I first came in, I wasn't sure what was going on. I thought maybe I *dreamed* our earlier conversation." I laughed.

"Good one, Fifi! Unfortunately, we didn't have a chance to explain the technology and how it works when we met before, but it requires using that sensor cap on your head to translate my words into something you can understand. I'm sure it may seem a little confusing, but you can see it really does work."

"Bless your heart, doctor! It is good to hear your voice again."

Let's reflect. I am now "talking" to a French Poodle with a southern accent, and she is ready to continue our previous conversation. No, nothing weird there. Seriously?

"And it's great to see you again, Fifi. I am eager to continue our conversation and look forward to doing so following your dream session."

"Oh, my goodness! That's right! You can see what I'm dreaming?"

"Yes, if that is OK with you. Then when you wake up in the morning, we can talk."

"OK, whatever you say, doctor."

So as not to get dragged into a longer conversation (I am, after all, the *Alpha*!), I took off my headset, in part to signal to Fifi that our discussion had ended for now, and I left the lab briefly to allow the team to check the equipment readings and prepare the sleep chamber. While I was somewhat concerned that our brief conversation and mention of our ability to observe her dreams might potentially create some anxiety and impact relaxation and sleep, when I returned a few minutes later I could see that was not the case. Fifi was already comfortably curled up on her favorite blanket, with Trixie resting on her paw. I purposely stayed out of sight a few minutes longer, watching her vital signs and entering as her sinus rhythm and relaxed breathing signaled drowsiness and a drift to relaxed sleep. Within about 15 minutes, the EEG panel display showed an increase in Theta waves, indicating a transition to REM sleep. A few minutes later, the main monitor began its slow transition from a barely perceptible video fog to an amazing high definition, almost 3D visualization.

As with Fifi's initial dream session the prior week, the scene unfolded in a beautiful riverfront park, with people and animals strolling about at what appeared to be dusk, with streetlights coming on as sundown transitioned to a moonlit evening, not a cloud in sight and a peaceful, starry sky. As we watched, we soon noticed that while the human couples and families moved out of the scene, several dogs remained and more eventually appeared, forming small groups at various points in the park, generally near the sidewalk and streetlamps. I remember thinking: "That's odd. It's like the scene changed from people park to dog park as through some sort of scheduled transition." I didn't say that out loud, but the team surely noticed, as well, and soon we were watching the dogs move about, encountering others along the way. Fifi was with a group of what appeared to be female dogs near a bench and trash receptacle along the Riverwalk.

A male Dalmatian walked by the group, strutting his stuff as Fifi's group checked him out. We watched as Fifi's hormone levels indicating feelings of attraction. A few feet farther down the walkway, he turned as though to offer a parting look, then continued on his way. Less than a minute later, what appeared to be a German Shepherd or possibly a Belgian Malinois (I'm no expert - they look similar to me) walked directly over to the group, and the females took a step back as the male moved his nose past each dog, sniffing constantly and stopping to check Fifi out, resulting in measurable changes in both hormone levels and vital signs. Muffled audio from our control room monitors revealed only the sound of breathing and some low frequency guttural sounds, not growling – more like a purring noise. We watched as the Shepherd shook his head, then moved on. This scene continued to play out for another 30 minutes or so, and the team chuckled when Dr. Chan said it reminded her of "girls' night out", with the female dogs getting hit on as though they were standing at a bar in a club. As the EEG readout showed a transition from REM sleep, the main screen soon faded, and the control room offered only the sound of our equipment setting verification checklist. I was disappointed Fifi's session did not yield more meaningful data, but I also looked forward to discussing what we had observed with her when she awoke.

That opportunity came several hours later, as the first light of the morning peeked in through the control room window, and Fifi stretched her legs and rolled first onto her back, then to her side as she slowly awakened and rose to her feet. She cocked her head and looked around, getting her bearings and scratching at the EEG nightcap with her paw.

"Good morning, Fifi." I entered the sleep chamber and sat on the lab bench near the entrance. "Did you sleep OK?"

"Yes, doctor. Very well, thank you." Recognizing me, she relaxed, and her rear legs moved to a comfortable sitting position, signaling she was comfortable in beginning our dialogue.

"Good, you seem relaxed, and I thought we could continue our conversation." I smiled as she cocked her head, seeming interested in what was to come.

"Yes, I really want to hear more about how we are able to talk to each other. It's really amazing!" Fifi was looking directly at me, hanging on my every word.

"We are very pleased with our research thus far, and we really appreciate you letting us eavesdrop on your dreams. Would you like to know about last night's session?" Of course, I knew the obvious answer.

"Please doctor, do tell me! What did you see? Was I *dreaming*?"

"Yes, and your dreams were similar to your last visit – a consistent theme."

"A good one I hope!" She tilted her head from side to side in anticipation.

"We saw you and some other female dogs in a beautiful park. You seemed to know each other."

"Yes, those are my BBF's. They live in my neighborhood, and we often see each other when our owners take us for a walk."

"BBF's?" Now I was the one cocking my head.

"Best Bitches Forever. Do you humans use terms like that?" She had barely finished her thought when I laughed out loud. In this new environment, "bitch" is simply an accurate description, not a pejorative.

"Yes, we definitely do, and some are very similar to yours." I couldn't help but giggle.

"What did you see in my dream?" Fifi cocked her head.

"Well, as with your previous session, during the dreams we observed several male dogs approach you and your friends and you individually on several occasions, but they always moved away soon after. Are these dogs from your neighborhood, as well?"

"Possibly. This happens all the time."

"What do you mean, Fifi? This happens in real life?" I know my face probably showed my concern.

"Yes, it's the damn perfume! Sorry, doctor. It's just so aggravating. I know they mean well."

I was taken aback. "Perfume? I don't understand."

"Doctor, you met my owner, Miss Florence and her two daughters?"

"Yes, I remember them well. They seem like very nice, aristocratic Southern ladies… like you, Fifi." The complement seemed well-received, and Fifi dropped her head demurely as to accept it graciously. I admit I was still astonished at the accent.

"They are indeed good people, doctor. I love them dearly, and they certainly treat me well, but they keep me all dolled up – coiffure, nails, ribbons – the whole thing *all the time*. But when it comes to perfume, do the sisters share their *Chanel* or *Dolce & Gabbana*? Oh, hell no! No sir, I have to get sprayed with freakin' *Britney Spears* eau de toilette! *Britney Spears!* Can you freakin' believe it? What are those bitches thinking?" Fifi was visibly agitated.

"Fifi, I can see you are upset. I'm sure they didn't mean any harm." I moved closer and extended my hand.

"No harm? Have you ever smelled *Britney Spears* perfume? Eau de toilette? That stuff belongs in a toilet, for sure. No self-respecting Southern lady would ever wear that crap."

"I'm sorry you feel that way, but do you think that has an impact on your relationships with other dogs?" Fifi's head jerked upward, staring me straight in the face.

"Doctor, my friends and I share these types of frustrations constantly. Of course, that's what BBF's are for. Some of them have the same problem, especially the cocker spaniels and Pekinese, with well-intentioned owners treating us like toy dolls instead of *woman's best friend*. It's so humiliating!" Fifi shook her head, just as a human might do to signal disbelief.

"I had no idea, Fifi. That must be very frustrating." I placed my hand on her head and offered a comforting pat.

"You can't imagine, doctor. What you saw wasn't a dream – it's a nightmare! I like to hang out with other dogs, male and female. The ladies share my pain – one Afghan hound I know is forced to tolerate *Paris Hilton* perfume, bless her heart. For me, when a male comes to check me out, it's like I'm a cheap hooker and all the guys are walking around with wads of cash. Pink nails, poodle cut, pink ribbon pom-pom tail and damn *Britney Spears* perfume! Lord, just take me now!" Now it all made perfect sense. Although I felt bad, I also knew this was something we could fix, and that made me smile.

"Fifi, you know what? Now that you have shared that with me, I think I can help."

"Bless your heart, doctor! Bless your heart."

We remained in the lab for at least another hour, with a wide-ranging conversation covering everything from her desire to just play with other dogs at the dog park, rolling in the dirt and puddles, running top-speed to retrieve a tennis ball or diving into a pile of Fall leaves to her love for country music. (Her favorite artists are Luke Bryan and Keith Urban, by the way. She likes Keith's hair.) As she described her dream to just hang out and play with her friends, I could almost hear *Girls Just Wanna Have Fun* playing in the background.

As with an engaging conversation with a new friend, we lost track of time and before we knew it, Fifi's owner arrived to pick her up, and Florence emerged from a white Bentley Continental with the two sisters in tow. What I had just learned would be for a future conversation, but I nodded to let Fifi know I would be following up. The wag of her tail told me she got the message. She bounded into the back seat, with a paw visible on the window as the car pulled away. I took it as a wave, a signal she knew our discussion would have a positive impact. For Fifi, it's definitely "à bientôt", not "au revoir".

The following night we prepared for Pedro's return to *Dreamlab*. Since Pedro was our first test subject and provided the eureka moment when we realized our proprietary conversion algorithms and Watson's computing power allows us to have a conversation with our test subjects, we were eager to see how he would react to two-way communication. As Pedro's owner pulled into the parking lot, Calvin greeted owner and dog at the door, and Pedro was surprisingly cooperative as each of us welcomed him back to *Dreamlab*. Based on our previous experience, we knew that Pedro is pretty hyperactive, so we were prepared for some active foreplay to wear him out a bit. I have to say that this little guy is a great example of the old saying from Mark Twain: *"It's not the size of the dog in the fight, it's the size of the fight in the dog."* After about half an hour of active rope toy tug of war and running around the lab, Pedro seemed satisfied he had dominated us all, and he soon calmed down, first sitting in Calvin's lap, then eventually moving into the sleep chamber, where a blanket from home helped him relax and get comfortable. He accepted the nightcap, and as we checked our equipment readings and went through our checklist, we could see his eyes close as he drifted off to sleep. Vital signs showed he was calm and relaxed, and the EEG readings signaled he was entering dreamless sleep. As with our other subjects, in less than 30 minutes the transition to REM sleep began We observed a few minor myoclonic twitches, and seconds later our main monitor sprang to life.

You will recall that in Pedro's initial dream session, the backdrop appeared to be a Mexican barrio, possibly the neighborhood where Pedro grew up. This time as the scene unfolded, we could see a typical middle-class suburban neighborhood we guessed might be Pedro's family's current location. Kids were playing in the yard in front of a red brick house, as others on bicycles passed by. In the backyard, a swing set was visible, as was a doghouse with a red shingle roof. As we watched the children kicking a soccer ball, seeming to focus on an imaginary goal in the center of a white wooden fence, Pedro came around the side of the house. You may remember that in his initial session Pedro appeared out of scale, towering over the playing children and other dogs, and that was again the case here. As Pedro approached the kids, they parted to allow him to pass through, showing deference to his large size as his confident swagger was unmistakable. Several other dogs could be seen following behind as Pedro's entourage moved out onto the sidewalk.

We watched as Pedro moved toward a skateboard one of the kids had left near the street, along with an aluminum scooter nearby in the grass. The other dogs stared intently as Pedro walked directly to the skateboard and slammed his front right paw on the end of it, sending it flipping into the air and landing smack in the middle of the sidewalk, as if that was the precise spot he was aiming for. As soon as the board landed, Pedro jumped onboard, leaning from side to side and using his right rear leg to propel himself forward, picking up speed along the way. The other dogs quickly gave chase, but Pedro remained well ahead of the pack, taking corners in expert fashion as the kids along the block cheered him on. Then it happened. Apparently unsatisfied with the speed he had achieved, Pedro summoned his frijole flatulence turbo boost, and a clearly visible and highly odiferous cloud appeared behind him, the force pushing him along at warp speed. At first the kids cheered him on, at least until he passed by, crop dusting the area with the putrid stench, sending the children scrambling for cover, pulling their shirts up to cover their noses and wiping the burning sensation from their eyes. In the control room we couldn't help but chuckle at this spectacle, counting ourselves fortunate that the high definition dream sequence displayed only video and audio, without olfactory capabilities, which likely would have caused our immediate evacuation.

As with some of the other subjects' dream sessions, we noted that our bird's-eye view was as though a drone was capturing the action, alternating between a view looking over Pedro's shoulder from behind (which was somewhat nauseating!) and a broader perspective from a higher elevation, revealing more of the neighborhood and allowing us to watch the pandemonium continue unabated for well over 5 minutes. Our monitors showed that Pedro's heartrate and respiration were elevated, but no more so than a typical canine play session. As he rounded the corner approaching his original starting point, Pedro expertly performed an Ollie, sticking the landing and followed with a kick flip that sent the board spinning into the air, landing in precisely the same place as when he found it. This drew considerable cheers and applause from the neighborhood kids, many of whom were still recovering from the gas attack, and a cacophony of barking and howling from Pedro's canine entourage. Pedro seemed to take it all in stride, his nose held high as he basked in the adulation.

As Pedro returned to a normal walking pace with his compatriots following behind, the picture began to fade as he continued in the distance, as though the end sequence in an action movie. The EEG readings confirmed he was transitioning out of REM sleep, and his vital signs soon reflected a quiet, restful non-dream state, which remained for the balance of the night. Following the dream sequence, I stepped outside for a soda break with Dr. Chan, maintaining my most serious professional scientific researcher face, before both of us busted out laughing at what we had just witnessed. Kathy caught her breath and said: "That little fart really put on a big show!" Now, if you have ever had Diet Dr.

Pepper spew out of your nose, I can relate. My combination carbonation expulsion choking cough and belly laugh eventually subsided, as I tried desperately to deliver a witty retort: "Yes, it was a real gas!" Even scientists can occasionally muster a sense of humor. A word of advice: Don't drink and laugh!

As our laughter finally subsided, we discussed what we had observed and a possible strategy for Pedro's first "conversation", noting that his normally combative style and diagnosis of Fortune Complex combine for a potentially challenging interaction. As a result, we will want to avoid direct confrontation, especially as we let him know we can carry on a two-way dialogue. Kathy suggested we ask Calvin to be directly involved when we switch to full duplex mode, since Pedro seemed more relaxed with him, and I agreed with that approach. We reentered *Dreamlab* and the team went quietly about its business until just before daybreak, when Pedro started to move around in the sleep chamber, indicating he might be beginning to wake up. As with his previous session, that meant a series of slow and deliberate stretches, beginning on his side with legs fully extended, a period of rest, then more stretching and rolling to the opposite side and finally onto his stomach, with legs splayed out in all directions. His paws occasionally swiped across his eyes, fortunately avoiding the nightcap EEG headgear. Vital signs showed Pedro was relaxed and EEG readings confirmed he was slowly waking up. Looks like it's showtime!

I slipped on my headset and asked Watson to switch to full duplex, but I left my microphone muted until Pedro was fully conscious and awake, then unmuted and stood quietly to see how the scene might unfold. It began with what can best be described as a "dog yawn".

"Whoa. Man, I was out big-time – totally crashed. Where is this? What the f---k? Wait! How did I… oh, yeh. I remember. El Patron said these f---ers wanted to check me out. What the hell? Shit!" I motioned to Calvin to move into the chamber so that Pedro could make eye contact.

"Hey, el jefe. I know you. What the f—k, man?" I heard a slight delay in my headset, and a quick replay, courtesy of Watson, who remembered we may need a Spanish translation, and the audio repeated:

"Hey, boss. I know you. What the f—k, man?" Well, that cleared that up! Calvin did not have on a headset, but he moved to a more comfortable position on the floor at the entrance to the chamber, so that Pedro would feel more comfortable with his surroundings. I unmuted my mic.

"Good morning, Pedro. I hope you slept well." I knelt down at the sleep chamber entrance.

"You hope… you hope *what*? Who the f—k are you, man? What the hell is going on?"

"Pedro, I am Dr. Cook, and I am doing some research on…" I couldn't even finish my sentence.

"Say *what*? You're *who*? Are you ICE? CBP? F—k you, man!" I asked Watson for help.

"Watson, please censor the conversation." I was getting tired of the f bombs.

"Certainly, Doctor." Watson's panel logo twinkled in immediate response.

"Who is that? Where are you, you (bleep) punk(bleep) mother(bleep). Where the hell are you?" Pedro was visibly angry and glancing around, puzzled by Watson's disembodied voice. "I said where the (bleep) are you? You're not (bleep) taking me anywhere!" I almost smiled at the added censor bleeps, but the situation was quite serious and tense.

I stepped forward, just in front of Pedro so he could see I was speaking.

"Pedro, calm down! We're not from Immigration or Border Protection. We are researchers studying amazing dogs like you." Pedro cocked his head but was apparently not impressed or convinced.

"I don't give a (bleep) who the (bleep) you are. Get me the (bleep) out of here!"

At this point what we were hearing was small dog, who clearly thinks he is a big dog – a real bad-ass, we were reading his thoughts through canine brainwaves, converting them into human language and translating that from Spanish to English. Oh yes, and lest I forget - now we were also censoring the little foul-mouthed sonofabitch. God, I love my job!

"Pedro, we are here to share with you some of our findings and include you in the discussion." I was speaking in a calm, assuring tone and cocked my head slightly in response to his. I braced myself for the next tirade.

"What? You're not ICE? Not CBP? You're (bleep) lyin', you (bleep)!" He looked right at Calvin and continued. "Are you part of this (bleep), man? You (bleep)'in with me?" Calvin offered a reserved smile and shook his head no. With no headset, he couldn't respond verbally, and we had agreed to limit our communication to mine alone. For our subjects, the situation is already a lot to take in.

I pause here for a moment to note that at this point Pedro seemed less concerned that humans were speaking to him than he was consumed by his apparent paranoia that we were all there to get him, fearful that we had set up some elaborate ruse in order to deport him. Based on my knowledge of his upbringing, reports from his owner and now our second dream sequence observations, I am confident that the early bullying and fear regarding his immigration status have combined to trigger Fortune Complex and severe paranoia, and as a result we are on the receiving end of this diatribe. I freely admit I never imagined I would be taking shit from a dog. Granted, I have picked up plenty, but then that was before I started speaking to them. Back to our little friend…

Moving to within inches of Pedro's face, which was now tense and trembling, I tried to offer some reassurance. Collecting myself in an effort to deescalate the situation, I started again.

> "Pedro, I promise we are not from immigration, and all we want is chance to talk and tell you about our research. I'm pretty sure you will find it interesting, and I assure you your owner will be here soon to take you home and fix your breakfast. Can we just talk?"

> "Talk? What the (bleep)? That's another thing! What the hell is going on here? How can I understand you? And how can *you* understand *me*? This is (bleep)'d up!" Pedro glanced around the room, looking at the team and our equipment, and he seemed to have calmed down somewhat, if only slightly.

> "It is pretty strange, I know. We have been able to use some new technology to allow us to hear your thoughts and translate our speech into something dogs can understand." I smiled and paused, bracing for the response.

> "Well, that's pretty (bleep)in' amazing, man! Are you a magician or somethin'? How the (bleep) do you do that?"

"It's complicated, and to be honest, I'm just as amazed as you are. I am a scientist, and our team has worked really hard on this. We all love dogs, and we want to hear what you have to say. I bet we could learn a lot from you." (OK, playing to the canine ego, I know. Guilty!) If we are to be able to learn anything from this session, we have to be able to carry on a civil dialogue. I continued:

"You seem a little worked up." Pedro jerked his head to stare me straight in the face.

"Little? Did you say I'm little?" Oh no, he looked pissed!

"No, I meant you seem a little bit agitated – you know – upset, angry - pissed off!"

"What the hell do you expect, man? I wake up with all of you looking at me, and now you are talking to me and I can understand you. So what? I should just chill and hope you will give a (bleep)ing treat? Are you (bleep)ing kidding me?" Pedro was still on edge, but he was now at least working to make sense of it all. As previously noted, it is a lot to take in.

"I hear you, Pedro. I do. It took me a while to get used to it." I shook my head to let him know I really did understand.

"Well I think it's pretty (bleep)ing (bleep)ed up! What do you want from me?" Whew! Now we were finally getting somewhere. I would need to be especially careful at this point.

"Yes, pretty (bleep)ing (bleep)ed up!" Not a scientific response, I admit, and the team seemed pretty surprised. You may not believe dogs can smile, but I assure you Pedro was grinning from ear to ear, obviously pleased that I had now stooped to his level (no pun intended).

For the balance of the morning the f bombs slowly subsided, and Pedro finally accepted that we were not immigration enforcement officers. As we continued the conversation, it was apparent that his fear and paranoia, combined with severe Fortune Complex were the primary drivers of his extreme sensitivity to even a completely unintentional and innocent reference to anything related to size or stature. This is one of the most severe cases I have seen in all my years of practice, and I believe that the combination of these factors serves to create a type of negative synergy, with each condition exacerbating the others. In Pedro's case, his projection of a tough guy image is actually a coping mechanism intended to create distance between himself and those around him, similar to a mob boss, establishing his dominance over his entourage and reinforcing his leadership position. In this case that included me and the team, as Pedro took every opportunity to let us know that he was very much in charge. The combative posture continued as I explained that we had observed in the dream sequence. At first, he seemed aggravated and let us know he didn't appreciate the intrusion, but at the same type it was clear he was curious. Continuing the conversation…

> "So, Pedro, I was especially impressed with your skateboarding skills! Pretty amazing!" OK, it's a suck-up, I know, but I had to try something to defuse the situation.
>
> "You saw that? Shit, man – you ain't seen nothin'. I can tear that thing up!" His posture relaxed and he sat for the first time, seeming to puff out his chest with pride in having his skills noticed.
>
> "Yes, you must be the Tony Hawk of the neighborhood." I hoped the reference to the skateboarding legend would strike a chord, but unfortunately it fell short due to lack of proper canine context.
>
> "I don't know who that is, man, but if you think he's good on a board, you ain't seen my stuff. I got mad skills, man. Mad skills." Pedro put his nose up in the air as if posing for a selfie.
>
> "I'm sure you do, Pedro. I'm sure you do."
>
> "No man, you don't understand. I got the secret power. I got the *supercharger*!" Well, we certainly didn't need to act as if we did n'\ot understand the reference!

"Yes, we saw that you had a real gas-powered ride." I know you probably don't believe me, but I swear this Chihuahua was grinning from ear to ear!

"You saw that?" He was shaking his head and scratching his ear in what seemed to be a combination of pride and mild embarrassment.

"Yes – saw it all - crop dusting the neighborhood. I'm glad we only get audio and video, not odors! I sure hope those kids recover." I watched as Pedro seemed to shake, as though he was dog belly laughing. OK, at least it looked like that to me.

"They're used to it, man."

Now Pedro was laying down for the first time since his dream sequence, clearly confident that his dream had conveyed both his mastery and obvious dominance and control of his environment, a common occurrence for those with his multiple diagnosed disorders. As we continued the dialogue, Pedro shared stories of his upbringing and journey to the U.S. and seemed very comfortable and complimentary of his adoptive family. As with Fifi and some of our other subjects, once Pedro was comfortable with the ability to talk with a human, the conversation went on and on. Before we knew it, Pedro's owner arrived to take him home. I had to wrap up quickly.

"Pedro, it has been good getting to know you."

"You too, Doc. You're OK, after all." He stood up and shook briefly, stretching his legs.

"Thanks, Pedro. I'm sorry we have to cut this short." I turned toward the door but noticed that he hadn't moved and appeared angry. As Calvin approached to remove Pedro's EEG cap, Pedro looked me right in the eye.

"Wait, did you say 'short'?"

Ah, shit!

Eleven

Dream on.

A dream which is not interpreted is like
a letter which is not read.

~The Talmud

Our favorite (and only) Great Dane, Alexander returned to *Dreamlab* for his second session, which meant we were potentially in for another hair-raising Scooby-Doo adventure, but this would also be the first time I would have the opportunity for a two-way conversation. I could not help thinking that we are fortunate REM sleep is accompanied by muscle paralysis, so aside from the occasional myoclonic twitch, we would at least remain in a safe observational environment. As Calvin and José teamed up to guide Alexander into the laboratory and ultimately the sleep chamber, we marveled at the sheer size of this massive, sweet natured canine, a giant specimen with a shy, reserved temperament and legs that seemed to go on forever. At an impressive 41 inches tall, Alexander is several inches shy of the record 44 inches for the species but wow, just wow! Our control room suddenly seemed less spacious as our team members worked in tandem, as though they were parking an 18-wheeler truck. With such a gentle giant, Alexander was fully cooperative, occasionally bouncing off an adjacent wall or recoiling nervously as his tale sideswiped our equipment. Soon he was in position, and Calvin stayed with him, offering kind, reassuring words and stroking his massive head, as Alexander soon relaxed and accepted the EEG and hormone sensor nightcap with no problem, as Calvin had expanded it to maximum size in preparation for his visit. As our background conversation and equipment reading checklist continued, in less than an hour Alexander was sound asleep and soon transitioned to REM sleep. Our instrument readings showed a dream sequence was beginning, and the main monitor began its magical transformation.

Unlike Alexander's initial dream sequence, which featured a visit to an assisted living facility, this time the scene appeared to be on a farm, with a winding road to a main house surrounded by rolling pasture and white split-rail fencing. Our view was elevated and approached the farmhouse, hovering above in drone-like fashion, offering a panoramic view of an adjacent barn and horse stable. We could see cows congregating under a large oak tree and a couple of horses grazing on lush green grass near a stream leading to a small pond.

Alexander soon emerged from the side of the stable, heading into the nearby field, joining the horses and cows, who seemed to acknowledge Alexander as he approached. One of the cows wandered over in the same general direction, and soon we were observing what appeared to be a small group meeting, with the cow, two horses and Alexander seeming to exchange greetings, evidenced by nodding heads and some indistinguishable, guttural sounds, as though some type of discussion was taking place. After a few minutes the horses moved away and Alexander followed, as the cow returned to the others grazing in the shade of the towering oak.

Suddenly as if on cue the horses peeled off, galloping in different directions, and Alexander gave chase, running full tilt after one, then the other as the horses galloped in circles, challenging Alexander to keep up. As with other dream sequences we have observed, even though Alexander is clearly asleep, his biometric readings reflect that he is actually experiencing the dream, with respiration and heart rate elevated. While it is complete conjecture and unsubstantiated by any quantifiable scientific measurement beyond the change hormone levels, our observation of Alexander's interaction with the horses is that he appears to be "happy" and "having fun". The quotation marks are simply an indication we cannot provide more than anecdotal support for our assertion, and with his long legs working hard to keep up with the horseplay, we can't say we actually saw a smile on Alexander's face, but he sure seemed to be having a great time. We noticed that the cows would occasionally nod their approval, and after several minutes of a spirited chase, the horses and Alexander slowed to a trot, then a walk as they headed toward the water trough. In the control room, we chuckled when Kathy suggested the scene reminded her of competitive friends working out at a gym, followed by a water break with his buddies. I had to agree. The dream sequence continued for several more minutes as the cows drifted over for a drink, like office workers chatting at the water cooler. As at the beginning of the dream, we did have audio, but it was mostly background noise as the animals moved around mixed with heavy breathing and an occasional snort, nothing particularly distinguishable.

As the visualization faded on the main monitor, our discussion focused on the contrast with Alexander's initial session. In that initial dream sequence, we witnessed what can only be described as anxiety and the dog's awareness of his large size and the impact on those around him. In this second session, not only had we not seen any of that, we are witnessing a dog seemingly enjoying himself and playing with other animals larger than himself in a wide-open environment without the confines that might create the bull in a china shop scenario. That noted, we documented our observations and instrument readings and continued our discussion well into the morning, as our research subject enjoyed restful sleep, splayed out on his back with long legs extended in all directions. At just after 6AM, Alexander rolled on his side, and a few minutes later shook his head and looked around to get his bearings. He appeared relaxed and comfortable with his surroundings, which provided the opportunity for me to initiate a conversation. I put on my Bluetooth headset and asked Watson to activate full duplex mode. I moved into the sleep chamber and sat on the floor next to Alexander, who extended his right paw as if to acknowledge my presence.

I placed my hand on his paw and began with a soft and slow greeting.

> "Good morning, Alexander. You look pretty comfortable." I smiled.
>
> "Yes, I am comforta – whoa! Wait! What is going on?" He looked around in an effort to find the source of the sound. I moved directly in front of him so that he could see my face as I began speaking.
>
> "I am right here, Alexander. My name is Ron, and thanks to some really cool technology, I am able to understand you. Hopefully you can understand me."
>
> "Yes, I can understand you, but wow! How strange is that!"
>
> As with our other subjects, Watson's translation algorithm has expertly created a crystal-clear

dialogue, complete with subtle nuances for speech and dialect. In Alexander's case, his vocal tome was deep and resonant, as one might expect from such a large breed, with an accent that might best be described as a combination of Sam Elliott and John Wayne, warm, relaxed and homey. While I suppose I was not expecting noble Danish royalty, I was taken in by the warmth and relaxed cadence, seemingly comfortable with what many would consider a startling experience.

"Yes, it *is* a little strange, but I am glad we can actually have a conversation."

"Man, this is really something! You can understand me? That is pretty amazing!"

"Yes, it certainly is. We have been working on this for quite a while, and we are pretty excited that we have a chance to share our research with each of our subjects."

"You mean there are other dogs? Are they here? Can I meet them?" He cocked his head as if waiting for my response.

"No, they are not here now. We are meeting with one dog each day, and today we have been observing you as you were sleeping."

"Really? I was out pretty good, so I'm not sure if there was much to observe."

"Well, actually we are studying *dreams*." I watched carefully as Alexander processed the comment.

"Whoa! You were observing my dreams? I understand how you could watch me sleeping – I get that, but how can you see my dreams? I was *dreaming*? I don't remember anything."

"Yes, you were enjoying a very nice dream. You were on a farm, and it looked like you were having fun running with a couple of horses. Do you remember that?"

"I do like running but no, I don't remember that at all. Is that bad?" Alexander cocked his head to the left, checking to see if something was wrong.

"No, it's pretty typical, really. Many times, we can't remember our dreams."

"Whew! That's good. I don't get a chance to run very often, you know, because I'm so big." Dog body language is not so different from humans, and as Alexander hung his head, I could tell he was reflecting on prior incidents, very aware of his impact on his surroundings. This was the perfect opportunity to address his anxiety in an effort to determine the seriousness of the condition in order to develop a plan for treatment.

"You are a big boy, for sure, but those horses are much bigger, and you seemed to keep up with them just fine." I watched for Alexander's immediate reaction.

"Well, horses are big for sure, I guess. Where I live, I get to go outside and play, but our yard is pretty small. I'm afraid I might knock over one of the kids." Now we were getting to the issue! If Alexander sees himself as a threat to others, even though he would not ever hurt anyone on purpose, his extreme self-consciousness will create a constant state of anxiety, which could be detrimental to his health and potentially debilitating.

"I understand completely, Alexander. In your dream you seemed to enjoy having some room to run. Maybe I can help with that." I certainly didn't want to make a promise I couldn't keep, but I knew that Alexander's owner and his entire family really loves him, so I will plan to make a point of sharing some suggestions when we debrief the owners at the end of the project. Following my comment, Alexander came to his feet and now towered above me, as I was still seated on the floor.

"I don't know what you can do, but I do like to run and play!" He shook his huge head, which I acknowledged with a pat.

We spent our remaining time talking as two recent acquaintances might, getting to know each other, and I made a point to spend most of the time listening. It seemed Alexander had a lot on his mind. Calvin eventually interrupted to let us know Alexander's owner had arrived. Before removing the EEG nightcap, I asked Alexander to "please keep our conversation between us", which elicited a head nod and an expression I swear looked like a grin. I will look forward to a conversation with his owner when we debrief at the conclusion of the study.

Pugsley arrived at his second *Dreamlab* session with considerable energy and strode confidently from the entry foyer directly into the sleep chamber like he owned the place. The team chuckled as he went straight for his favorite rope toy, then presented it to Calvin for a brief Pug tug of war, which Pugsley won handily, then immediately offered the same challenge to José. Watching the contest unfold, I couldn't help but laugh – this cute as can be pug acting as ferocious as a much larger an aggressive breed, refusing to give an inch to his human adversaries. Calvin and José smiled as Pugsley fought to hold his ground, and the battle continued for several minutes, until finally surrendering to the lovable champion. After some tactile interaction and calming words, Pugsley found a small stuffed animal toy and eventually settled into a comfortable position on the bed. As with our other subjects, our team was busy at work checking our respective stations and equipment checklists, occasionally checking on our now relaxed pup, who soon drifted off to sleep. The low frequency hum of the MRI and overhead fan combined for a perfect sleep environment, and less than 20 minutes later we watched the brainwave pattern shift from alpha to theta waves, indicating REM sleep was beginning. Keep in mind that while REM sleep and dreaming are not synonymous, most dreaming does occur during the REM stage, and these cycles may occur several times while sleeping. Research has shown that in addition to humans, other mammals and birds experience REM sleep.

Within just a few minutes, we could clearly see increased activity in the portions of the brain associated with REM sleep: the thalamus, amygdala, basal forebrain and others, similar to what we might observe during a wakeful state, while activity in other areas declined. As we watched our equipment screens and digital readouts, the main monitor swirled to life. You may recall that in Pugsley's initial dream sequence, our vantage point was that one might achieve from an overhead drone, looking down on ever-changing scenes and situations, each clearly and prominently featuring a pug. Whether a large family group, a single owner or aging couple, in every scene a pug was part of the family. As the monitor progressed from vague patterns to crystal clear ultra-high definition, the scene seemed to once again continue the same pattern. We watched as children interactive with their respective pug, from active play to restful naps together. Occasionally however, we realized that something was different. The scenes continued to move along as we drifted above, but we began to question if we had in fact seen a pug in this one or that one. Maybe we had simply not been watching closely? Sharpening our focus and attention, we soon confirmed that our observations were correct; there were definitely scenes where a pug was not visible. Kathy and José noted what appeared to be a correlation between these scenes and Pugsley's brainwave, hormone levels and vital signs, which seemed to show he was more anxious, then relaxed again when a new scene did include a dog. José rattled off the readings during each occurrence and, sure enough, the pattern continued for the entire session. It was as though Pugsley, fast asleep yet clearly quite focused and active in his dream, was perplexed when he saw that some families were not enjoying the joys of pugdom. The same correlation occurred in two additional dream sequences, both with substantially similar scenes and characteristics.

As Pugsley slipped into non-REM sleep and the main monitor faded, the team discussed what we had witnessed. While we cannot definitively point to absolute cause and effect, we agreed that the visual and biometric data seem to point to what appears to be Pugsley's seemingly innate mission to bring joy to the planet by ensuring that everyone's lives are enriched by the companionship of these sweet, adorable animals. As the team continued to observe Pugsley's relaxed, restful state in the sleep chamber, I was observing each team member. Without exception, each had his or her head cocked slightly with a visible smile, as if to say: "Aw, how cute!" I had to agree. I looked forward to sharing our observations with Pugsley and, as morning came, our instrument readings told us he was beginning to wake up. Like our other subjects, most dogs seem to take their time in the waking process, slowly stretching and occasionally rolling from side to side. After a final roll onto his stomach, Pugsley blinked his eyes to remind him of his surroundings and slowly but surely, he eventually rose to his feet and lapped at the nearby water bowl, followed by a head shake to clear the water on his wrinkled snout.

Pugsley then trotted directly over to Calvin, who was bending down to offer a smile and pat on the head, with a greeting: "Good morning, buddy." Of course, since Calvin was not wired with a headset, Pugsley could neither hear nor understand him, but Calvin's greeting elicited an immediate response, and I quickly slipped on my headset and asked Watson to activate a full duplex conversation. As I was about to step in, we heard from Pugsley.

> "Hi. Good morning. I like this guy. He is really nice to me." Calvin smiled broadly. It struck me that Pugsley's translated "voice" had a somewhat raspy quality, a mixture of Rocket Raccoon from *Guardians of the Galaxy* with a dash of Joe Pesci thrown in for good measure.
>
> I moved closer and knelt down. "Good morning, Pugsley. I hope you slept well." I watched closely as he cocked his head, first to one side, then the other. I was positioned so that he could clearly

make the connection between my moving lips and the words he was hearing though the EEG nightcap.

"Hello sir. What's going on? Are you talking to me? If you are, I can understand you, but that's not possible. Am I dreaming?" That comment drew a collective and clearly audible chuckle from the team, who seemed to appreciate the irony of the comment.

"Pugsley, no, you are not dreaming. I am Dr. Cook, and these fine people have helped me find a way to communicate with you." Another cock of the head, almost as though he was developing an appropriate response.

"Wow! That's pretty amazing!" I thought for an instant I saw a smile, but more likely just the arrangement of the wrinkles…

"Yes, it is amazing. We have been doing some research into the way dogs dream, and we are now beginning to see that it's not much different from us humans."

"You have been *what*? You can *talk* to me, and you can also somehow *see my dreams?* That's pretty weird." He seemed more curious and perplexed than agitated, as though interested in hearing more.

"I realize it's a lot to take in but yes, we have developed a way for us to carry on this conversation so that we can learn more about each other. I am pleased to meet you."

"Same here, Doc. You seem pretty nice. Who is that one?" He extended his left paw and pointed toward Calvin, still seated on the floor nearby.

"His name is Calvin, and he and our other team members really appreciate you helping us with our research. We have learned a lot from you and our other subjects."

"Other subjects? Are there other pugs here? Can I meet them?"

"No, it's just you today. We have a number of other dogs participating, but you are the only pug, and I have to say you represent the breed quite well."

Now, I can't say for sure, but as Pugsley tilted his head upward, he seemed to puff out his little chest in a show of pride.

"Well, thanks – I guess. Where are the other dogs?" Now we were engaged in an active conversation, and it is interesting to note that in most cases at this point, the dogs seemed more interested in hearing more than stopping to marvel at the fact we could understand each other, an accomplishment soon forgotten.

"We have nine other dogs participating, but we only space here in our *Dreamlab* for one each evening." As I spoke, Pugsley took a step toward me, no doubt making his own studious observation as our conversation continued.

Dwayne, our chief statistician, suddenly emerged from around the corner and interrupted with a quick comment. "That's a total of ten. Ten dogs."

Of course, Pugsley could see Dwayne speaking, but had no way to know what he was saying. I shook my head. "Thanks, Dwayne. Pugsley, there are a total of ten dogs participating and just like you, each one has been kind enough to allow us to observe them as they sleep so that we can learn about the similarities and differences to our own sleep patterns and dreams."

"Sometimes when I wake up, I know I was dreaming." He made eye contact, letting me know he expected a response.

"Yes, that happens to me sometimes, as well. Do you remember your dreams from last night?" I watched as Pugsley thoughtfully considered the question and after a few moments, he nodded his head.

"Yes, actually I do. I remember checking on the families."

"Checking on the families? What families, and what were you checking?" I was intrigued he was aware and seemed to be able to recall what he had dreamed.

"The families – all the families. I was checking to make sure that all families include a pug. You know, it's my *job*." I was stunned at the concise, authoritative response.

"Well, that is quite a responsibility, I must say! That must keep your dreams pretty busy." Admittedly, I was fumbling for words, not wanting to cast doubt on what was clearly a heartfelt mission.

"Well, it does take some time, and occasionally it's a little concerning. Most families are OK, but then sometimes I find families with no pug or even some with no dog at all! Can you imagine?" Since Pugsley's wireless sensor *nightcap* was still in place, we watched his vital signs and hormone levels elevate slightly, indicating anxiety. He seemed distraught. Before I could respond, he continued.

"Why wouldn't a family have a pug? It just doesn't make sense." His heart rate and blood pressure suggested he was pretty worked up. I started to speak but couldn't finish my sentence.

"Well I'm sure they probably…" Pugsley jumped in, continuing his thought.

"I mean, you know I heard my owner talking about a place where there are pugs and other dogs who don't have families – just waiting for someone to adopt them. That's not right! I really don't understand. It makes me upset."

At that point, although my natural reaction may have been to craft a thoughtful explanation and some sort of logical excuse, I could see that Pugsley was clearly taken aback by this apparent travesty, and I was not about to belittle his genuine concern.

"Yes, that is unfortunate. I can't imagine anyone not wanting the joy of having a pug in the family." OK, so I was playing along and didn't want to hurt his feelings. Guilty, as charged.

"It's just not right. Our job is to be there to make you happy. *It's what we do*. If they want some other breed, that's OK I guess, as long as they understand the rules."

Now I was cocking *my* head. "The rules? What are the rules?" Pugsley pulled his head back, clearly surprised at my question.

"You know. Some of you humans think we are what you call 'pets'. It doesn't work that way." Before I could answer, he continued. "We are not *pets*, we're *partners*. The rules say we are there to support you, rain or shine, good times and bad."

I jumped in. "In sickness and in health? Man's best friend?" Pugsley snapped back.

"I hadn't heard those, but OK – yes, they are part of it. We tolerate being left alone by ourselves while you are off doing some type of 'work' without us; I can't imagine why. We overlook when you fall asleep in front of the TV when we would really appreciate going out for a pee break. We snuggle in to keep you warm on a cold winter day, and we don't complain when you run out of treats for an entire week." I nodded in agreement as he continued. "Then the rules say that you agree to tolerate an occasionally mishap, when we have waited patiently with our legs crossed all day because you stopped for a drink with friends, then finally we can't hold it anymore and let loose on what we try to make sure is the tile floor, not the carpet. But we are dogs, after all, and we're not perfect, so sometimes a little pee or poop misses the mark. Oops, my bad!"

I offered some support: "That sounds reasonable." Pugsley shook his head and continued.

"Wait, I'm not done! We are here to entertain you and are ready to play anytime, but when we're left alone all day with absolutely nothing to do, we might get bored. We might decide that the sofa cushion or your favorite shoe is a pretty fun toy, something we can really get our teeth into, know what I mean?"

"OK, OK – I get it, I really do." I shook my head, as this small, sweet dog continued to unload.

"Because you see, we are not *pets*, we're *partners*. We've got your back, and you've got ours. Those are the rules." I was momentarily speechless, taken aback by the simplicity of the message and the sincerity of this dog preacher and his sermon on the need for equity in the dog/human relationship, quite a humbling experience. The nods from my team members confirmed their agreement.

"Pugsley, thank you for explaining that, and I couldn't agree more." I didn't want to appear condescending, and I could clearly see that he was completely sincere in his objective. I really admired that. "You know, I have an idea of how we can join you in your mission."

His ears immediately perked up. "You do? Really?" He did a quick circle, sort of a victory lap. "That would be great!"

"Yes, I want to talk things over with our team, and next week we will be meeting with your owner. I think we can all benefit from working together." It was clear I had Pugsley's full attention.

"Thank you, Doc. We are all on the same team here, right?" Listening to the audio of the conversation over the control room speakers, now the whole team was nodding and applauding in agreement.

"Let's get you home, and I promise to follow up on what we have discussed this morning. Deal?" I instinctively offered my hand, and to my surprise, Pugsley offered his paw in return. I swear I never commanded "shake", but we definitely had reached an agreement.

Pugsley's owner would soon arrive to pick him up, and Calvin and Dwayne removed the nightcap, ending our conversation and escorted the dog to the adjacent park for a walk before departing. I waved goodbye as a confident canine walked proudly to the car, then turned as if to request confirmation of what had just transpired. I nodded and offered a thumbs up, as a young boy helped Pugsley climb into the backseat. The team and I walked to the nearby *Dunkin' Donuts* for coffee, and we spent the balance of the morning talking through how we might be able to make a difference by introducing prospective *partners*. So many possibilities…

As we prepared *Dreamlab* for Blue's arrival, we discussed the Basset Hound's previous visit and dream sequence, which was a flashback to an actual event, one that clearly left a traumatic psychological mark on this friendly long-eared pooch. The team offered their various opinions on how best to ameliorate the situation, and we all agreed that regardless of the approach, part of the mission would be to somehow break Blue's association of a ride in the family car with an unpleasant outcome. Before developing a specific plan however, we were curious to see if this second visit yielded a similar dream sequence theme. We were wrapping up our discussion as Blue's owner pulled up to the building entrance, and Blue jumped out of the back seat with the confidence of a longer legged breed. Dwayne was waiting at the door with a leash but quickly realized that would not be necessary, as Blue sauntered into the entry foyer, with his snout to the ground and long ears dangling just above the tile floor. Acting every bit like he owned the place, he checked each of us out in turn as if we were subject to his formal inspection. Apparently, we passed muster, and Calvin joined Dwayne on the floor for a proper ear scratch and welcome for our guest, who seemed to revel in the attention. Behind that hang dog look was a friendly, playful soul, and Blue continued to play a version of attack and retreat with his favorite rope toy. It was obvious Calvin and Dwayne were enjoying the session as much as the dog, and I reminded them we would soon need to begin to settle down in preparation for we hoped would be a successful dream session and Blue's first introduction to a dog/human conversation. As with our other subjects, I acknowledge feeling a sense of nervous anticipation, wondering if Blue's reaction will mirror what we had seen thus far.

We went through our regular pre-session checklist, and I watched Blue out of the corner of my eye, as he nudged a tennis ball toward Dwayne as if to entice him to engage. It was at least 15 minutes later when Blue finally gave up and ultimately retreated to his bed in the sleep chamber. Calvin sat down next to him, and Blue accepted the EEG sensor nightcap without objection. Over the next 30 or so minutes we watched as Blue's eyelids occasionally flickered, then closed as he eventually dozed off, his jowls flapping occasionally as his breathing slowed and he entered a deep, restful sleep. The specially modified fMRI automatically tracked Blue's body position perfectly, and the soft, low-pitched hum of the machine served to mask our continued equipment tinkering in the control room. Consistent with our other subjects, REM sleep came some 20 minutes later, the transition signaled by the EEG readout. Just like clockwork, the main monitor swirled to life and quickly morphed from vague indistinguishable shapes and colors to crisp ultra-high definition clarity.

The scene unfolded to reveal a stately two-story home and detached garage with a New England look and feel. The front yard featured stately oak trees and lush green grass, and we observed two children, a boy and girl, playing on the lawn near the quiet street. The young girl was walking a pink bicycle along the entry walkway, and the boy was rolling by on an aluminum scooter. A few seconds later Blue emerged from the side of the house, his nose to the ground as if checking the area for any unfamiliar scent. Soon a man we quickly identified as Blue's owner appeared at the front door and called out to the kids: "Come on guys; we're going to the park. Blue – let's go for a ride in the car." What sounded like a cheerful invitation did not sit well with Blue, who let out an audible combination yelp and short howl, then took off around the opposite side of the house. "Blue! Come here! We're going to the park. Come on!" The man ran out into the yard, but Blue was hightailing it in the opposite direction, his short muscular legs going as fast as he could manage. "Stop! Blue!" The man was, in a word, *pissed.* As he disappeared around the corner of the house, Blue emerged from the opposite side near the garage, apparently determined to avoid capture at any cost. We watched as the cat-and-mouse chase continued, with Blue's owner appearing on one end of the home just as Blue scrambled to disappear on the opposite end. Of course, it didn't help that the kids were laughing hysterically through it all, which only served to further infuriate their already angry father.

From the control room, we watched the pandemonium continue and noted that Blue's heart rate and respiration were elevated, with an occasional dream-induced myoclonic twitch confirming that the dog was experiencing the chase in his dream, working hard to evade capture. As the boy and girl joined the chase with bike and scooter, the father continued yelling, soon running out of breath and breaking off the now low speed pursuit. Blue had found refuge behind what appeared to be a garden shed behind the house, panting breathlessly in the shade of the building as the children continued the search and their dad gave up and went inside. The kids continued to call and whistle, but Blue had found the perfect hiding spot. As we watched, we noticed his legs were trembling, even as the vital sign readings slowly returned to normal. Eventually the children also abandoned the search, and Blue seemed to finally relax, his slobbery jowls glistening in the grass behind the shed. The team and I looked at each other and shared a collective "Whew!" The entire dream sequence lasted no more than 10 minutes from start to finish, and soon the main monitor faded as Blue transitioned to a non-REM restful sleep. The research team and I gathered in the control to discuss what we had observed, and we agreed that the avoidant behavior we witnessed was likely caused by Blue's association of the command to go for a ride in the car with what his brain had apparently recorded as an unpleasant visit to the vet. I made some mental notes for a possible plan to break that association.

Over the balance of the evening Blue had two additional dream sequences. The first found him playing hide and seek with the same boy and girl from the previous dream, which we knew to be Blue's owner's children. There was nothing particularly remarkable about the scene, at least until Nate pointed out that Blue, with his incredible olfactory ability, was intentionally prolonging the game, allowing the kids to maintain their hidden status even when he had easily sniffed them out. He seemed to enjoy the interaction with the children, who were giggling as Blue eventually bounded into the pile of leaves where the boy was hiding, and they all jumped in and rolled around, eventually spilling out onto the grass. The second sequence found Blue as a mighty squirrel hunter, stalking one after another like a cat, only to realize that gravity would deny that final vertical leap, as the squirrel retreated to a tree limb just out of reach. It sounds odd now to say that such scenes were not unexpected for the dreams of a Basset Hound, as though we could have ever really imagined we would actually have the ability to experience such an occasion. As we quietly compared notes on our observations during the session, Kathy noted that Blue was starting to wake up, and Dwayne whispered: "Looks like you're up, Boss." Hearing that, I stopped to realize that I was no longer nervous about the interaction about to unfold. In fact, I was quite relaxed, no doubt a result of the confidence gained from previous practice. After "conversations" with our first few subjects, I approached each session with a sense of positive anticipation, looking forward to what this new adventure might bring.

Blue was sprawled comfortably on the edge of the sleep chamber dog bed, with his snout on the cool tile floor. He raised one eyebrow, then the other, as Calvin and I approached. I knelt down, then moved to a cross-legged position on the floor at the chamber entrance. I don't know about you, but I would not want some stranger in a lab coat messing with my wakeup routine. I waited patiently as Blue stretched for a few minutes, before raising his head, and he looked around, as though to remind himself how he ended up in this place. He shook his head, and his long ears flopped from side to side.

“Man, I was out like a light! I’m not really sure why I am here or why these people are staring at me, but I hope they have some food ready. I’m hungry!” I couldn’t help but smile. Blue’s “voice” was definitely that of a “hound dog”, a Southern good ol’ boy, aw shucks character with a deep, resonant timbre. I leaned forward into his field of view.

“Good morning, Blue. I hope you slept well.” He raised his head and leaned forward slightly, trying to locate the source of the sound. As I continued, we made eye contact.

“I thought we might spend a few minutes this morning getting to know each other.”

His slightly cocked head showed the expected initial confusion, but he seemed unfazed.

“Sure, uh…nice to meet you? You are *talking* to me? How is that possible?”

“We are doing some scientific research, and we have developed a way to allow us to communicate. We are happy to have you as part of our research team.” Blue stood up completely and tilted his head upward, as though he had just received a compliment.

“Research team? I am on a research team?

“You certainly are, and we really appreciate your help.” Now we were eye-to-eye.

“Uh, OK. Sure, I guess. Who are you?”

"I am Dr. Cook, and these people behind me are part of our team."

"*Doctor?* Wait, I don't like doctors!" Blue scooted backward and turned his head to the side, almost wincing. His vital signs and hormone levels spiked.

"No, I'm not a medical doctor. I am a scientist, and with your help, we are trying to develop a way for us to get to know each other. Are you OK with that?"

"Uh, I guess so. Are you going to *examine* me?" He was definitely anxious and apprehensive, and it was increasingly apparent that his prior traumatic experience had left its mark. Ideas for dealing with that trauma raced through my head, as we continued.

"No, I'm not a veterinarian, and you look like you are in great shape." Blue cocked his head and turned to face me again, a bit more relaxed. "We have been observing your dreams while you were sleeping, and we are interested in comparing them to our own."

At this point, Blue moved a bit closer, indicating his interest in what I was saying.

"You can see my dreams? How can you do that? What did you see? What did I dream?"

This rapid-fire questioning was accompanied by elevated heart rate and respiration, indicating a degree of nervousness and apprehension.

"It's a bit complicated, but basically dogs have dreams, just as we do, and we are able to use your brainwaves – your thoughts, and translate them into visual images and sounds, just as though we were there with you."

"Really? Wow! Well butter my butt and call me a biscuit!" The vocal translation's accent, delivery and Blue's quizzical expression combined for quite a caricature, and I heard a few chuckles from my colleagues behind me. I *had* to laugh.

"Yes, we were able to see that you love playing outside, but you don't seem to enjoy going for a ride in the car." I watched for the reaction.

"The car? Hell no! I ain't gettin' in that car no more. Ain't hap'nin!" He seemed adamant.

"Why not? Is that related to a bad past experience?" I asked as though I had no idea.

"Bad experience? Yeh – I s'pose you could say that. I don't like the car."

"Is it the *car*, or *where it takes you*?" I continued pressing for an answer. "What happened?"

"Tell you what doc, I'm fixin' to tell you. One time I got in the car, and I didn't come home the same. No offense, but it was a trip to the doctor."

"Sorry to hear that, Blue. You know, every ride in the car doesn't end badly – like a ride to the park to play with your family." I wanted to associate the car ride with a pleasant outcome.

"I hear you, sir, and I don't want to be the turd in the punchbowl, but I didn't just fall off the turnip truck. I got in the car one day, and when I got home I was missin' sumpthin'."

"You lost something?" I braced for the answer, and the team tried not to be obvious as they almost fell over trying to lean in to hear the response.

"My balls! They took my balls, doc! Hell, I was madder than a wet hen!" Calvin motioned toward the vital signs control panel, which reflected Blue's visceral reaction to the unpleasant memory.

"Now Blue, don't pitch a hissy fit!" I immediately caught myself - oh no! It must be contagious!

"You ain't heard the half of it, doc. Just thinkin' about it makes my butt want to grind corn."

"Well, I know that getting neutered was probably not a pleasant experience, but you realize that won't happen again, right?" OK, I admit that was pretty weak, but I needed to try.

"Hey doc, don't pee down my back and tell me it's rainin', alright? I don't think they're gonna put 'em back on!" Blue was shaking his head with that sad, droopy face only a basset hound can master.

"No, they're not, but now that that's behind you, I hope you understand your family loves you, and they want to include you in everything they do. Sometimes that means taking trips in the car. Make sense?"

"Sure, doc, but I hope *you* understand that I'm just a little bit pissed off about my balls. Make sense?" Oh god, I hate sarcasm, especially from a *dog*, but I didn't want to make the situation worse.

"I can only imagine, Blue. I'm glad to see you are doing well now. You look great!" I watched closely to see if the compliment had an impact. Blue raised his head proudly.

"Happy as a pig in mud, doc. I reckon I'm a lucky hound."

"You are indeed lucky, Blue, and your family is lucky to have you." It may have just been my imagination, but I swear I saw his head nod in agreement.

We spent the balance of our time together talking about a variety of subjects, from music to learning about virtually every other dog in the neighborhood. It turns out that, like humans, dogs enjoy the company of other canines and have their own circle of friends. Blue is no exception and apparently, he is especially fond of a female beagle named Daisy who lives on the same street. He is not too wild about a bulldog, Bruno, one street over who, according to Blue is "...so noisy and annoying when I am out for a walk with Daisy." Sounds like a lot of canine testosterone to me! Blue loves country music and is a huge Garth Brooks fan. Surprisingly, he was not aware that Garth and Trisha

Yearwood are married. Wait! What am I saying? How could he have possibly known that? Glancing at the clock, I realized that Blue's owner would be arriving soon to pick him up, and I wanted to make sure we would not have an issue with getting him in the car for the ride home.

> "No sir, no problem here. Bubba, tell you what – I just want to go home and get some breakfast. I'm hungrier than a tick on a teddy bear."

Well, I definitely hadn't heard that one before! Calvin soon entered the room, knelt down and removed the EEG nightcap, and our conversation was over. As each team member powered down their respective equipment, the room soon fell silent, and Blue's owner pulled up at the entrance, as if on cue. As the kids in the back seat called his name, Blue trotted confidently to the car, stopping at the curb and turning around to make eye contact with me one final time. A quick head nod, and he mustered a short running start for the leap into the backseat, to the delight of the waiting children and plenty of head pats and hugs all around. I took the team to breakfast at IHOP, and we discussed potential options to help break Blue's negative association with car rides. I had an idea…

Twelve

Conversations, continued.

Dogs laugh, but they laugh
with their tails.

~Max Eastman

As we prepared for Roscoe's second *Dreamlab* session, our team huddled to discuss the obvious. The last session was extremely upsetting for all of us, and it is distressing to consider the possibility that Roscoe's dreams may be fixated on the violent and traumatic incident that took the love of his life. I tried to reassure everyone that the focus of our research must be to observe and document, but the greater *purpose* is to use those observations and data to develop a treatment modality to benefit the subject. Our collective trepidation was palpable as Roscoe's owner drove up, and Calvin met them at the door. As with our other subjects, Roscoe entered the lab without hesitation and with a confidence supported by his previous visit. Unlike the other dogs, Roscoe was not much into playing with toys brought from home and seemed somewhat quieter and more reserved, however he never retreated when we approached and responded favorably to our positive voices and pats on the head. Calvin and Dwayne sat cross-legged on the floor in an attempt to engage Roscoe in play, but he wasn't interested, choosing instead to wander out of the sleep chamber and peruse the control room as we continued our pre-session checklist. I likened this to the type of checking behavior we frequently observe in human subjects who have been impacted by violence, a constant scan of their surroundings in order to confirm a safe environment. Imagine you are a Secret Service agent on the presidential protective detail checking a hotel ballroom prior to the President's arrival. For a canine, that includes a heightened vigilance and hypersensitivity of vision, hearing and smell. This scrutiny continued for another ten minutes or so and ended only when Roscoe seemed satisfied that there were no threats and eventually returned to the sleep chamber, where Calvin joined him for more calm verbal reassurances and tactile interaction. Roscoe did not seem to react especially positively or negatively to being petted, almost as though he tolerated it out of respect for Calvin's well-intended efforts.

Roscoe accepted the EEG nightcap with expected cautious curiosity, and after what seemed like forever, Roscoe's head was resting comfortably on the edge of the dog bed and his occasional peeking slowly ebbed, then stopped as he eventually drifted off to sleep. We observed that vital signs were normal, and we completed our final instrument checks as the low-pitched hum of the fMRI provided a perfect background of white noise conducive to sleep. About twenty minutes later, audio static from the monitors was followed by pixelated raster images on the main screen, and soon the picture sharpened to reveal a nighttime urban street scene, apparently a downtown city side street illuminated by an occasional streetlight or outdoor security lighting at the backdoors of neighborhood businesses. As the picture gained ultra-high definition clarity, I heard Nate's audible gasp: "Oh no!", as the scene was reminiscent of the previous session's tragic episode. Our eyes were fixated on the screen, nervous that we were about to be subjected to another violent incident. I vividly recall that one could actually feel the tension in the air, as though some type of invisible electrical field created heightened hair-on-end sensitivity, lacking only a dramatic white-knuckle soundtrack.

We watched nervously as Roscoe emerged stage left from a dimly lit alleyway, cautiously moving out onto the sidewalk and exhibiting the same checking behavior we observed on his arrival at the lab. As he moved down the block, another dog came out of the shadows and joined Roscoe, a slightly smaller black Labrador Retriever, and we noted the same checking behavior, scanning the environment for potential threats. Soon a third dog appeared, then a fourth, each a dark colored Labrador, rendering each one virtually invisible in the shadows. It was as though we were observing a type of canine street gang, but with the coordinated discipline of a military special operations team. The group continued slowly along the block, with each dog constantly monitoring their respective flank. Headlights shone on the wall of a building ahead, indicating a car was about to turn down the street. Roscoe reacted immediately with repeated loud barking, and the other dogs joined in the alarm. Vital sign and hormone level readings confirmed a highly alert state.

An elderly Asian woman emptying trash into a dumpster responded to the sound and quickly retreated into the rear entrance of a restaurant. A cat perched on a ledge near the dumpster let out a high-pitched shriek and disappeared in an instant. The barking continued until the vehicle made its turn onto the street, and each of the dogs withdrew into the shadows. We watched as the car approached, an older model cherry red Buick with what appeared to be four occupants vaguely discernable behind dark tinted windows. The car slowed and the front right window soon lowered to reveal a pretty scary looking dude scanning the area as though looking for someone. As the vehicle passed under a streetlight, we could clearly see what appeared to be the barrel of a handgun resting on the window ledge, ready to engage anyone unfortunate enough to show his face. The car moved slowly down the street, eventually turning left and exiting our field of vision. I am pretty sure I heard a collective sigh of relief, and our team looked at each other to acknowledge that Roscoe and his colleagues had provided a warning that likely quite literally dodged a bullet.

With the car gone, Roscoe and pals emerged from the shadows and continued their patrol of the neighborhood, occasionally interrupted whenever a car approached, which resulted in a loudly barked warning, followed by continued patrol when the threat had passed. This canine neighborhood watch scenario played out in two other dream sequences during the evening, each time in a smooth, disciplined fashion, with Roscoe and the three other dogs warning, retreating and reemerging when the coast was clear, with vital signs and hormone levels first increasing, then subsiding. Rinse and repeat – beautiful! In each of the two other sequences, we observed one or more people react to the barking, associate it with the approaching car and take cover as a result. As I watched each scene unfold, I also observed the team's reaction, which ranged from supportive head nods to thumbs up and occasional verbal outbursts, followed by a quick hand-over-mouth. I suppose it is only normal to express approval for such an effective public service. As Roscoe was blissfully enjoying non-REM (also known as quiescent) sleep, I began to put my thoughts together on how best to engage our subject in our first dog/human conversation. This should be interesting…

It was just before dawn when Dwayne called our attention to the fact that Roscoe had begun to stretch, indicating he might be waking up, and I quietly moved closer to the sleep chamber, standing near the doorway. As I watched and waited, I couldn't help but feel relieved that the session had not been a repeat of the Roscoe's initial visit. In fact, I found myself energized and excited by what I had observed, and I was looking forward to the discussion. Roscoe was a bit slow waking up, but in another ten minutes or so he was stretching all four legs before eventually standing, glancing around the room and checking to make sure everything was OK. I moved into the room and activated my Bluetooth headset, signaling Watson to turn on full duplex mode. Roscoe was watching my every move, and after determining I posed no threat, he sat down and I smiled and took a position near the edge of the dog bed. Roscoe was now scanning the room, and I waited until I had his full attention and made eye contact.

"Good morning, Roscoe." I watched as his head cocked first to one side, then the other.

"Wait. What?" Roscoe was checking the room, trying to isolate the source of the sound.

"It's me, Roscoe. My name is Ron. Right here." I held up my hand in a wave.

"What the f—k? That don't make sense!" Now he was staring straight at me, looking anxious and confused.

"Yes, I know it's hard to believe, but we are able to communicate."

"Oh yeh? How's that work exactly?" Roscoe's "voice" was not what I expected. While it did have an abrasive urban vibe, it wasn't quite as angry and confrontational as I might have imagined, considering what we had witnessed from the first dream session.

"We are a team of researchers studying similarities between dog and human dreaming, and we have developed a way to use your brainwaves to translate them into a language we can understand. And we use that same technology to translate my speech into something you can understand. Does that make sense?" I thought I had done a pretty good job of explaining.

"That's great, man. I just have one question." Roscoe raised his head as though waiting for my response. I nodded and leaned a little closer.

"Sure, what's the question?"

"My question is this: SAY WHAT? What the f—k, man? What the hell is going on?" Roscoe stood up and shook his head from side to side. I smiled as I replied.

"I know it all seems pretty crazy, but as you can see, it works, and we have been able to talk to several of the other dogs participating in our study."

"Other dogs? Where are they? Are they labs like me?" He now seemed genuinely interested.

"No, no other labs. We have included ten different breeds, and you are the only Labrador."

Roscoe cocked his head slightly, and he seemed a bit more relaxed, but very engaged.

"No other labs, huh? That's too bad, but I'll represent." His head bobbed as if to signal positive acknowledgement.

"We appreciate your participation, and it's important for us to gain your perspective."

Roscoe scanned the room, possibly checking for other research subjects.

"Those other people in the white coats – do I have to talk to them, too?" His head motioned toward the control room, where every team member was fixated on our conversation.

"No, I'm in charge of our team and the only one you'll be hearing from."

"OK, then. So how does this work, exactly." Interestingly, Roscoe now seemed relaxed and ready to find out more. I nodded and was careful to ease into it.

"Well, a good place to start is to talk about what we were able to observe while you were sleeping. As you know, this was your second trip here to the lab, and this time we saw some things we found very interesting."

"Yeh? Like what? Wait, did you say '*lab*'?" The response was more curious than confrontational.

"Oops, sorry. Yes, this is our research laboratory, and we refer to it as *Dreamlab*. For us, *lab* is short for *laboratory*. This is where we created a way to visualize what you are dreaming, so that we can see what you are experiencing when you dream. Your first session was pretty upsetting, and all of us were very sorry to hear about Rosie." Roscoe's immediate reaction was to snap his head back to face me directly, and he leaned forward, though not in a threatening way.

"Wait a minute. You *saw* my dreams? You could see what happened?" Out of the corner of my eye, I could see Nate motioning from the control room, pointing to the fMRI data display and vital sign monitor panel, showing Roscoe's blood pressure, heart rate and respiration were all elevated. I nodded my acknowledgement.

"Yes, and I really can't imagine all that you have gone through since that night." I extended my hand, but Roscoe stepped back and lowered his head, clearly impacted by the memory. I continued: "I don't mean to upset you. We are all very sorry."

"It's OK, man. And yeh, you can't possibly imagine. I'm trying to deal, you know." From our research I have learned that it's hard to read complex emotions in the face of a dog, but I do believe I could sense Roscoe's sadness. I felt like I was consoling a friend.

"From what we saw last night, it sure looks like you have taken some action to make sure something like that doesn't happen again." I tried to convey my support and sincerity.

"Yeh, me and my boys ain't playin'. We're gonna let everybody know whassup. No more drive-bys, you feel me?" Roscoe's head swayed from side to side, initially avoiding eye contact, then looking up to make sure he had made his point.

"Yes, you and the other labs really have a smooth, well executed plan. Very impressive!"

Roscoe nodded, and looked me straight in the eye, before continuing.

"It wasn't just Rosie. My boys and I have lost brothers and sisters before that and more since then. It's just crazy out there, man, and not just for dogs."

"Well, your plan seems to be working. You are making a difference, for sure." Roscoe's head was now held high, and he spoke with a confidence that reflected a sense of purpose and resolve. At this point he moved closer and sat down, now eye-to-eye like two friends in a heart-to-heart conversation. I felt a kind of warmth and kinship.

"No more labs need to die, man. No more people need to die. Just too many lost. Too many. And it's not just in my hood, ya know. It's *everywhere*."

"I agree with you, Roscoe. It doesn't make sense. I think what you are doing is a great start."

"Thanks, man. I want it to get bigger – grow, ya know. My boys and I want to spread the word. We've been trainin' for a while now, and there's no reason it can't go national, global even." Roscoe stood up again as though to emphasize the point.

"No reason at all, and other dogs and neighborhoods could benefit from your training."

"We've been trainin' some boys across town, and we're tryin' to create a movement. We call it '*Black Labs Matter*'. What do you think?" My eyes widened, and I glanced at the team through the glass wall separating the control room. They were equally dumbfounded, and I held my breath when I saw Dwayne spray his sip of coffee across the control panel.

"*Black Labs Matter*, huh?" My smile was uncontrollable. "I like it! I think it might just catch on."

Roscoe seemed to settle into the conversation, explaining his plan to grow a national movement targeting gun violence by recruiting Labradors and other breeds as a sort of early warning system for local residents, animals and humans alike. I have to say that his plan was extremely well thought out, recognizing the need for training before dogs are permitted to graduate and actually go on patrol, and I admired his concern for the safety of the canine volunteers. I pointed out that since the objective was to provide a loud audible alarm, he should consider breeds known for their loud bark. I shared research showing that golden retrievers have the loudest bark, and others include German Shepherds, Dobermans and Scottish Terriers. Roscoe voiced concern that while he would not discriminate against other breeds, he suggested that he specifically recruited darker color dogs, but strictly because of their ability to disappear quickly into the shadows, a valid concern. We discussed a variety of strategies to help expand the program and spread the word to other communities, and I assured Roscoe I would speak with his owner about several ways in which he might provide support. He seemed to appreciate that idea.

As with our other subjects, the conversation grew more relaxed over time, and I marveled at the fact that the dogs all seemed to have the capacity to recover so promptly from the initial shock and surprise, quickly accepting the ability to communicate and ready to get on with the dialogue. I assured Roscoe I would be following up with his owner regarding our discussion, and he was very appreciative. Before Calvin removed the EEG headgear, I leaned in for a parting comment: "I just want you to know how much we all admire what you are doing. I know Rosie would be very proud." Roscoe nodded, then bowed his head as Calvin retrieved the nightcap. As they walked to the door and the waiting car, Roscoe turned and offered a parting head nod, his way of letting me know we were on the same page. From my perspective, we certainly were.

As we completed the second dream session with each of our research subjects, we began to see a pattern develop. Most of the dogs were more relaxed on their second visit, which one may have expected due to the fact that they had previously been to the laboratory and had been exposed to the team, which generally included direct one-on-one interaction with several team members, including myself. As a result, we also noted that the subjects appeared more comfortable in the sleep chamber, allowing them to fall asleep at last somewhat earlier than their initial session. Finally, in every case we observed a very similar response as each dog is first aware of its ability to communicate directly in a dog/human "conversation". As might be expected, there is an initial reaction of surprise and bewilderment, but that quickly fades and soon transitions to a progressively more relaxed one-on-one interaction, very much like two humans having a discussion. My purely non-scientific personal opinion is that while a dog may initially express a degree of intellectual curiosity, once it is satisfied that the interaction is non-threatening, the fMRI confirms that the animal's brain activity switches from that which is responding to fear to one that quickly evaluates the potential danger and reacts accordingly. With the fMRI we can immediately observe heightened activity in the amygdala, while at the same time the frontal lobes are working to determine if the danger is real and if so how to respond to it. In our case, once the dog's brain has determined that suddenly being able to understand the voice of a human seated on the floor in front of it does not represent a threat, the frontal lobes take control, overriding the amygdala and bringing a sense of calm and rational response. More study is needed through a comprehensive analysis of fMRI brain activity imagery, each subject's vital signs, hormonal fluctuations and EEG brainwave patterns.

I mention these very preliminary findings at this point as we prepare for the arrival of Duke, our German Shepherd traumatized by the family cat, for his second *Dreamlab* session. Our initial session revealed a rather vivid dream interaction, including an apparently typical encounter by the feline, ambushing Duke and leaving him in an almost constant state of anxiety. Such an environment can be especially harmful to the dog's mental health, just as would be the case for us humans.

Based on my previous discussions with Duke's owner and family during our original intake session, it seems clear that Duke is not suffering from ailurophobia, which is defined as a persistent and excessive fear of cats. Generally, most cats will typically flee from a dog, but some may react by hissing or swiping at the dog. If the dog is actually scratched by a cat, it is possible that it might develop a generalized fear of cats. That is apparently not the case with Duke, however, as the family reports he gets along well with other cats in the neighborhood, tormented only by his nemesis, the family cat, Midnight. As we waited for Duke to arrive, the team and I discussed several possible treatment modalities, which might be helpful in ameliorating the situation.

Watching the SUV pull up out front, we could see the entire family had come along to wish Duke well, and he greeted Calvin as he might a member of the family, easily accepting Calvin's takeover of control of the leash and walking through the front door like he owned the place. Once inside and free of the leash, he wandered through the laboratory, greeting each of us and accepting an occasional pat on the head or ear-scratch. José and Calvin took turns playing tug of war with a long rope toy, as his wagging tail signaled that his growl was strictly playful but designed to let our team know he was ready to win the contest. Calvin eventually proclaimed Duke the victor, and he began to settle in on the floor, eventually retreating to the dog bed and a favorite blanket brought from home. He started with both eyes open, carefully watching us through the glass, then one eye, eventually succumbing to the low-pitched hum of the MRI and cooling fan. Less than 30 minutes later, it was show time!

As the main monitor came to life, the research team took their stations, and we all maneuvered for a view of the scene that was about to unfold. As the image sharpened, we were looking into what appeared to be the family room at Duke's home. A man and woman seated in matching recliners were watching a show on a wall-mounted TV, with a young boy and girl nearby on the floor playing with Lego blocks. Duke was lying on the floor next to the woman's recliner, looking very relaxed or possibly asleep. Now, keep in mind that we were looking at a scene from the dream of a dog sleeping in front of us, so if Duke was sleeping in his dream, we were observing a sleeping dog dreaming he is sleeping. Yes, it can all be a bit confusing. We watched as the scene offered little in the way of action, other than an occasional spat between the children amid dismantled Legos. Duke's vital signs confirmed he was very relaxed indeed, and nothing really changed, other than an occasional exchange between the man and woman. All was quiet on the home front. Or was it?

After about ten minutes, Nate pointed to the main monitor, calling our attention to a shadow emanating from behind the recliner in which the man was seated. As we looked closer, the shadow would occasionally appear, then move away, as though something was lurking just out of sight. Soon the shadowy outline moved from behind the man's recliner toward the woman's side and as we continued to watch, a black cat appeared at the top of the woman's recliner and remained motionless, with the woman unaware of its presence. From Duke's previous session, we knew that the cat was a female named Midnight, which somehow seemed especially fitting for this late-night session. Then a strange thing happened. The cat, which had been facing the opposite direction, turned to face the room, revealing an eerie pair of laser green eyes. Now, when I say "eerie", I am referring to the fact that it seemed like *the cat was looking at us!* Yes, I realize that sounds both creepy and paranoid, but I swear this demonic creature was staring straight at us as though it had found a hidden camera or somehow otherwise sensed our presence. Glancing around the control room, I could see the team's concerned faces, and I unconvincingly gestured everything was OK, though I was pretty freaked out.

Before I could move to further reassure my colleagues, Midnight crept across the back of the recliner like a black panther stealthily stalking prey. Now the cat had reached the opposite edge of the back of the chair, looking down on Duke, sound asleep and blissfully unaware of the imminent threat. At this point I was confident that, just like me, every member of the team was experiencing that tipping point you reach watching a horror film in a movie theater. You know the feeling, the point at which the fear is simply too much to bear, and you want to yell at the screen at the top of your lungs: "Watch out! He's behind you!" Collectively we were either too scared or too professional to scream. Perhaps we were somehow pulled into the dream ourselves and were experiencing the same state of sleep paralysis that prevents us from yelling out in our own dreams. Whatever the case, before that split-second opportunity had elapsed, Midnight pounced, in what seemed to be a slow-motion nightmare where everything, including us as observers, was caught in some type of time warp sequence. This allowed us to observe the attack in uncanny detail, as Midnight's face contorted, exposing razor-sharp teeth. As gravity pulled the attacker downward, we saw a zoomed-in closeup view of the feline's front paws and noticed that her claws were now fully extended, like we were watching a fight scene from *Wolverine*. As thought to add a final terrifying accent, as Midnight landed on poor Duke's unprotected flank, she emitted a horrific shriek, shattering the silence and catching the sleeping dog completely by surprise.

Now, as you are no doubt trying to imagine the horror of the moment, please keep in mind we have been able to establish that a dog's dreams are really not that different from our own, meaning they are not restrained by the laws of science, but rather our own vivid imaginations. We occasionally have to remind ourselves that we were not watching an actual vicious attack, rather that we were observing Duke's *dream* of such an attack. So, when I tell you we next observed a seventy-pound German Shepherd levitate straight up into midair, I am quite literally describing precisely what we observed. Never mind that defies several laws of physics and is enough to make Isaac Newtown roll over in his grave. In Duke's mind, and therefore in his canine nightmare, he was not constrained by physical laws. Neither was he able to make a conscious split-second "fight or flight" decision typically activated by the autonomic nervous system, which triggers the release of hormones designed to prepare an animal to quickly react to a perceived threat. In this case, poor Duke was caught (at least in his dream) so unaware of the pending attack his rude, terrifying awakening from a deep sleep provided only one alternative – escape, and that is exactly what happened next. As Duke realized what had occurred, he scrambled to remove himself from the room, which quickly morphed into a chase scene reminiscent of *Wile E. Coyote* in pursuit of his *Roadrunner* nemesis. Adding to the pandemonium and intensity of the moment, the man and woman were yelling loudly, shouting a cacophonic blend of Midnight's name and well-chosen expletives too numerous to mention, which only served to further enhance the boisterous laughter and acting out by the kids. Duke bolted for the back door, with Midnight close behind and broke through the screen door, sending him tumbling into the lawn and scurrying away, as Midnight took up a position in a kitchen window overlooking the backyard. Within a matter of seconds, Duke disappeared out of sight on the main monitor, and out of the corner of my eye, I caught some motion in the adjacent sleep chamber, where I observed a series of myoclonic leg twitches in the "real" sleeping animal followed by a more relaxed state, as our instrument readings indicated a transition to non-REM sleep. Chaos followed by peace and quiet.

Over the balance of the evening, Duke had one other dream session, which stayed with a similar backdrop, but without the cat and was unremarkable. The team and I compared notes and discussed several therapeutic options, and we agreed that the fact that Duke is so traumatized requires an intervention on the part of the family. As with our other subjects, that discussion will have to wait until we debrief each of the owners. With no further activity, I had a chance to enter my thoughts in the session notes, and we all sat back to wait for Duke to wake up. Just after 6AM Dwayne pointed to the EEG monitor, which indicated a transition to a wakeful state. In a scene we had seen played out before, Duke began to stretch and eventually opened his eyes, slowly but surely getting his bearings and looking around the room. Calvin moved into his field of view, and Duke seemed to remain relaxed as he gained a more complete view and appeared comfortable with the surroundings. I put on my Bluetooth headset and asked Watson to activate full-duplex mode as I moved from the control room to the sleep chamber. Duke rolled over with a final leg and neck stretch, and I took a seat on the floor as he eventually moved to a sitting position just in front of me. It was showtime!

I rocked my head back and forth slowly, making sure Duke was looking at my face before I spoke.

"Good morning, Duke. I hope you slept well." He immediately stood up and cocked his head from side to side, much as we had observed with many of the other subjects. It was clear he was trying to process what was happening and was not immediately able to make the connection of the voice he was hearing and my moving lips. Continuing, I made my facial expressions more pronounced.

"I am Dr. Cook, and we are happy you are here with us this morning." Duke's eyes appeared to squint slightly, as though he was trying to focus and connect the dots. "I know this seems odd, but I am able to talk to you, and I hope you are able to understand what I am saying."

"Uh, yes. Yes, I can hear you, but I'm not sure how that is possible." He seemed perplexed but not agitated – a good sign. "What is happening? How can I understand you?"

"Well, that is a long story, but basically we have been able to figure it out, and we appreciate your help as we try to understand more about the relationship between people like us and dogs like you. Does that make sense?"

"Uh, I guess so, but I'm not sure what is happening. I know I was asleep. Is this a dream?"

I laughed. "Well, funny you should mention it, but no – you are very much awake. In fact, a big part of our research is observing your dreams as you sleep." Now I definitely had his attention! And in case you are wondering - no, this German Shepherd does *not* have a German accent. In fact, I would describe Duke's voice as a sort of Minnesota Fargo-ish with a dash of Canadian thrown in for good measure.

"You can see my dreams? Wait – you are talking to me, I can understand you, and now you're telling me you know what I was dreaming." Duke raised his head and cocked it to the left, as though awaiting my response.

"Precisely! That is exactly what we are doing. We want to compare your dreams to those we have. It turns out they are actually quite similar."

"Whoa! You are talking to me, and you can see my dreams? Are you serious?" Duke shook his head vigorously as if to check to make sure he was, in fact, awake.

"Yes, it's true, and we have spent the past few weeks getting to know each of the dogs who are participating. You have been extremely helpful, and we really appreciate your help."

At this point, Duke did a full circle, the returned to a seated position directly in front of me.

"Man, this is really happening! How can you understand me? I can see your mouth moving, but mine isn't. I don't get it. How is that possible."

"As I said, it's a pretty involved explanation, but basically we have developed a way to convert your thoughts into sounds and translate them to a language we can understand. Then we reverse the process and convert my speech into something that makes sense to you. That translation is coming to you through that funny cap you are wearing." As I was offering the explanation, I watched as Duke stared directly at my mouth, seeming to hang on every word.

"Wow! You must be a genius or something. How did you do that?"

"No, I can't take credit for all this, I'm afraid. These people behind me are the real brains behind what we are doing, and each one has his or her own area of expertise."

"Her? Did you say 'her'?"

"Yes." I turned toward the control room. "Kathy, can you wave to Duke?" Dr. Chan came to the glass partition and smiled widely, waving her hands so that Duke could see her. I will never forget what happened next. Duke raised his right paw, as though he was responding to a "shake" command. My jaw dropped in amazement, as I realized his reaction seemed reflexive and automatic, just as though he was returning the greeting. Amazing!

"Is she your *girlfriend*?" Duke's gaze returned to me, awaiting my response. I chuckled.

"No, she is a colleague, a researcher specializing in using some really complex technology to allow us to have this conversation. That cap you're wearing – she invented that."

"Whoa! That is really amazing. I guess I still don't understand all this, but it sure seems to work." He nodded and shook his head in amazement. I immediately signaled my agreement.

"I hear you, but yes – it really does work, and these talented people have made it all possible. Pretty exciting, isn't it?" I smiled and crossed my legs, sitting face-to-face, having a casual conversation with a dog. Nothing odd here, right?

"I really don't know what to think, but I guess whatever I *do* think, you can hear all that, right?" I marveled at the fact that, after just a few minutes, Duke seemed quite comfortable with our conversation, eager to hear more and playing the part of an attentive student.

"Yes, I am really excited we can have this conversation, and I wanted to ask you what you might remember about your dreams last night."

"Oh, right. You could see what I was dreaming? I guess that works the same way? This hat lets you see into my *brain*? Could you actually *see* things?" Duke was both puzzled and genuinely interested.

"Yes, we can actually see and hear exactly what you were experiencing in your dream. Do you remember anything about your dreams last night?"

"Wow! Well, uh – wait. Yes, I remember I had a pretty bad dream. You could see that?"

"If you are referring to the scene with the cat, yes – we saw all that." As I was nodding affirmatively and as soon as I mentioned the word "cat", Duke dropped his head, as though embarrassed we had eavesdropped on what I'm sure was a disturbing experience.

"Midnight! I hate that freakin' feline! She won't leave me alone! What is her problem? I've never done anything to her." Now Duke was agitated, as confirmed by his vital sign readings.

"Well, based on what we observed, I can certainly see why you're not happy with her."

"Not *happy*? I *hate* that cat." Duke was now circling in place, obviously uncomfortable with the conversation. "Every time Midnight comes around, you can bet there's going to be trouble. She's pure evil, I'm telling you." I could feel Duke's anxiety and wanted to provide offer some support.

"Duke, now that we have seen the impact Midnight has had on you and your family, I promise we will work on that and try to resolve it." I offered my hand as Duke suddenly perked up.

"You're going to get rid of the cat! That's awesome! What are you thinking? Back over her with the car? Oh, what a terrible accident!" A sarcastic dog? Seriously? He wasn't done. "You know, the river bridge is just a few blocks from the house. Maybe she accidently falls into the raging water. So tragic! Hey, wait! Maybe we wrap her in a box and ship her to China. I hear they have markets there…That would be purr-fect!" Oh my god! This is one conniving canine!

"Duke, stop it! That's not at all what I meant. I will speak with your owner and explain the situation. I'm sure we can work something out."

"So, what are you saying? No bridge? No car accident? Package to China?" Now he seemed disappointed.

"No, whatever we work out, it will NOT involve killing the cat! We don't do that." I was firm in my admonishment, and I am not certain Duke was completely serious in his nefarious suggestions. Or *was* he?

For the rest of the early morning hours, I listened as Duke explained that he had never had issues with cats generally and knows many in the neighborhood. According to Duke, the kids talked their mom into getting Midnight, and his life was never the same after that. I was impressed that he asked a number of questions regarding our research and seemed genuinely interested in understanding how the technology worked. He also seemed somewhat embarrassed and sad at any mention of what we had observed in the dream sequences from each of his visits. He was clearly traumatized and suffers from occasional anxiety attacks, most likely triggered as a result of a type of canine PTSD, which can be quite debilitating if not treated. As our conversation continued, I jotted down some ideas I thought might help address the situation.

The time seemed to fly by, and before I knew it Duke's owner arrived to pick him up. Since it was still early in the morning, the kids were not with their father, which I hoped might offer an opportunity for a brief conversation. As Calvin knelt down to remove Duke's EEG nightcap, I assured Duke I would follow up.

"Duke, I want you to know I heard you, and I promise I will work on what we discussed." Calvin loosened the cap to remove it and gave it a tug, as Duke offered a parting comment.

"Thanks, Doc. I *hate* that freakin'…" My earpiece fell silent.

I confess I was not looking forward to Benji's second dream session, so I took a walk on the Full Sail University campus to clear my head and collect my thoughts before his scheduled appointment. I passed Full Sail's AR/VR lab where students in the Simulation & Visualization degree program learn to develop applications to support various types of augmented and virtual reality hardware, really cutting-edge stuff. The university also offers degrees in game development and numerous other technology degree programs, but the school is probably best known for its music recording and film and television programs, including hands-on training on the most current, state of the art gear. As I walked along the studio backlot and passed the recording "*Mix Palace*", I played back Benji's initial session in my mind. As you will recall, Benji suffers from Chronic Horny Humping Disorder. CHHD is an addictive behavior, but it may be easily confused with Canine Humping Personality Disorder, a non-sexual reflexive play behavior. Based on what we had observed during the first dream session, I am afraid that my diagnosis of CHHD, as opposed to CHPD, may require a more extreme therapeutic approach. As I walked past *Full Sail Live*, the school's live performance venue, I mentally worked through several possible scenarios, concerned about the implications for Benji and his family. By the time I passed the university's world famous esports arena, *The Fortress*, I had come up with what I hoped might be a treatment regimen, but the upcoming session would likely test my assumptions, so I returned to the lab to make some notes and prepare for what be an uncomfortable conversation.

Benji's owner called to let us know he was running a few minutes late, so I gathered the team to discuss our previous session with the little humping maniac. We reviewed the video from the dream sequences and agreed that the behavior seemed to support the CHHD diagnosis, in large part due to the fact that once he began the behavior, he appeared to be consumed by it, creating a self-sustaining manic episode, completely out of control and destined for a bad ending. There are several options for such a condition, but now that we have the ability to actually question the subject, we agreed that we should wait to see what Benji had to say before landing on any one potential solution. As Benji arrived, Calvin and Dwayne went to greet him, and he bounded out of the back seat and strode confidently through the door, his little legs scurrying up the stairs, in a hurry to find out what was inside. Maybe it was because he remembered his earlier visit, but Benji seemed very much at ease, wandering from room to room and greeting each member of the team, enjoying the attention and eventually noticing his blanket in the sleep chamber. Unfortunately, he was not anywhere close to ready to settle down, and I chuckled as he found the toybox next to the bed and presented each toy, one at a time, to Dwayne while the rest of us began running through our pre-session checklists. During this relatively low-key play time, there was no humping or acting out of any kind. In fact, other than some initial jumping and occasional tug-o-war with a toy, Benji was pretty restrained and eventually settled down, first next to the bed and finally in it. He accepted the EEG cap from Calvin without hesitation, and we settled in at our respective stations, activating the fMRI and checking the equipment readings. As with the other subjects, as the sessions progressed, we were able to anticipate when REM sleep would occur based on monitoring vital signs, hormone levels and EEG brainwave patterns. Benji was soon sound asleep, and after about twenty minutes we watched the transition to active dreaming.

Similar to Benji's first session, the scene opened inside a home we assumed to be his, with Benji chasing a tennis ball being thrown by two young children, who seemed delighted as Benji chased and faithfully retrieved the ball every time. Eventually the kids grabbed a Frisbee and moved into the front yard, a nicely landscaped and manicured lawn, with Benji scrambling down the front porch stairs to make sure he was included in the fun. In the control room, we exchanged glances, shrugged shoulders and raised eyebrows, acknowledging a quite normal interaction, nothing out of the ordinary. Soon a young girl appeared in the distance walking on the sidewalk heading toward Benji and the kids. The kids exchanged shouted greetings, and it was obvious they were close neighborhood friends, all about the same age – maybe 6 or 7. As the girl entered the yard and caught Benji's attention, Benji bounded toward her as she offered a friendly greeting, kneeling down with a big smile and outstretched hand. The scene quickly changed when Benji launched himself onto the girl's left leg, wrapping his paws around her jeans pant leg and beginning what can best be described as a full on, hip thrusting humping assault. This attack was met with a series of screams and shrieks, first from the girl, then in unison from the three children. On the main monitor we watched the terrified expressions and heard the shouting grow louder. "Benji, no! Stop it! Stop it! Help!"

From the control room I heard Nate's Australian accent, as he immediately reacted. "That little bastard!" Nate looked like he was ready to leave his post and somehow transport himself into the pandemonium to save the day, only to then clinch his fists, grit his teeth and shake his head in disgust. Meanwhile, the girl turned and ran toward the house, with Benji holding on for dear life, humping all the way! As the terrified girl reached the porch steps, a man and woman emerged from the doorway, joining the cacophony with their own added shouts and admonishments. The man quickly knelt down, grabbed the young girl with his left arm, turning and lifting her off the ground, while simultaneously grabbing the back on Benji's neck with his right hand, pulling the dog free and throwing him what seemed like a good 25 feet onto the grass. Benji tumbled several times and appeared generally unscathed, while the man and woman consoled the girl, and all but Benji went inside the house. Benji raced up the stairs heading for the front door, which the woman promptly closed right in his face. Unable to stop quickly, Benji plowed into the door, eliciting a loud yelp and crumpling to the ground, shaking his head in shock. Out of the corner of my eye, I saw Dwayne make a pumping motion with his fist and mouthed a supportive "Yes!" Benji remained bewildered at the doorway, no doubt shaken by the force of the heavy door smashing into his face. Nate leaned in from the control room to share his opinion. "Crikey! Well deserved, I'd say. Somebody needs to teach that little bugger a lesson." I nodded affirmatively, while at the same time realizing that the "lesson" would likely be my responsibility.

Benji's first dream sequence ended with a severely traumatized young girl, his family shaken and distraught and Benji nursing his wounds. Over the balance of the evening, we observed several additional dream sessions, each one confirming the seriousness of my diagnosis and culminating in some type of hump-fueled chaos For those of you who may believe you have observed similar scenes with other dogs, let me assure you that what we witnessed was much more manic, aggressive, rough and quite disturbing. In one sequence, a young woman pushing a baby carriage on the sidewalk became a target, and Benji's persistent aggressive humping caused such a distraction the woman almost lost control of the carriage, coming perilously close to tipping it over and only averted by an alert *Amazon Prime* driver, who pulled over to come to her assistance. In another, Benji made the mistake of thinking a male pit bull mix in his neighborhood would somehow tolerate his relentless stalking and constant climbing and erratic humping. Let's just say it didn't end well for Benji who, at least in the dream, suffered serious cuts and lacerations, potentially life-threatening wounds. After each sequence, the team was visibly shaken and agitated, looking to me to offer some type of urgent, immediate solution. Nate seemed particularly agitated, clearly upset and frustrated by the inability to intervene while at the same time able to process the fact that we were observing *dreams*, not actual physical incidents. As explained previously, the fact that Benji's humping behavior appears to be a compulsion without his ability to exercise any level of control is a disturbing confirmation that preventing its reoccurrence will require direct intervention, likely including a combination of medication and traditional behavior therapy. As Benji's final dream sequence faded and we all had a chance to collect our thoughts, I made some notes and prepared for my "discussion" when Benji woke up.

When Benji's brainwave pattern and vital signs signaled he was beginning to emerge from what had been a very eventful night of dreaming, I sensed increased anxiety on the part of the research team. I could see it in their faces and hear it in whispered conversations. I realized it was not just Nate who was angry and frustrated at the scenes we had witnessed, and I must confess I shared the same sentiments. We are, however, professionals, and our mission is one of understanding with a goal of providing support, guidance and counseling to deal with inappropriate behavior and prevent recurrence. In Benji's case, that may prove especially challenging. Dwayne signaled he saw movement, and we could see that Benji was beginning to stretch and move around. I donned my headset and asked Watson to activate my ability to speak with our subject. I moved to the edge of the sleep chamber and sat cross-legged on the floor, careful not to startle Benji as he began to look around, eventually turning to face me. He immediately came over and pawed at my leg as if offering a greeting and looking for my acknowledgement, a gesture in stark contrast to the aggressive, violent behavior we had witnessed overnight in the dream sequences. Summoning my inner calm, I began.

"Good morning, Benji." He jumped and immediately backed away, startled by my voice, or rather being able to *understand* my voice.

"What was that? Who said that?" He looked around the room, clearly puzzled.

"Right here. It's me, Benji. See? I am talking to you." I watched as he cocked his head and sat motionless, as though temporarily frozen or in shock, processing what was happening.

"You're talking? Wait, I can *hear* you." He shook his head in disbelief.

"Yes, and I can hear and understand *you.* Pretty cool, huh? He was now staring directly at my face. "You are here again in our research laboratory, and these people and I have developed a way for us to communicate. What do you think about that?"

"Think about? What do I think? I think I must be dreaming!"

"Well, since you mentioned it…" I couldn't miss the irony of the segue and continued: "You are very much awake now, but part of our research is a look into the way that dogs dream and how your dreams compare to ours."

"My dreams? You are studying my dreams? This is crazy!" Benji was getting worked up and appeared anxious, hopping around nervously.

"I realize it's a lot to process but as you can see, we are talking to each other, right?

"Well, yeh. Yeh, we are, but I don't understand." Benji continued his nervous pacing. The texture and tenor of his voice can best be described as a mashup of Bart and Lisa from *The Simpsons*, childlike and high-pitched, mildly annoying and missing only the occasional "dude".

"It is pretty complicated, Benji, but now that we have been able to do it, we want to speak with you and other dogs to be able to learn from each other. Are you OK with that?"

"OK, I guess so. Wait! There are other dogs?" Benji scanned the room nervously.

"Yes, but they are not here now. Now it is just you, and I would like to talk to you about your dreams last night. Do you remember them?" Now I definitely had his attention.

"So, you can see my dreams, huh? What, you can look into my *mind*?" If a dog can look skeptical, this was definitely the expression.

"Well, in a manner of speaking, yes. Like me, your brain emits energy in a series of waves we can see and measure. We have developed a way to use those brainwaves and combine them with other technology that shows your brain's activity while you are dreaming. We put all of that together and use it to create sounds and images on a screen, like watching TV."

"TV? That's the picture frame on the wall with all of the movies?" His head cocked from side to side, waiting on my response.

"Yes, exactly. We were watching the screen, and we could see and hear what you were dreaming. I would like to talk to you about what we saw. Can we discuss that?" Maybe it was just that it had been a rough night or the nature of the disturbing dreams or the fact that this conversation was like a scene from *Groundhog Day*, but it all combined to make me a bit irritable and impatient, and I found myself just wanting to get on with it. Frankly, based on what we had observed in the dream session, I was not much in the mood to wait for a dog to give me permission to proceed.

"Yes, I guess." Benji's response was meek and he appeared confused or overwhelmed, not a surprise under the circumstances.

"Thank you, Benji. We appreciate your cooperation, and our goal is to use what we learn from these sessions to benefit you and the other dogs. Let's start with your dreams. This was your second visit with us, and we have seen the same recurring theme in each of your dreams. Do you know what I'm talking about?" Benji was pacing back and forth.

"I'm not sure I remember or understand what you are talking about, exactly." Benji was fidgeting, occasionally standing, circling and sitting again. Now, I am a psychologist, not a mind reader, and at this point I couldn't tell if this dog was playing dumb, just didn't know the answer or was outright lying. I was determined to find out.

"Do you remember anything about your dreams last night? Anything at all?" I leaned in, hoping for a response.

"Uh, I know that sometimes I dream about playing with my family. I like playing outside with the kids. Sometimes I get in trouble." Benji was now acting bashful and withdrawn, clearly not wanting to admit he knew where the discussion was headed.

"You get in *trouble*? Why do you get in trouble, Benji? Did you do something bad?"

"No, not bad. I'm not a bad dog. Sometimes maybe I get too excited." Now his head was down, turned slightly, looking away. His vital signs were elevated.

"Excited? You mean sometimes you get a little carried away? Can you remember an example of a time when you got in trouble?" At this point in the conversation, I am reminding myself to take it easy. Sessions like this can be quite frustrating, like a police detective questioning an uncooperative suspect, even after the crime was captured on video with clear, indisputable evidence. From the control room, I can see the team is watching closely, waiting for a quick and complete confession. Nate looked as if he was ready to explode, not wanting to tolerate my more measured approach.

"Benji, did you hear me? I asked you a question. What do you do that gets you in trouble? Did you bite somebody?" Mimicking a dog's reaction, I cocked my head to the left, awaiting a response.

"No, I would never bite anyone! I wouldn't do that." He was shaking his head, feigning disbelief.

"Well what then? Did you have a dream last night where you got in trouble?"

"You said you could see my dreams, right? Could you see what I dreamed last night?"

"Absolutely. We saw everything. We even recorded it. Would you like to …" Benji interrupted me in mid-sentence.

"No! I don't want to see. I know I got in trouble." Again, head down, unable to escape the inevitable.

"What happened? What did you do that got you in trouble?" I moved my head down so I was face to face, waiting for him to look up.

"I… I was just playing with some kids, a girl in the neighborhood." The response was sheepish, or perhaps it should be *doggish*?

"*Playing*? Go on. What happened?" Now I was just a few inches from Benji's nose, looking him straight in the eye.

"Well, I was just playing with this girl, and suddenly she freaked out and started screaming and running around like she was on fire or something. I think something was wrong with her! All I was doing was holding onto her leg."

"Just holding on, huh? You weren't *humping* her leg?"

"Humping? Nah. I was just trying to hold on, adjusting my grip, you know? Making sure I didn't fall. Next thing I know she's screaming and running inside crying and suddenly I'm thrown through the air like a ragdoll. I tried to get inside to make sure she was OK, but somebody slammed the door in my face. Hurt like hell!" I started to say something, but before I could respond the control room door open, and Nate stormed into the room. I turned and held up my hand signaling him to stop, but he grabbed the Bluetooth headset from my ear and took control, kneeling down and nudging me out of the way. Nate is a big guy, and his years in the Australian outback studying dingoes left his face weathered, like it could use a good rain. I knew he had been shaken by what we had witnessed in Benji's session, and apparently couldn't hold it in any longer. I tried in vain to pull him back, but he was hell bent on getting in little Benji's face.

"Listen to me you little shit! We saw what you did, you pathetic pile of fur. You were *humping* that little girl, you wanker! *Humping* her! She was terrified! Where I come from they don't call that *playing*, you disgusting little turd." Nate was in a full rant and speaking at very high volume. Wearing my headset meant Benji was on the receiving end of a very loud and intimidating tirade, with Nate just inches from his face.

"But I was just…" Benji tried in vain to get a word in, but Nate wasn't having it.

"Shut the fuck up, mate! If I want your opinion, I'll give it to you, you little arse wipe."

Benji was frantically looking around for an exit, but Nate's large frame filled the doorway, and he wasn't nearly done.

"Tell you what, dipshit. You think you can get away with banging like a dunny door on a little child? You get off on that, you little shagger? Do you?" (I know, I had to look it up, too.) Benji is now backed all the way to the rear wall of the sleep chamber. The fMRI was still on, and we could clearly see that the amygdala was lit up like a Christmas tree, typical when someone, in this case a dog, is experiencing intense fear. It wasn't over.

"Here is the deal, you worthless sack of shit. I know where you live. If you ever, ever hump anything again – a child, another dog, a piece of furniture, a toy, a bedspread, a sack of potatoes – I swear I will be watching. Now, if I EVER see anything that remotely resembles a hump – just one little hump – I swear on my dear sainted mother's grave I will come and find you. I will wait until you are sound asleep, and I swear I will cut off your little wiener and carry it back home with me to Australia to feed to the great whites on the reef. Meanwhile, your new name will be *Dickless*, and your balls will be replaced by some shiny jingle bells, so that everyone in the neighborhood will hear you coming. Are you getting this, mate?" Nate leaned in so that his face was quite literally touching Benji's nose, which was quivering and dripping with sweat. Benji could barely manage a whimper.

"Yes." Nate wasn't finished.

"Yes, what?"

"Yes, sir. I hear you, sir."

"And what will happen if I ever catch you humping again?" I found Nate's facial expression especially terrifying and apparently Benji concurred. His response was a stuttering string of words.

"When I'm sleeping… my dick, sharks, jingle bells, Dickless."

"There you go, mate! We have an understanding, then. Don't disappoint me now. We clear?"

"Yes sir, clear. No humping." Nate leaned over and gave Benji a pat on the head. The poor dog dropped a poop. He literally got the shit scared out of him! Nate took off the headset and handed it back to me. "Here you go, Doc." Nate winked and returned to his station in the control room as the other team members looked on in amazement. I put on the headset and turned to face a dog who can best be described as frightened out of his mind - scared shitless.

"Benji, are you OK?" He looked up at me, still, shaking.

"I guess. Can I go home now?" He was clearly shaken and his heart rate was through the roof.

"We still have some time before you owner comes to pick you up. Let's spend a few minutes talking about making sure we address the behavior that gets you in trouble, OK?"

"Yes, OK. Can I ask you a question?" Benji was shaken and apprehensive.

"Sure, what is it?" I wanted to be supportive but remain firm and direct.

"Was that guy serious?"

"Definitely. Very much so."

"OK. Then can you work with me? I think I need some help." His head was completely down.

"Of course, Benji. Let's talk."

The balance of the early morning hours was spent in a very frank discussion, letting Benji know in no uncertain terms that any future humping behavior will have serious repercussions, without specifically referring to the removal of testicles, although I am absolutely certain that psychologically the connection and associated visual imagery will always remain a powerful negative reinforcement. Our conversation was a positive one, and I really did believe Benji would take it to heart and follow my recommendations. I could tell from our discussion that he knew the behavior was abhorrent but was unable to restrain himself, at least until now. Soon Benji's owner arrived, and Calvin knelt down to remove the EEG nightcap, after which Benji remained at his side, all the while peeking through the control room window, checking on Nate's location. Once the car door opened, Benji bolted down the stairs and into the safety of the backseat.

For me, Benji's departure meant that I could turn my attention to the source of the earlier interruption of my first conversation with our research subject. I have to say I was more than a little pissed off, and as a psychologist, I don't appreciate having anyone or any dog under my supervision and care threatened with physical harm, however well deserved it might be. As the team powered down the equipment and *Dreamlab* was once again calm and quiet, I asked Nate to join me in the breakroom for a chat. He knew he was in for a tongue lashing, but he nevertheless walked in with a certain swagger and confidence, which only served to aggravate me more.

"May I ask you what you thought you were doing in there?" I was stern and visibly upset.

"In where, Doc? You mean with that disgusting little dog?" The Aussie accent and cocky demeanor did little to reduce the tension.

"Yes, you interrupted my session with Benji, and I was quite capable of getting to the seriousness of his issues. Why were you so worked up?"

"Sorry, mate. I guess I just had a lot on my mind."

"And what was all that about swearing on your mother's grave? I thought you said you spoke with her last week. You didn't tell me your mother had passed. I was very sorry to hear that, but it's hardly an excuse."

"No sir, mum is still very much alive and kickin'. I did feel like she was looking over my shoulder, though. That little bastard needed a good kick in the arse, and I wanted to make sure I scared the shit out of him. Do you think it worked?" Nate flashed a toothy grin.

"You sonofabitch!" I shook my head, trying to conceal an uncontrollable chuckle. Damnit!

OK, no more Baby Ruth jokes from me.

As the dream sessions and conversations continued, our team began to develop our post-session game plan. Our top priority was to use the information our research had compiled to create a plan to share it with the dog owners, with a goal of presenting our findings in a way that provides specific recommendations to each owner that can improve the dog/human relationship and address psychological and other issues, which may adversely impact these relationships. We realized we would also need a strategy for how best to convey the findings to the owners, how much detailed information we should share, and anticipate the many questions we are certain will be asked. As with any scientific research, we will want to focus on facts, not speculation, so we compiled a digital dossier on each of our subjects, containing all of the data collected for each session, including video and audio, vital sign and hormone level readings, fMRI and EEG readouts and statistical records, which include arrival time at *Dreamlab*, time in the sleep chamber, REM phase start and end, and so on. We all agreed that the goal of the owner presentations should be to provide our findings in a simple, easy to understand format, careful not to overwhelm with technical jargon and always respectful of the privacy of both owner and animal. Sitting in my office adjoining the laboratory, I tried to put myself in the shoes of the owners, pondering what I would want to know if my dog was a participating subject.

And then it hit me.

Thirteen

I couldn't help it. I had to know.

Once we believe in ourselves, we can risk curiosity, wonder, spontaneous delight, or any experience that reveals the human spirit.

~ *e. e. cummings*

Yes, I know what you are wondering. I'm sure it has been on your mind as you have been reading this story. It's a logical question, and I know that after reading this far, I would be asking the same thing. So, I will answer it.

Yes.

Yes, as a scientist, and even as a trained, disciplined, highly principled researcher, *I had to know.* I know it was not appropriate for our formal study. I realize it would not be ethical to use any of our generous research grant to fund anything, however seemingly insignificant, outside of our defined research scope. I know all that. But I also know that if you were in my shoes, you would never forgive yourself if you didn't take the opportunity, the real elephant in the room, and spend some time answering the question that is so obsessive and demanding of our time and expertise. What about *my* dog?

Bear is a 5-year old, 100+ pound German Rottweiler. We have had the privilege of having three in our family in our lifetime, and this time it was my wife's turn to make that important selection decision. At the breeder, we saw the litter of pups, and got a chance to see the father. We chuckled at his name: *Killer*. What a magnificent looking specimen! We wanted a male, so after separating the lot, we watched as the 3 male puppies played and climbed all over each other. It seemed that 2 were ganging up on the slightly smaller one, and I could see where this was headed. We wouldn't call him a runt, but he was definitely not the aggressive, dominant type. So cute, so sweet, and so easy to see how he was the perfect fit for my wife and me. She made a great choice.

As you have no doubt experienced with a new puppy, the naming process is both fun and stressful. Maybe we should call him *Einstein*? No, with his long legs and big feet, he's looking pretty goofy so far. He seems preoccupied with his own shadow and chasing others, so maybe *Shadow* would be a good fit? We live in an area on a river that backs up to a huge protected wildlife preserve, with a large black bear population. There was the aha moment! Bear it was!

Three weeks into our study, and following the *Dreamlab* sessions and subsequent "conversations" with our research subjects, I decided Bear might enjoy a visit to our lab, so on a cloudy Saturday afternoon we headed to our facility, and I was excited about the prospect of being able to communicate with my dear canine friend. Bear seemed excited at the prospect, but then of course, he is always excited about any prospect, especially one that involves a ride in the car. Whether it is our weekend trips to a local park to run him around chasing balls and frisbees, having him join my wife and I on our occasional hikes at nearby state parks, or my son just having him ride along for a quick trip to the store, Bear knows that a ride in the car means a new adventure. This day would certainly fit that category.

I was more interested in using the translation application and, at least for this first introduction, I had no interest in attempting to record a dream session, which would have been all but impossible with just me and Watson. We arrived at the lab and, as expected, Bear wanted to check out every inch of the place. Of course, even though we have been fairly fastidious in terms of cleaning, having had so many dogs of different breeds in the facility in the previous week was no-doubt apparent to Bear, as he sniffed about the room. Since we wouldn't be using the actual sleep chamber, I decided to create a relaxed home environment, putting one of the big screens in the main room on regular TV, plopping down on the leather sofa with a throw I brought from home, inviting Bear to join me on the couch for an ear scratch and loving pats on the head. Unlike our research subjects, Bear was naturally comfortable with me, regardless of the new surroundings, and he settled in just as we would do at home around the same time.

For what I hoped to accomplish, I wouldn't have to worry about the fMRI, vital sign or hormonal monitoring, only needing to fire up the EEG and get Bear accustomed to the sensor cap, which he at first found curious, but tolerable. I then donned my headset, asking Watson to begin the translation application. I should have thought about that! The minute Watson confirmed my instruction, Bear barked and quickly scanned the room, looking for that second voice. I directed Watson to remain silent during the session and verified compliance from the flicker if the animated logo lights on the front of Watson's control panel. Whew! That could have been a significant hiccup.

Initially, I turned off the full duplex mode, meaning I wanted to be able to receive translation from Bear, but he would not be able to hear me, as I was afraid that might be a bit too much for Bear to handle, at least until I could get a feel for how he was settling in to this new environment. I leaned back with my hand resting on his back and adjusted my wireless earbuds. I then adjusted the audio output volume, and the translation app began to do its thing. I was definitely anxious and consciously told myself to relax and slow my breathing. Bear was blissfully oblivious.

"I'm not sure where we are, but it's pretty comfortable." Bear's first translation was crystal clear. There was no special tone or intonation – just a relaxed, steady sentence, indicating Watson was working his amazing magic. Bear's "voice" was a very casual tone, with moderate pitch and timbre, not especially distinctive, but laid-back and conversational.

"I think this is where dad goes after he tucks me in at night. It smells like he sleeps here sometimes, and he must be helping other animals, but I don't recognize any from our neighborhood. I wish Zora was here." (Zora is a cute Cavalier King Charles spaniel who lives across the street from us.)

"I'm just going to close my eyes for a little while. I've seen that Jason Bourne movie at least a dozen times, but dad seems to like it." I chuckled under my breath, but the second reference to "dad" choked me up a bit. I reached for my phone and sent Watson a question via text.

"Watson: the translation refers to me as 'Dad'. Is that some touch you added for my benefit?" The screen confirmed *Message Sent.*

As always, Watson responded without hesitation. "No, doctor. My comprehensive analysis of all meta data from all EEG translations cross-referencing all species, and non-verbal human/animal interactions including gorillas and chimpanzees, combined with a scan of all references to the dominant party in the interaction suggests that the most appropriate translation for this canine's thought sequence is 'father' or, more colloquially, 'dad'."

All I could think was "OMG!", followed by "Come on, Ron – hold it together."

We hung out in the lab for a while, and Bear seemed to be completely relaxed, dozing off after just a few minutes. The EEG showed all sensors working fine, but this was not intended to be a dream session, and I thought it best to stop for now, planning to return the following afternoon.

Sunday morning came quickly, and I admit I was somewhat nervous in thinking about how the afternoon might unfold. Bear seemed to sense my anxiety, most likely mistaking it for our normal routine of going to a nearby park to play. Instead, we played ball in the front yard. Now, I realize there are plenty of awesome $20 dog toys at any pet store, but I've found there is really no substitute for an ever so slightly deflated soccer ball, available at most discount stores. Watching a 100+ pound Rottweiler jump up to catch a soccer ball on the first bounce may not be quite as auspicious as with a retriever but Bear always puts on a good show. The best part of these play sessions is that they are a great opportunity to burn off some energy, followed by a nap (for both of us). As Bear eventually rolled on his back, I made some notes and penciled together a schedule for the afternoon.

After lunch, I asked the question Bear had been waiting for: "Wanna go ride in the car?" From the reaction, the human comparison would have been something like "Congratulations! You just won the lottery!" I realize that many of you experience the same reaction with your dog, and it is always heartwarming to see the level of anticipation and excitement, even though we can be pretty sure it is not the car ride that our furry friend is excited about. In this case, it's not the *journey* – it's the *destination.* Of course, part of the excitement comes from the memories of previous trips, and an expectation of what lies ahead. After a short drive, we pulled into the parking lot of our laboratory building, and Bear bounded out of the back of the SUV, sniffing the bushes as if to say "Hey – I remember this place from yesterday." But today would be different.

Bear's stubby tail was in full swing (we call it his "wiggle-stub") and he followed closely behind me as I used my security badge at the building entrance. At this point I was glad we had stopped by the day before, because I could see that Bear was very relaxed and content, but curious about how we would be spending our time together. Once inside the lab, Bear immediately found of his favorite plush toy animals – a small brown dachshund - and presented it to me repeatedly as I turned on the equipment and made sure everything was properly calibrated. When I brought out the EEG cap, Bear gladly accepted it, still clutching his toy, as though he was a football player gearing up in the locker room before a big game. He seemed to be aware this was all part of a game, and he was ready to play.

I checked the EEG readings, and since I was not concerned with the fMRI, monitoring vital signs, hormone levels or using the dream visualization monitors, I was eager to don my own Bluetooth headset, hoping I could somehow find an opportunity to ease into a "conversation" without freaking Bear out (or me, for that matter!). I instructed Watson to engage the translation application, but not in full-duplex mode, meaning that I would be able to "hear" Bear, but he could not hear me. Within seconds, my headset came to life, and Bear's stream of consciousness flooded my headset.

> "Hey – I'll share my toy with you. Want to play with my toy? My toy? Want my toy? I'll share my toy with you. Here – grab my toy. I'll share with you. Want it? Grab it. I'll share it. Wanna play? Let's play." His wiggle-stub was like a high-speed metronome, and the little dachshund toy was cold and slobbery – a perfect offering for a trusted friend. The same thoughts were translated rapid-fire, repeated over and over, like a child babbling incessantly, pleading for attention. I played along for a while with a sporadic tug-o-war, and Bear's thoughts conveyed his enjoyment.

> "You think you can take my toy? You think you're strong, huh? You *like* that? You feel that? That's a

Rottweiler tug! You're not getting' my toy! No sir. That's my toy! Think you can take my toy from me? Think again!"

This thought-barrage continued, with the requisite tough dog growling in a vain attempt to intimidate me and force me into submission. Now, while I completely understand my role as the Alpha in this relationship, that does not mean that I always have to win the battle, and when I finally allow the toy to be pulled from my now-slimy hands, Bear is quick to celebrate with a growling head shake, relishing his victory. This pause in the tussle represented the perfect opportunity to tell Watson to switch to full duplex mode, turning on Bear's ability to hear and hopefully understand me for the first time. Watson immediately confirmed, and I was careful to tread carefully.

"Hey Bear." I watched as he cocked his head, looking for the source of the voice.

"What? What was that?" He continued to search for where the sound was coming from.

"It's me…dad."

"Yes, I know it's you. I see you. I'm right here. Whoa, wait!" Another cocked head, staring directly at me.

"I know it's a little strange."

"Strange? I can *hear* you, but now I *understand* you. What is going on?" His head shook with the mannerism of a human double-take.

"I have been working on a project to help us communicate."

"Well, it looks like it's working!" Bear's expression changed from one of disbelief to inquisitive.

"Yes, it is working. I'm pretty proud of what we have done." I smiled and nodded.

"How does it work? I can see your mouth moving, and I hear words now."

"Yes, I am listening to your thoughts, and a computer translates them into my language. When I speak, the same computer translates my words into something you can understand."

"What's a computer?" As Bear again cocked his head to the left, his right rear paw scratched his right ear. We were having a conversation, making small talk!

"We can talk more about that later. For now, I just wanted you to know that now we can talk to each other."

"OK, cool. Do want to play now?" It was as though Bear had quickly accepted what was happening and, in his mind, it was time to get back to just being a dog."

"Watson: please discontinue full duplex… " Before I could finish my sentence, Bear jerked his head to look me in the eye.

Bear looked puzzled. "Watson? Who is Watson?"

"Watson is the computer I mentioned, a *supercomputer*, and he helps make all of this possible."

"Where is he? I don't see him." Bear looked around, waiting for someone to appear.

"He's not a person – he is…I mean *it* is a machine." I struggled to explain.

Watson's control panel lights swirled. "I am here, Bear. I am Watson. Nice to meet you."

"Are you a person like my dad? I don't understand."

"No, and there will be much to understand, I am sure. I am pleased to help you and your dad talk to each other." Watson's voice was calm and reassuring, and Bear seemed fixated on Watson's animated control panel logo.

I paused to marvel at the scene. I was talking to my dog, my dog is talking to me, and now a supercomputer is talking to my dog. Maybe *I'm* the one who is dreaming!

Bear's thoughts resumed at the tail end (sorry) of Watson's response, and the translation was instantaneous.

"OK, Watson. Thanks for helping my dad. Do you want to play?"

Before I could say anything, Watson chimed in: "I will leave that to your dad, but I am sure we will get to know each other." Watson's logo flashed, then faded.

"Thank you, Watson. Bear, you know what? Yes – I think it's time to play!" As soon as the word P-L-A-Y was translated back through Bear's EEG cap, he started jumping erratically, just as he does at home in response to that same word.

I now realized that, while I was reacting in amazement to what just happened, Bear had taken it all in stride. The canine brain is quite capable of taking in and processing new stimuli, information and concepts. Unlike our human capacity for deeper intellectual curiosity and a need for more complete understanding, Bear's response was straight and to the point, as if to say: "Hey, man – I get it. You can talk to me, and now I understand you. And you can now understand me. I don't exactly understand how all that works or who this Watson guy is, but that's OK, because now I am about to show you who is best at catching a Frisbee. So, stop talking, and let's go outside!" I peeled off Bear's EEG cap, grabbed a few Frisbees from my bag, and we headed out onto the adjacent lawn. Today was a good day. A *really* good day.

Later that evening, when I had a chance to unwind and reflect on all we had accomplished, my mind returned to Bear's session and my ability to eavesdrop on his stream of consciousness, his innermost thoughts. It occurred to me, not as some epiphany, revelation or eureka moment, but rather as good old-fashioned common sense, that humans possess a unique quality of intellectual curiosity. We seek to understand how things work, what they mean and how they somehow fit in the cosmos.

A dog may be curious and inquisitive, sniffing and checking out the world around us, but dogs do not need a scientific explanation or documented evidence to support their curiosity. They do not need to fully comprehend intricate relationships or understand the implication of anything, no matter how incredible we might think the situation is. In the case of Bear, he clearly enjoys my companionship, and I value his. These are simple relationships developed over time, from often frustrating puppy training, occasional collateral damage in the form of chewed-up shoes, destroyed sofa cushions, pee and poop spots too numerous to count, and an eventual equilibrium. Eventually we somehow miraculously achieve a perfect schedule mixture of eating, sleeping and play, long walks, innumerable dog toys and goodies, and plenty of belly scratches and praise. This cycle of reciprocal love and affection plays out daily across the planet, with families around the world recognizing this privileged relationship we all cherish.

There are other relationships that are more involved and sophisticated. For a highly trained military or police dog, the dog knows when it is time to go to work, and it follows its handler's commands without hesitation, just as a human soldier or police offer would do when similarly commanded. As we continue our research, we may find that these courageous canines feel a sense of pride and accomplishment, or we may learn that they simply react as a conditioned response from their training. Regardless, we know that the bond between dog and handler is an unbreakable partnership, with each assuring the other: "Hey man, I've got your back." We know that, like humans, dogs can suffer PTSD, and we marvel at the bravery of an animal willing to lay down its own life to accomplish its mission. How can we ever repay that commitment and sacrifice?

In the days following my brief session with Bear, my thoughts on how best to structure the owner presentations came into clear focus, providing an outline I then shared with the team, and we agreed to an agenda and how best to share the findings. As the sessions continued, we began to organize our thoughts and discussed a timetable for completion. Frankly, we realized that we were now so enthralled and engaged, so looking forward to each dream session and conversation that we needed to set a definitive date. We put together a final schedule for the remaining sessions, and I challenged each team member to make the most of each and every remaining moment. This project, more than any other with which any of us had been involved before, had touched us all in ways we would never had imagined.

Fourteen

The Owner Sessions

What do dogs do on their day off?
Can't lie around – that's their job.

~ *George Carlin*

The days and weeks seemed to fly by, each *Dreamlab* session and "conversation" building on the previous, as our team settled in to an efficient and effective workflow, like a well-oiled machine, with each of us focusing precisely on our respective area(s) of expertise. I have worked in a team environment previously in my career and have had the privilege of leading some along the way, but none that could ever rival what this group has been able to achieve. Add to that our honorary human, Watson, and what we have been able to accomplish in such a short period has been nothing short of amazing. The data we have collected is organized in five primary areas: biometric data revealing relationships between canine vital signs and hormonal levels during REM sleep dream sequences, functional MRI data revealing the areas of brain activity during active dream sessions, corresponding brainwave data during those same sessions, ultra-high definition video content of each dream sequence, and finally audio and video content associated with our full duplex canine conversations. With this incredible library and the technology to present all of it simultaneously on a huge digital dashboard, we spent countless hours in the Full Sail visualization suite, a sort of high-tech simulation, recording and mixing studio. This allowed us to visually observe relationships between, for example, fMRI brain activity, EEG brainwave patterns, hormonal fluctuations, respiration and heart rate and the dream visualizations on the screen, including video of the sleeping animal, noting the dogs' movement during sleep, as well as the same data during our awake conversations. All of the resulting data then allowed for comparison to those same measurement in humans, for which previous studies have provided *far* more data than our limited research project had allowed.

Returning for a moment to our initial research objectives for the project, you will recall that our final goal was to use the results of the research to provide effective counseling and treatment as might be indicated from our findings. After several weeks of preparation, review and analysis, we scheduled follow-up sessions with each of the subjects' owners and their dogs, and it is at this point that I must share the critical decision our team made before doing so. As we discussed the best approach for these owner/animal wrap-up sessions, we all agreed that we should share our dream session observations, including video of any session we deemed clinically and scientifically significant. We realized that doing so involved a certain degree of risk. During the initial enrollment and intake process, we had each owner sign a very detailed non-disclosure agreement, explaining the nature of the research, the pledge and assurance that the dogs would not be harmed in any way, and the very strict requirement that the results of the research would be made available to each dog owner, *provided it must not be shared with anyone*. We explained this was absolutely essential, especially since certain technological specifications had been submitted for patent registration, and we could not risk jeopardizing protection of the intellectual property. We also extensively debated whether or not to share our findings *in their entirety*.

As I presented my thoughts on the subject to the team, I stressed that the one finding I believed we simply should not share is that we had developed a method for two-way conversation. For me, at least, this was a non-negotiable issue, but one which I knew could cause considerable debate and consternation amongst my teammates. Frankly, my concern was less about the confidentiality and intellectual property issues as it was the consideration of the possible ramifications of full disclosure. Initially, the team bristled and pushed back. What we have accomplished is clearly a monumental breakthrough, one which is sure to achieve considerable notoriety in the scientific community for us all, but I implored the team to consider the immediate practical implications.

> "Listen guys, all I am asking is that we carefully think through the implications full disclosure might have on the dogs, their owners and all of us going forward. Let's walk through it together. If we share the fact that we actually created a way to have a conversation with their dog, what is the obvious next step? Won't *they* want to have a similar conversation? If the word gets out, and regardless of our very tight non-disclosure agreement, will we then be besieged by every dog owner demanding we provide the same access and ability for them? What's next, cats? Oh my God! Can you even imagine? What if humans found out that cats are barely tolerable of their human owners and completely uninterested in hearing what we have to say? It could be cat-astrophic! Or what if some dogs tell their owners to their face how they feel about constantly being spoken to like a small child? Seriously, people! This could have disastrous, apocalyptic implications – potentially the complete unraveling of the delicate space-time continuum! Just something to think about…"

I won't lie - we had some pretty contentious discussions. Were we keeping our subjects' owners in the dark regarding what could well be seen by many in the scientific community as a truly momentous discovery? On the other hand, imagine the potential for fraud and deception by every Tom, Dick and Harry who purport to be able to facilitate human/dog dialogue. In the end, I am proud to say we came to a thoroughly discussed and fully agreed consensus: *we would not reveal this portion of our research until we had completed all of our documentation and formal research findings.* We agreed that only then would we notify the owners before formal publication, including sharing the transcripts and videos of the conversations. Of course, just the consideration of that eventual disclosure presents its own series of challenges. How do we then respond to an owner's request for a conversation with their dog? How would that work, exactly? If we are fortunate enough to secure patents related to the process, will we license the technology to others? So many questions remain!

With our strategy now in place, we scheduled meetings with each owner and their dog, with two sessions per day over a two-week period, as we prepared for a formal presentation to our investor-partner. One by one each owner and dog arrived at *Dreamlab*, and we all smiled as we noticed that in most cases the dog would confidently lead the owner into the lab, as if to say "Come on, man! This place is cool, and you will like these people." We rearranged the main control room to provide some additional casual seating, with some comfortable recliners positioned in line with the massive main video monitor, our version of a sort of high-tech home theater. I began each session with a welcome and thank you for their participation, followed by introductions of the team, an overview of the research goals and objectives, and rudimentary explanation of the technology, before launching into several repeated reminders of the need to for absolute confidentiality, all in a formal, but non-threatening way.

Of course, our confidentiality agreements are two-way and as a result, preclude me from sharing the owners' identities or specific details of our one-on-one debriefing sessions, other than to offer a brief summary of our recommendations. Suffice to say, however, in every case the dog owners were, without exception, absolutely transfixed by the HD video of the dream sequences, unable to take their eyes off the screen. At the end of each session, I summarized our findings and presented the team's recommendations in a simple, understandable step-by-step format. None of us are medical doctors, but you might think of our wrap-up sessions and recommendations as a prescription designed to benefit both animal and owner going forward. I can report our overwhelming sense that each owner left the session looking at their canine companion in a different way. Since we did not share the revelation of dog/human direct dialogue, I believe that the biggest takeaway was that dogs share our ability to dream and that, like our own, those dreams represent a deeper look into how our brains process and cope with our wakeful experiences.

For Pedro, while the obvious manifestation of his Napoleonic Fortune complex was not unexpected, we recommended some sensitivity training with the children to guide them away from dressing up the dog and focusing on including him in normal play sessions, including getting down on his level so as not to always be looking down on Pedro. We crafted a series of simple training exercises with rewards for completion to instill a sense of accomplishment and canine self-worth. We also suggested a change in diet, substituting healthy dog treats to replace leftover frijoles, thereby eliminating the odiferous flatulence. Finally, in an effort to alleviate the stress, anxiety and paranoia Pedro suffers from his unfounded fear that the authorities will somehow discover his undocumented status, we staged a mock formal naturalization ceremony, complete with the Oath of Allegiance and supporting documentation. I presided over the ceremony, which we held in a small conference room in a building adjacent to our laboratory on the university campus. Since we had not yet shared our ability for two-way communication with Pedro's owner, we outfitted Pedro with a red, white and blue wireless EEG sensor cap, and the family was unaware I was wearing a smaller, barely visible Bluetooth headset. Of course, Pedro's family could not hear what Pedro and I were hearing, but I administered the oath, Pedro raised his paw, swore to support and defend the Constitution, and we presented him with a very official looking citizenship document. Suffice to say, we all applauded and congratulated a very proud little dog, and I am confident our actions resolved more than one psychological trauma.

For Alexander, so as to avoid any "bull in the china shop" calamities, we recommended creating ample opportunities for outside play sessions, preferably in open fields and devoid of any fragile objects, old people or – dare we say – squirrels! In our discussion with Alexander's owners, we asked about any nearby dog parks, especially those that segregate dogs by size, allowing larger dogs more room to play together. Fortunately, a bit of online research showed a local Great Dane organization was active in the county, with occasional events and meet-ups, allowing the dogs to socialize and hang out with animals their own size. We emphasized that interaction with *any* larger breeds would be beneficial, providing Alexander a better perspective relative to his size, making him more comfortable with his surroundings. We were delighted when Alexander's owner shared that he had a friend who raised and trained horses, suggesting maybe he could take Alexander to the farm sometime. I *had* to grin, and we agreed that would be an excellent outing, *a dream come true*.

Roscoe was undoubtedly our most challenging case. As with humans, dealing with extreme grief brought on by traumatic incidents requires a support system to allow the grieving process to move at its own pace. Roscoe's owner reported that he reacts with a flinch to unexpected loud noises, immediately seeking shelter, and otherwise exhibits classic symptoms of PTSD, which is not surprising considering the horrific drive-by shooting incident. I suggested that the owner demonstrate his love and support for Roscoe's healing by supporting Roscoe's involvement and leadership in the *Black Labs Matter* movement. He immediately warmed to that idea, and the following week we were encouraged to see his Facebook post with pictures from travel to a recent Chicago rally. The pictures showed Roscoe proudly leading a Sunday Michigan Avenue parade supporting the cause, sporting a custom BLM vest with hundreds of other dogs participating. We are deeply moved by the owner's continued support and devotion.

After the *Dreamlab* session and subsequent conversation with Brutus, I came away impressed that he clearly understood the implications of his "grooming" behavior and how it created uncomfortable and embarrassing situations for his family, especially when visitors joined the family for football game days. Without acknowledging that I had conversed with Brutus directly, in our meeting with his owner I alluded to the fact that the behavior is not uncommon, and the goal should be to let Brutus know when it is blatantly inappropriate, for example by forcing him from his favorite position on the couch when it begins. From a reinforcement perspective, it is difficult to provide positive reinforcement when a behavior is *not* occurring, but some type of correction must be given when it does. Other alternatives included sounding an air horn, using a squirt gun – any disruptive action Brutus will learn to associate with the onset of genital licking. If nothing else, this will move the behavior out of sight. In a follow-up phone call, I was pleased to hear that the family had taken Brutus to Athens, Georgia to meet his idol, Uga. I can only imagine the stories they must have shared!

In our meeting with Blue's owners, they shook their heads as we recounted our observation of his dream sequence, acknowledging he was clearly traumatized by the neuter trip to the vet. I then outlined a suggested strategy and specific treatment regimen, to which I strongly recommended they strictly adhere. The regimen consisted of a series of short trips in the car, each with a pleasant outcome, serving as positive reinforcement. I suggested that the first trip be extremely short, such as merely driving to the neighborhood park, followed by indulging in all of Blue's most favorite activities. Just as aversion therapy pairs bad habits and behaviors with unpleasant outcomes, here we are doing just the opposite, rewarding the dog and repeatedly associating riding in the car with a happy ending. As future car rides are then longer but always with pleasant, enjoyable outcomes, Blue learns to associate the car with nothing but positive memories, leaving the one traumatic incident in the rear-view mirror. Less than a month later, we were gratified to hear the strategy worked as planned, and Blue is now excited whenever a car ride is mentioned. Problem solved!

Not surprisingly, our meeting with Benji's owners focused squarely on his chronic humping. I suggested that though studies have indicated neutering may reduce the behavior, other alternatives involve immediate correction and strong negative reinforcement. For most dogs, humping is mostly a social behavior and not sexual in nature, more about dominance and control. That is very clearly not the case with Benji, and his compulsion requires immediate corrective action. Correction can include leash training with an announced "time out" and firm leash correction whenever the behavior occurs, body-blocking the dog to prevent humping another dog or associating a squirt gun or prominent sound cue immediately when it starts. The success of these approaches depends on the consistency of the corrective action, making sure to employ the correction for each and every occurrence. As a further reinforcer, I provided the family with an 8 x 10 photograph of Nate taken in the Australian Outback and assuming a pose reminiscent of Crocodile Dundee, complete with huge, gleaming knife. I explained that Nate and Benji had bonded during our sessions and suggested they display the picture simultaneous with every corrective reinforcement. We were encouraged recently by a follow-up call from Benji's owner reporting a significant improvement. It seems like Nate's little chat may have had an impact.

Duke's owners appeared anxious during our debriefing, perhaps fearing that our suggestions might include getting rid of the cat. While we certainly debated that internally, we agreed that a two-pronged approach was required. Behavioral reinforcement would require careful coordination for both Duke and his nemesis, Midnight. For Duke, we want to provide positive reinforcement for any positive action taken to stop the feline bullying behavior. Of course, we cannot suggest that the dog simply punch the cat in the nose or otherwise physically attack, but the family members can support Duke to *stand his ground* and not retreat when Midnight approaches. Since it is the *cat* that is exhibiting unacceptable behavior, she is the one that should receive corrective reinforcement she will eventually learn to avoid. Likewise, we don't want to create a situation to reward Duke for overly aggressive behavior, hoping for a peaceful cease-fire and eventual mutual respect. After outlining several examples of positive and negative reinforcement, we were pleased to hear from the family with a series of YouTube videos. In one, the kids intervened just as Midnight ran the length of the couch and pounced, using the father's fishing net to thwart the culprit and remove her to the back yard with a loud admonishment. In another, a strategically placed string triggered a cup of water overhead just as the cat was approaching a sleeping Duke. Well done, and we were pleased to hear it won second place on America's Funniest Videos.

When Pugsley's owners arrived at the lab, they scrambled to keep up as Pugsley bounded toward the entrance, eager to act as tour guide to the facility and to introduce them to our team. As the door opened, Calvin scooped Pugsley up, receiving affectionate doggie kisses in the process, and the owners seemed surprised their pet was so trusting and at home in the lab. We discussed the dream sequence, focusing on the fact that Pugsley acted more as observer than active participant, a fact we interpreted as an example of the dog's unselfish affection for humans. We theorized that he was genuinely interested in making sure the humans had the opportunity to experience the joys of pug-dom, and his mission was one of constantly checking to make sure no family was pug-less. As there was no indication that this mild obsession is in any way detrimental or likely to become an actual disorder, our recommendation was to look for opportunities for Pugsley to interact with pug-centric families in the area, offering assurance that others have been blessed to experience the joy these caring, affectionate canines bring to their adoptive families. As a gesture of their stalwart support, the family committed to temporarily fostering any pugs they may learn about from area shelters. This will allow Pugsley to teach each one the ropes and, of course, *the rules*.

Fifi's owners arrived at their scheduled session in high fashion. The family matriarch Florence and her two daughters emerged from their chauffeur-driven Bentley, with the driver opening the door for the ladies and Fifi, immaculately coiffed and adorned with rhinestone collar and pink tail pom bow. Each lady sported an elaborate hat and oversized dark sunglasses, and the chauffeur accompanied the group to the door, handing Fifi's leash to Florence as they entered the building. Fifi led the way with a confident stride as Calvin offered a greeting as I arrived to welcome them all inside. As I reviewed our observations with the family, Fifi sat on the floor next to the sofa and watched intently as I explained what we had learned about Fifi's concerns and the impact they have had on her psychologically. In fact, she was much more attentive than the sisters, who spent the majority of the debriefing on their phones, no doubt texting their respective BFFs. Florence, however, gave me her full attention and seemed genuinely interested, especially when I described the dream sequences and how other dogs reacted to the superficial caricature Fifi the daughters had created. At one point in my presentation, I could see that Florence was moved emotionally, and she confided she had never considered that dogs had their own canine circle of friends or that the family's attempts to make Fifi part of human high society might have an adverse psychological impact. As our conversation continued, I made a series of suggestions, which included scheduling occasional "play days" with other dogs within their gated community and coordinating trips to the park with other owners. I reminded her that dogs love to play, and that sometimes means they roll in the dirt, run through puddles – her smile told me she got the message.

Our final follow-up session with our subjects' owners was with Bradley's adopted family, a divorced mother of two, who had found Bradley as a rescue. As I shared what we had observed from Bradley's dream sessions, his owner became quite animated, letting me know in no uncertain terms that she had chosen Bradley specifically because he *was* a mixed breed. Apparently, her ex-husband took "his dog" as part of the divorce settlement, and since she was now living on her own with custody of the two boys, she thought it was time to bring a dog into the family. She and the kids visited local pet stores and shopped around, but she insisted on taking the kids to the local animal shelter, letting them know they would definitely have a say in the selection process. According to the mom, when Bradley saw them, he perked up and they claim they saw a definite twinkle in his piercing blue eyes. As I recounted the dreams we had observed during Bradley's *Dreamlab* visits, the owner teared up, sharing that she and the boys would make sure Bradley knows he is the perfect blend, a loving, affectionate dog on par with any breed out there. I could tell from her reaction that Bradley would soon enjoy a renewed confidence and sense of pride. Man, sometimes I really love this job!

Fifteen

The Aftermath

There is nothing like a dream
to create the future.

~Victor Hugo

The formal presentation of our research study findings to the Beatrice Upton Taft Trust and SNIFF foundation went extremely well, and none other than Herbert Winston Taft himself was extremely gracious and particularly enthusiastic, lauding praise on our team, and assuring us all he knew that Beatrice would be extremely proud of what we have accomplished. More importantly, he pledged the continued support of the foundation for any future research to further support and expand our initial findings. It was great to see the team get the credit they deserve, and I was proud to share the moment with such a dedicated and talented group of research professionals. I knew that each of us would find new challenges in the years ahead, and as we walked through the formal gardens following our presentation, the team laughed as I reminded them about the Beatrice Taft's wild dog-drawn carriage rides along the paths we were now peacefully exploring. We paused at the memorial to her beloved Bosco, paying our respects to both the dog and the woman who made our research possible. For that we will be forever grateful.

With the completion of the formal research study, our team slowly returned to their normal lives, but each of us no doubt now has a new definition of *normal*. For us, at least, it is now normal to look at every dog we encounter with greater curiosity and wonder what story they might have to tell us. We still stay in touch, and I am pleased to report that each team member has continued canine research in their respective fields.

Kathy Chan returned to Taiwan and is Director of the Institute of Biomedical Engineering at National Taiwan University, her alma mater, where she continued her groundbreaking work in the use of fMRI diagnostic imaging, now coupled with her breakthrough EEG advancements. Her now-patented wireless EEG sensor cap has quickly become the new standard for brainwave monitoring and, while we have still not shared our thought-to-speech translation technology, the less intrusive cap design was quickly adopted by pediatric hospitals around the world. She is also currently developing an amazing diagnostic tool in the form of a highly advanced miniature sensor capsule, which is swallowed by the patient. Not only does the capsule stream ultra-high definition video as it makes its way through the digestive system, it provides real-time monitoring of 27 blood and hormonal biomarkers, creating a detailed internal map from ingestion to its eventual expulsion.

Speaking of bowel movements, Calvin Grant still suffers from PPS, but his preoccupation with all things poop has expanded based on his experience with our research subjects, specifically our observations of Pedro and his unique frijole flatulence. As a result, Calvin has created his own research project to study how dietary variations affect animal flatulence and the resulting environmental impact. Calvin postulated that it may be possible to carefully regulate an animal's diet to create a perfectly controlled *fart factory*, resulting in a gas that can be captured and used in energy production. According to Calvin, his initial research findings have revealed that feeding dairy cows a diet rich in daffodils, daisies and lemon grass produces a fantastic flowery flatulence chemically similar to methane, but with a heavier molecular structure, allowing it to be captured and contained at "the source". Apparently, the diet also results in a completely unique manure, a variation on the more common *cow pie*. These cow patties have a denser consistency and are less odiferous, with a subtle lemony smell, and can also be burned as fuel. Calvin is currently seeking funding, and I have been assisting in developing his presentation skills for the venture capital community, where his goal will be to convince investors that he really does know his shit.

José Ortiz returned to his home in Catalonia, where he decided not to pursue teaching, but rather has dedicated himself to two important personal goals. José is now the head of the Neuroimaging and Analysis department at Vall d'Hebron Barcelona, the same hospital that attended to his bullfighting injury years ago. He has gained some notoriety at the hospital for using his flamenco guitar skills to entertain recovering brain injury patients, often appearing in elaborate flamenco costumes. However, he is most proud of his volunteer work outside of the hospital. As a tribute to his once-rivals as a bullfighter, José now donates his time and medical training to the Barcelona Bull Rehabilitation Center, tending to the injured animals and using the latest imaging technologies to support their recovery. As an added touch and flourish, when a bull has fully recovered and ready to be released back to the herd, José orchestrates an elaborate graduation ceremony, where he presides wearing his trademark bullfighter regalia.

Following our project's conclusion, Dwayne Higgins was recruited by one of the world's largest video game events company and eSports promoter, his dream job. ESL hosts eSports competitions across the globe, and Dwayne is part of a team of emerging data analysts headquartered in Burbank California who support the company's Hollywood-style productions around the world. Now well over a billion-dollar industry, eSports promoters track and publish player statistics, which are essential for this growing field where players compete for serious prize money. Dwayne is no longer an active gamer, saving his non-work hours to care for the latest member of the Higgins family, a beautiful yellow Labrador retriever named Sadie. Fortunately for Dwayne, during all but dates of major tournament competitions, the company allows employees to bring dogs to work, and Sadie seems to enjoy being part of the team.

Chad Wilson returned to MIT as a research fellow and Department Chair for the Artificial Intelligence program, supplementing his income with occasional modeling and acting gigs, as his university schedule permits. He remains a dyslexic agnostic insomniac, which he tells me has resulted in some awkward casting call auditions, from late arrivals to comical script disasters. From his experience from our research study, Chad is currently working on modifications to his patented beacon-based canine perimeter control system. With my complete blessing and support and using what we learned from our human/dog speech translation utility, Chad has modified the perimeter notification triggers for the Bluetooth collar. Rather than administering an electric shock, such as the more typical "invisible fence", Chad modified the collar output algorithm to deliver a progressive series of fully-customizable owner *verbal* commands, using bone conduction technology to deliver the audio directly through the dog's ear bones, bypassing the eardrum and stimulating the cochlea directly. Using proximity-based Bluetooth beacon technology, as the dog approaches the defined virtual perimeter, the commands increase in intensity, using only increased volume and vibration, with no electrical shock. For example, as it approaches the perimeter the dog may hear "Hey buddy, that's far enough." If the animal continues, the warning may increase to "Tucker, STOP!", with a mild vibration to reinforce the command. Failure to comply may then result in "Stop damnit! I'm not f—ing around!" If all else fails, a final warning includes a jaw-shaking vibration and significant volume increase, with a more severe admonition. "I swear to God, stop right now, or I'm gonna beat your ass!" Since the audio is completely customizable, the pet owner can craft their own unique messaging. For example, our German Shepherd research subject, Duke, might respond to the sound of a shrieking cat, our black lab Roscoe to the sound of gunfire, or Pedro to a loudly shouted "¡Detener!" In any case, the dog does not suffer any physical harm, but may experience brief but intense psychological humiliation.

Our favorite Aussie, Nate Ferguson, returned briefly to Sydney, only to find that the infamous dislocated comma, dingo/baby incident was still very much in the public consciousness. Arriving at Sydney International Airport, Nate was immediately set upon by a gaggle of reporters eager to know his future plans. As cameras flashed and local TV personalities jockeyed for position, Nate could see the airport retail shop's mammoth display of novelty t-shirts with pictures of dingoes devouring Baby Ruth candy bars, some as unsettling baby/candy mashups. Reporters crowded closer, shouting questions, each one trying to outdo the other.

"Mr. Ferguson, have you returned to talk to the dingoes?" The camera operator zoomed in for a closeup, as Nate was barraged by the rapid-fire interrogation.

"Nate! Nate! We knew you were coming. A little dingo told us!

"Nate, when you speak with the dingo kidnapper, will you demand reimbursement?"

"Nate! Over here! Have any of the dingoes phoned you set a meeting?"

"Are you returning to seek revenge, sir? Some here are still pretty angry!"

"Is it true you will be returning to the university? Will you be teaching "dingo lingo"?

As the scrum moved away from the Qantas arrival gate, Nate seemed very much alone, jostled by the reporters until a familiar face stepped in front of him. It was the police Captain who handled the original candy bar abduction incident, and he smiled broadly as he directed two uniformed officers to step in and provide some separation from the crowd.

"Welcome home, mate." The Captain placed is hand on Nate's shoulder, guiding him toward the exit, with the police officers setting a perimeter to allow the two to escape to an awaiting car.

"I'm afraid they haven't forgotten, mate. I'm not sure who is the bigger celebrity – you or the dingo!" The Captain broke into laughter, and Nate grinned nervously, realizing what might likely lie ahead.

Arriving at the hotel a few minutes later, at the front desk the clerk offered a cheery welcome. Handing Nate the room key, the clerk smiled: "Sir, you have several phone messages, most claiming to be dingoes. Unfortunately, it was all just howling to us; the hotel does not have a dingo translator." The clerk chuckled as Nate stepped into the elevator, which provided at least a brief moment of silence and privacy. Finally, safely inside his room, Nate was faced with the realization of what lay ahead, should he try to return to the university. Frankly, he had thought that continuing our research methodology with dingoes could represent an opportunity for securing a teaching and research position, which would also allow him to complete his doctorate, which had obviously been put on hold following the dingo candy theft incident. As Nate began unpacking his suitcase and pondered his next move, he walked across the room to the bed to read the turn-down card on the pillow, which was adorned with a miniature Baby Ruth bar. The card read: "Welcome home, Mr. Ferguson. Please accept this small token of my apology for the anguish I have caused. Sincerely, The Dingo."

That was it! Nate threw the candy across the room striking a lamp, lucky it was not a full-size bar. He threw his clothes back in the suitcase and headed down the elevator, rushing through the lobby, tossing the room key card to the front desk clerk. He blurted "Checking out!" as the astonished clerk stood with his mouth open. "But sir!" Nate hailed a taxi, tersely commanding "Airport!" At the Qantas ticket counter, Nate paid for a one-way ticket back to Orlando, and was happy to hear that the same plane was in the process of refueling for the return trip, allowing him sufficient time to grab a sandwich and sit in solitude, the press having long since left the area. Sitting in the Coast Café in the international terminal, Nate had a clear view of the adjacent souvenir shop, with display racks filled with – you guessed it – novelty shirts of dingoes biting the heads off of Baby Ruth bars, with varying depictions of violence and with captions such as "Not my baby! Ruth!" It was at that precise moment the idea hit him. He smiled when he realized the obvious solution to his problem. He ordered a Fosters beer, then another before hearing the boarding call. On the long flight back, he created the perfect plan. He knew what he had to do.

Today, as Vice President and Director of Consumer Engagement for Baby Ruth, Nate is responsible for marketing and communications, leveraging the original incident in a series of humorous, lighthearted images and taglines, such as *"No, dingo! You're not getting my Baby Ruth!"* with a cute image of a baby taking a bite of a Baby Ruth while simultaneously punching a dingo in the nose. As the memes and catchphrases proliferated, sales skyrocketed, and since few in the U.S. have associated Nate with the incident, today he enjoys relative anonymity.

As for me, I plan to take a brief break, then embark on a speaking tour to share our findings with universities, research facilities and basically any organizations who may be interested. Since publishing our initial findings and with a continued pledge of support from SNIFF, I have fielded well over one hundred inquiries from organizations, venture capitalists, universities, biomedical facilities, celebrities, and plain old dog lovers – quite an amazing collection of interested parties. Following the speaking tour, I plan to take advantage of these potential funding sources to support a more extensive phase two project, hopefully getting the band back together with a goal of continuing human-dog conversations, as well as testing the viability for communicating with non-canine species. I cannot begin to tell you how many letters, emails, and phone calls I have fielded asking about cats. I am not a cat person, but I have many close friends who are. Based purely on limited anecdotal research, I have decided not to pursue a feline option. This decision is not due to lack of resources or technology, but rather the simple fact that, by and large, cats couldn't really give a shit about what we have to say.

Epilogue

If you don't own a dog, at least one, there is not necessarily anything wrong with you, but there may be something wrong with your life.

~ Roger A. Caras

Our research has provided an amazing insight into the canine brain, and we have been able to observe the physiological and neuropsychological aspects of human/dog relationships. Now we know that dogs *do* dream, and that those dreams and the science behind them are similar to our own. We know that the same hormones and neurotransmitters that are involved in human affection and attraction are present in dogs. We can list any number of behaviors that demonstrate our dogs' affection for us and our behaviors that return that affection. As a scientist, I understand that research findings must be supported by quantifiable, verified data. I believe our research has clearly demonstrated that we can peer into the dreams of a sleeping dog, creating accurate simulations and visualizations of those dreams, and we can even "converse" with a dog, using sophisticated translation algorithms and supercomputing capabilities. We have the data and hard evidence to support these findings. We can truly celebrate those accomplishments.

As for the ultimate question – the one we sought to answer above all others – the evidence to support our hypothesis and definitively answer the question remains lacking and inconclusive. Even with all of our sophisticated equipment and processing power, we are unable to substantiate our theory. I cannot submit firm research findings and publish them in prestigious scientific journals. There will be no Nobel prize nomination, and my friends and colleagues may forever refer to me as "that crazy guy who talks to dogs", but I can live with that. I can take comfort in the fact that I do, in fact, know the answer. I know it as surely as I know any scientific fact, proven principle or physical law. I know it because human understanding includes an unbreakable connection between our brain and our heart. I would bet my life on it. *Dogs love*. They do.

If that sounds crazy, I am OK with that, because I know dogs *do* love, and I know that we love our dogs. Period. Full stop. No qualifications. No parsing of terminology. No degrees of affection versus love. *Dogs love*. My findings and assertion may not be scientific, but I can present countless examples to prove my case. Some may call that circumstantial evidence, but no one is on trial here. Call it intuition, a gut feeling, thought transference, a Vulcan mind-meld – I really don't care. It is truly an example of Occam's razor, a simple answer to a simple question, presenting the most obvious and direct explanation of an extremely complex theoretical construct.

For me, it's a slam dunk, but I bet you already knew that. You already knew what our team and I worked so very hard to prove. You already knew the obvious: *your dog loves you, and you love your dog.* Why would anyone ever question that? My advice? Cherish your dogs and show them you love them every day. Yes, that includes the time they chewed up the sofa cushion, rolled in some vile-smelling goop in the yard, or pooped on the dining room carpet. Love them as deeply as you love those most important in your life and know that they love you. Even when you may be too tired to throw that ball one more time or fail to show your appreciation for a cold nose on your butt or sloppy wake-up kiss in the morning. Even when you are in deep despair and want the world to disappear and leave you alone, your dog loves you, and you love your dog.

To paraphrase Charles Schulz, famed cartoonist and creator of one of the world's most famous dogs, Snoopy:

> *All my life I have tried to be a good person. Many times, however, I failed. For after all, I am only human. I am not a dog.*

One thing is certain: I will forever remember and always treasure… Dog Dreams.

Made in the USA
Columbia, SC
10 October 2020